LITTLE KNOWN FACTS

A Novel

CHRISTINE SNEED

BLOOMSBURY

NEW YORK • LONDON • NEW DELHI • SYDNEY

Chapter 1, "Relations," appeared in *The Southern Review* 38, no. 1, Winter 2012; chapter 2, "Flattering Light," appeared in *The Southern Review* 38, no. 2, Spring 2012; chapter 4, "The Finest Medical Attention," appeared in *New England Review* 33, no. 1, 2012.

Published by Bloomsbu

All papers used by Bloor̶ ... are natural, recyclable products m̶ ̶ le from wood grown in w̶ ... es conform to the environ̶mental regulations of the country of origin.

LIBRARY OF CONGRESS CATA̶

Sneed, Christine, 1971–
    Little known facts : a novel / Christine Sneed. — 1st U.S. ed.
        p. cm.
    ISBN 978-1-60819-958-7 (alk. paper hardcover)
    1. Actors—Fiction.   2. Celebrities—Fiction.   I. Title.
    PS3619.N523L58 2013
    813'.6—dc23
                                                    2012034227

First U.S. edition published in 2013
This paperback edition published in 2014

Paperback ISBN: 978-1-60819-967-9

1 3 5 7 9 10 8 6 4 2

Typeset by Westchester Book Group
Printed and bound in the U.S.A. by Thomson-Shore Inc., Dexter, Michigan

FOR ADAM TINKHAM

Let feelings bring about events, not the contrary.
—Robert Bresson, *Notes on Cinematography*

CONTENTS

RELATIONS

*M*ore times than he would care to count, Will has witnessed his father's ability to silence a room merely by entering it. He has seen his father's expression change in an instant from utter exhaustion to the bright, sometimes false pleasure of being the center of attention, the person on whom every pair of eyes is fastened, some with desire, others with envy. His father has won coveted annual awards and routinely earned millions of dollars for a few months' work in front of a camera and has attracted the admiring, sometimes slavish attention of some of the world's most powerful men and beautiful women. Despite his own early marriage, he has achieved the goals that many men set for themselves in adolescence but abandon when they marry young and begin to produce children and acquire mortgages and jobs they aren't thrilled with and wives who, after a few years, can barely tolerate their bullying insipidity and dispiriting lack of imagination. Will's father, Renn Ivins, is in his early fifties and divorced from two women who did not tire of him before he tired of them. Will is shorter than his father by two inches and at twenty-six already witnessing his hairline's recession, whereas his father still has a full head of movie-star hair. Will believes that even his name is less interesting than his father's: Billy, though he has asked people to call him

Will since his second year of college, and now it is only family—his parents and his sister Anna, and a few childhood friends—who still call him Billy.

His mother was the first woman to marry and be left by his father. She is a pediatrician and for a long time was furious to have been discarded for a younger woman with no obvious merits other than her witless adoration of Renn and the supposed ability to suffer more gracefully the sex scenes that he has pretended since the beginning of his career to dislike—his claim has always been that he submits to them only to avoid an argument with the director. Sex scenes, he has said, are his least favorite scenes to film because they aren't at all sexy. If you actually paused for a moment to consider it, how could you believe that the actors are enjoying themselves while choreographing intimate acts in front of a film crew, most of them little better than strangers? How many people, in any case, want to be studied and critiqued while making love?

The first Mrs. Ivins has told her children that she was too smart for him, that from the beginning, she saw through his selfishness and self-obsession. Behind it, there was a simple message scribbled on a dingy wall: Pig. Over the intervening years, Will's sister has tried to defend their father by telling their mother that she thought he was the nicest man she knew, that she missed him when he was gone, that she thought he was more fun than anyone else. Twelve years old when the divorce went through, Will kept his opinions about their father mostly to himself. They weren't as generous as his sister's, but they weren't as unkind as their mother's either.

Despite his easy access to casting agents and directors, Will has not followed his father into a career in film. Four years postcollege and he still has not come across anything that fills him with suspense or a sense of purpose for more than a few weeks at a time. He has everything he needs materially, and on some mornings when he wakes in his three-bedroom condominium that sits within view of an imposing hilltop museum, a home that he paid for with one check drawn on his trust account, he feels restless and out of sorts. The unearned spoils of his comfortable life, the European stereo system, the nearly weightless down comforter, the copper cooking pots he almost never uses, all seem incidental, as if he has awakened in a privileged stranger's home. He has used his father's money but has not wanted to use his influence to sign with an agent and begin the process of auditioning for roles he would never previously have imagined himself pursuing. He is not interested in gaining weight to play a paunchy stoner or an unshaven flunky in a biker movie. He does not want to be cast as the waiter with two lines who serves the film's stars their lunches. As a witness to and a sometimes-grudging admirer of the great roles his father has played—the noble statesman, the tragic 1920s film star, the human rights worker murdered for his ideals in a deadly, faraway land—Will understands that he would want immediately to be cast as the hero.

"I thought you were going to start applying to law schools," his sister says when they meet for dinner to celebrate her twenty-fifth birthday. It is mid-October, the weather perfectly mild, the famous southern California smog less dense than usual because of winds off the Pacific. Their mother is in New York attending a convention on new pediatric allergy treatments, their father in New Orleans filming a script he co-wrote with a friend about the aftermath of Hurricane Katrina. Anna is unmarried and boyfriendless. Will has a girlfriend, but she is in Hawaii for a week with two college girlfriends to celebrate their thirtieth birthdays. Danielle is four years older than he is, already divorced. He has never been married and wonders if he will ever want to be.

"I'm still thinking about it," he says, meeting his sister's clear green eyes. She is pretty and kind and could have a boyfriend right now if she wanted one, but claims she is too busy. "I took the LSAT two months ago."

This news surprises her. "Seriously?"

He nods. He hadn't told her that he was studying for it; he wasn't sure how he would do.

"How did it go?"

"All right. I got a one sixty-four, which is good enough for a lot of schools, but I think I want to go to Harvard or Yale."

"You could get in," she says, cutting a big piece from her steak. It is red in the center, shockingly so. He has always ordered his steaks medium well. They are both meat eaters, she more guilty about this than he is. She has tried vegetarianism several times since their teens. He has never tried it, knowing he would give up within a week.

She's right; he could get in. It is because of their father. The Ivies like the offspring of the famous. Most everyone, especially the non-famous, do. But he wants to be admitted based on his own talents, not his father's.

"I don't know," he says. "Maybe. I think I'm going to retake the LSAT anyway."

"You're sure you want to be a lawyer?" she says.

"I think so."

"Why?"

"I just think it'd be interesting." He likes the idea of under-standing something arcane and potentially tricky, of being a person other people go to for answers.

"Do you want to stand in a courtroom and argue for murderers' lives in front of a judge and jury?"

"Alleged murderers," he says. "I don't think I want to do crimi-nal law."

"But that's where the action is."

"I don't need to be in on the action, Anna. Whatever that means."

She looks at him for a few seconds. "You say that now, Billy, but—"

"But what?" he says, impatient.

"I just think you'd probably want to do something a little more interesting than sit in an office all day surrounded by affidavits and filing cabinets."

She has always been the better student. She is in her last year of medical school at UCLA, very close to earning her diploma, as their mother did over twenty-five years earlier, but she does not want to practice pediatric medicine; instead, she intends to specialize in family medicine so that she can offer everyone primary care, particularly those who can't afford it. She has told him that she might even go to Africa someday to volunteer in a clinic. She isn't interested in the big paychecks that many of her classmates seem to be chasing, in part, Will supposes, because she already has money. Nothing is certain yet, but she will do her residency after she is placed in a good teaching hospital, and then she will decide where to go next. Will does not want her to go to Africa or some other place where he would not want to visit her. For a while it bothered him that she has done something so different with her life than anything he has ever considered doing, but over the years, his adolescent jealousy has turned to reticent admiration.

"Do you plan to start next fall?" she says.

"Probably. There's still enough time to apply. Most of the deadlines aren't until December or January."

She cuts off another piece of her steak and looks at it on the end of her fork. "Dad's flying back from New Orleans on Friday and staying until Sunday night," she says quietly. "He probably told you. This is the only time he'll be here until they're done shooting *Bourbon at Dusk*."

"I haven't talked to him in a couple of weeks."

"You should call him more often, Billy. He says you don't unless you need something."

He feels anger prickle his scalp. "That's not true."

She hesitates. "Don't get mad. He was probably just in a bad mood when he said that."

"I called him last week. He's full of shit if he says that I only call when I need something." It sometimes takes him a week or more to get through to his father. They are both in the habit of waiting two or three days to return each other's calls. Anna always seems to have more success reaching him, but she also calls more often.

"He asked if we'd have dinner with him on Saturday. Can you?"

"I don't know. I think I have something planned already."

"Reschedule it. I bet you haven't seen Dad since his birthday."

She is right, but he doesn't admit it. Their father's birthday is in April. It has been almost six months since their last dinner together, at his favorite restaurant, an Italian place in Santa Monica where the ardent and merry owners refuse to let him pay for his meals and only ask permission to take his photo, to have him sign autographs for their relatives back in Salerno. It is their pleasure, their honor, to have him eat their humble lasagna, their minestrone and sweet cannoli. Their smiles split their handsome, aging faces, and Will can barely look at them, he feels such a painful mix of shame and pride.

"I'll let you know, Anna."

She purses her lips but doesn't say anything.

After he drops her off at her house in Silver Lake, he calls his friend Luca, who was supposed to have returned two days earlier from several weeks in Australia. Luca is his closest friend from high school and prone to devising practical jokes that involve convincing impersonations of celebrities and politicians. He has almost perfected Will's father's voice and sometimes calls pretending to confess to a fetish for lawn mowers and athletic girls wearing men's underwear. To Will's mind, Luca fits the stereotype the rest of the world seems to have of southern Californians—happy, never anxious, half stoned. When he calls Luca's cell number, he is routed directly to voice mail and his friend's lazy voice declares that he's "hanging in the land down under until November 1." Will is disappointed that he has decided to stay on the other side of the world for another month. It is likely that he has found a girlfriend, which a year earlier kept him in Paris at his father's place for two extra months.

Will knows that he could do the same thing—disappear overseas for months at a time—but the idea has never appealed to him. He likes California, his apartment, his sister and mother's proximity. He spent a semester in Scotland during college and drank too much and slept with girls who liked him because his father was Renn Ivins. Luca once asked him, "Wouldn't it be worse if you had a famous brother? Your dad at least is twice your age. It's not like you can go on a double date with him."

"Why couldn't I?" Will had said.

"I guess you could, but why would you? He's your dad, you freak."

He dials his father's number now and is surprised when he answers. Renn sounds tired and deflated for a few seconds before his voice rises to its usual breezy conversational pitch. "I just talked to Anna," he says. "She said you took her out for her birthday. That was nice of you."

The compliment makes him feel shy. "It wasn't a big deal. She went out with Jill and Celestine for lunch, so it was just us at the steak place she likes in Pasadena. Mom's in New York. Anna might have told you." He is the dutiful son, filling in the blanks for his absent father. He can't help it. He has always wanted to be good, to be applauded too for this goodness. But Anna's comment that their father thinks he only calls when he wants something rankles. Still, he can't find the nerve to confront him, not so soon.

"How's Danielle?" his father asks.

"She's in Hawaii with a couple of friends."

"Why aren't you with her?"

"She didn't invite me."

His father hesitates. "I want to ask you something."

Will feels his stomach sink. "Okay."

"We've had a couple of people quit down here, and my assistant is taking a leave of absence. Her mother just found out she has cancer, and she asked Trina to come home for a while. I wondered if you'd be interested in flying down here to fill in for her until we're done shooting. You'd be making phone calls and running errands for me. We've got about a month left. Unless you're busy."

It has been several years, since his second year of college, that he has worked on a set doing odd jobs for his father. The last time was for a film that had an enormous cast of extras, which Will had been hired to assist with, and was shot partially in Kenya, partially in Kashmir. He developed digestive problems in India and had to be sent home early. His father had asked him two years later to help with a shoot in Romania and Russia, but Will had declined. This is the first time since then that Renn has offered him work. "I don't know, Dad. Can we talk about it when you're here? Aren't you coming home on Friday?"

"No, not anymore. There's too much going on right now."

"Can I at least think it over for a day or two?"

"No, I need to know tonight. If you can't do it, I have to make other arrangements."

"Can you give me an hour?"

He sighs. "All right. One hour. That's all I can afford."

Before they hang up, Will says, "I thought I was the one who called only when I wanted something."

His father laughs softly. "You called me, Billy."

"I don't call you only when I need something."

"Did I say that you did?"

"That's what Anna told me."

"I don't remember saying that. I'm sorry if I did. I must not have meant it."

After they hang up, Will sees that his sister has sent him a text message: *Dad not coming. No dinner Sat. Ur off the hook.*

In the morning he catches a flight from LAX to New Orleans. His ticket is waiting at the airport, the machinery of his father's life well lubricated by his fame and large bank account.

His sister says she's happy that he'll be helping their father again, but asks in the same breath about his plans to retake the LSAT.

"I can still do it when I get back," he says.

"Don't you have to study?"

"I will."

She laughs. "In New Orleans?"

"Why not? If I don't apply this fall, I can always do it next year."

It takes her a long time to reply. "Yes, you could," she finally says. "If you still feel like it."

New Orleans is much warmer than he expects when he steps out of the terminal and into the town car his father has sent for him. The outlying areas of the city have a stunned look, the effects of the hurricane still visible, despite the years that have already passed. He feels both guilty and relieved to have been living so ignorantly elsewhere, unaware of the scope of the city's troubles. His father's interest in it, his research and his four visits in the years since the storm, had until now only seemed to be a businessman's pragmatism: here was a beleaguered region that could enhance his reputation and earn him more money if he managed to fashion something cinematic out of the ruins.

He is taken directly to the Omni Hotel on St. Louis and Chartres by a silent driver, an older, completely bald man in a dark gray suit. His father and a few of the film's actors are also staying at the hotel, his unit production manager having negotiated a good rate on a block of rooms, but no one is in the reception area to greet him. The Quarter looks as he remembers it, largely unscathed by the storm, its black wrought-iron balconies glistening in the sun, their hanging ferns and flowering potted plants as effusive as he remembers them from a trip during his junior-year spring break, several months before the hurricane. His father's film is being shot in the Quarter as well as in Metairie and on a shrimp boat in the Gulf. Will read the script early in the morning before he got on the plane; his father had given him a copy months earlier, but he had only glanced at it then. It is genuinely good, a story about a brother and sister trying to recover their livelihood after the storm and to keep their mother's health from failing.

It is two in the afternoon, and he is struggling to stay awake. He didn't sleep well the previous night and couldn't sleep on the plane either, but after hanging up the few pairs of pants and the nicer shirts he has packed, he lies down and drops off immediately.

Fifteen minutes later, he is awakened by the hotel phone's strident ring. His father's voice is on the other end of the line. "You didn't pick up your cell, Billy," he says, not bothering with hello.

"I must not have heard it," he says, his voice cracking.

"You sound like you were sleeping."

"I was."

His father hesitates. "I'd really like you to be down in the lobby in five minutes. George will be there, and he'll take you over to the set. We're almost done setting up the street scene outside the Ursulines, and we'll start shooting in the next half hour. I'd like you to be here before we do."

"Who's George?"

"The same person who picked you up at the airport. Didn't you introduce yourselves?"

"We shook hands, but he didn't tell me his name."

"You might have asked him."

Will is silent.

"Five minutes," his father says again. "Can you be ready?"

"Yes."

George is sitting on a sofa reading the newspaper when Will appears in the lobby ten minutes later. The driver stands up and folds his newspaper when he sees Will. His father's reprimand still stings, and he doesn't ask the older man his name when they face each other for a moment before George directs him outside to the car. He sits in the front instead of the back seat this time, guessing that the driver finds this preference strange, but neither of them says a word. There are dozens of tourists in the streets, some moving slowly in the heat with their heavy bodies and melting frozen drinks in plastic souvenir glasses shaped like a naked woman's torso, but the drive takes only a few minutes, the convent only eight or nine short blocks from the hotel. He could easily have walked but knows that his father told his driver to take him so that he wouldn't dawdle in his room.

Before he gets out of the car, George looks at him and says, "I think your dad's grateful that you could be here right now."

Will stares at him. He would sooner have expected the driver to reveal a humiliating affliction than to comment on his effect on his father's well-being. "He is?"

"Yes."

He falters. "Okay, well, thanks for telling me."

George nods. "You're welcome."

He wonders if the driver is his father's confidant. His father's friends, for the most part, are other actors, but Will wonders how close most of these friendships really are, if jealousy keeps them from confiding in each other.

There is a small crowd of spectators near the set, several of them members of a sunburned family dressed in New Orleans Saints T-shirts and ill-fitting shorts. They stand squinting on the sunbaked sidewalk near the white utility trucks that have been transporting the movie equipment from one end of the city to the other for the past four weeks. The catering van is surrounded by a half dozen crew members, each sweaty and tired-looking and holding a bottle of water or Diet Pepsi. His father isn't in plain sight, but Will's phone rings as he walks toward the crew.

"I'm here, Dad," he says. "By the catering van."

"Can you come around to the west side of the convent? I'm over here with Marek and Elise, getting ready to start shooting."

"Okay, I'll be—" But his father has already hung up.

Marek and Elise are Bourbon at Dusk's stars, the brother and sister trying not to self-destruct. Will has met Marek once or twice, but not Elise, who is just beginning her career and is two years younger than he is. She is from Dallas and has a southern accent that she only reveals in interviews. He doesn't think that she has been allowed to use it for this film either; if so, Marek would also have to speak with an accent. Elise is beautiful, tall and slender with strawberry blond hair and hands that gesture animatedly when she talks. Will watches entertainment news shows and other junk TV that his sister doesn't have time for and his mother says that she has no interest in, though he knows she follows his father's career closely. She sees his movies in their first week of release, but rarely has anything good to say about them. After fourteen years, it bothers him that she is still bitter about the divorce, but Anna sees it differently. "I think she feels like she failed him. She would never admit it, but I do think it's true."

He didn't call his mother before he left for New Orleans, not wanting to bother her in New York with news that was likely to annoy her. He could imagine her pretending not to mind Renn's offer and Will's acceptance of it, but she would mind. She has never remarried but has had male companions. None have lasted for more than a year. It must be hard on them, Anna once mused, to feel like they could never measure up to Dad.

His father is standing on the sidewalk in shirtsleeves and khaki shorts, sweating in the afternoon heat as he talks to Marek and Elise. His chest hair is visible in the V of his green cotton shirt, and he wears sunglasses, Ray-Bans that look like the ones Will gave him for his birthday the previous April. The cameraman is several feet away, making adjustments to his complicated and expensive device. Two sound guys with the boom mic that they'll hold above the actors' heads, just out of range of the camera, stand a yard or two away. There is also an electrician inspecting one of several cords snaking out of a power strip, a makeup artist powdering Marek's face and neck, and a couple of older men, one heavyset, the other tall and almost gaunt. Will guesses they are the film's producers. He sees Elise staring up at his father, her tanned, perfect face rapt, and his breath catches. It looks like she is in love with him, a man who is probably older than her own father. Perhaps she is already his girlfriend.

His father glances away from Elise and spots him. He smiles and motions for Will to come closer, hugging him briefly and hard before introducing him to Marek, then Elise. The actor has professionally mussed hair and three days' worth of whiskers. Elise's hair is in uneven braids, and there are dirt smudges on her chin and right cheek. Her hand is damp in his when he shakes it. She smiles and says, "You look just like your father."

He doesn't think that he does, but feels his heart leap at her words. Maybe to her they do look alike. Or else she is a canny liar. "Thanks," he says. "It's very nice to meet you. I'm a fan."

Her smile widens. "You're so nice to say that."

"We're getting ready to do the scene with the argument about the money Tim lost in the card game," his father says. "Tim is Marek's character."

"I remember," says Will, feeling his face flush. "I reread the script this morning."

"Let me talk to them for a couple of minutes, and then I'll tell you what I need you to do."

Will smiles at the ground, incensed that he was ordered to rush over to the set in spite of his exhaustion. He goes back around the corner to get a drink from the catering truck, feeling his father's eyes on him, but he doesn't turn to say he's not going far. He thinks that he has made a poor choice, that he would have been better off staying in L.A. and waiting for Danielle to come back and do what they usually do together—eat in restaurants and shop and see movies and the occasional play. He knows that he should be studying for the LSAT and researching law schools, making plans for his future that are more solid than any others he has made in the past. But he isn't sure if he wants to be a lawyer. He doesn't know what he wants to do tomorrow, or the next day either. It is a problem that has plagued him since childhood—there have always seemed to be so many choices, a fact that strikes him as more oppressive than having no choices at all.

He takes a bottle of Gatorade from the ice chest at the foot of the folding table, where a scattering of apples and plums lie on a bed of rapidly melting ice. A few of the crew members smile at him, but no one tries to talk to him. He doesn't want to talk to anyone either. He can feel the approach of a headache, and the heat is a heavy sheet that sticks to him like a suffocating second skin.

His phone rings. His father again. He walks back around the corner without answering. Marek and Elise have taken up positions on the sidewalk a few yards from where they were standing earlier. The makeup artist, a ponytailed woman wearing a jean skirt and red Converse hi-tops, is now dabbing at the smudges on Elise's face. Will's father hands him a piece of paper with several names scrawled on it. Underneath each one is the name of a periodical. "Can you call Fran and ask her to call these people and try to schedule phone interviews for me for Saturday from seven to ten p.m.? I can give them each fifteen or twenty minutes. She knows that I've talked to them all about past projects. They'll do some advance press for *Bourbon*."

Will blinks. "Fran?"

"My publicist. Her number's at the bottom of the sheet."

"I thought your publicist was named Barbara."

"No, I had to hire a new one last year. Barbara retired with all the money I've paid her over the years and moved to Florence." He pauses, smiling. "After that, I want you to have George take you to buy me ten pairs of white running socks. The short ones, ankle-length, and a dozen white V-neck T-shirts, a hundred percent cotton, extra large. Nothing fancy. He knows where there's a Target. I need some sunblock too, sixty SPF or more. Four or five bottles should do it. Neutrogena, not Coppertone. I can give you some cash right now." He reaches into his front pocket and removes a small wad of folded bills. "Here," he says, pulling loose three fifties. "This should be enough. If you need anything, you can use whatever's left over." He also hands Will one of his two cell phones. "Use this to call Fran. She won't pick up if she doesn't recognize the number. If you get any calls on this phone too, let me know. Someone at Sony called me twice yesterday from a general line but he wouldn't say who he was or what he wanted before he hung up. I don't think I gave anyone there this number either. Maybe he'll tell you what he wants if he calls again."

"Okay," says Will. "I guess I can try to get him to talk to me."

"He probably won't call, but just in case," his father says.

On the way to the store, Will dozes instead of calling the publicist. George doesn't try to talk to him as they drive out of the city toward the commercial sprawl on the outskirts, but when they arrive at the store's bustling entrance, Will asks him a question that he abruptly wishes he could withdraw. "Is my dad dating Elise Connor?"

The driver doesn't turn to look at him. "I don't know," he says.

Will studies the back of the older man's gleaming, hairless head, feeling his face turn hot. "Sorry if I put you on the spot."

"You don't have to apologize. She is beautiful. She's a nice lady too."

"Yes, I guess she is."

George hesitates. "You'll have to ask him if they're dating. I really don't know."

The store is crowded, its fluorescent lights overly bright. Parents of whining children listlessly push carts filled with boxes of cookies and chips and diapers. He finds the things his father wants and picks up some Oreos and cashews for himself. For what feels like the hundredth time that day, his phone rings. His father's, however, has been silent.

"You're in New Orleans, aren't you," says his mother.

"Yes. As of a few hours ago."

He hears her sigh. "I hope you won't let him boss you around too much."

"Lucy, I'm supposed to be working for him." He knows that she dislikes it when he uses her first name, but he can't keep himself from goading her.

"Yes, child," she says. "I know that, but don't let him take advantage of you."

He looks down at the bag of Oreos in his basket and sees that he has gotten double-stuffed instead of regular. "When are you coming back from New York?"

"Tonight. I was hoping you or your sister would be able to pick me up from the airport."

"Anna's probably working."

"She is. I'll take a cab." She pauses. "How's your father?"

"He's fine. Maybe a little stressed, but since this is only his second time directing, I guess it's—"

"I remember The Zoologist, Billy. Maybe he'll have better luck with this one."

"I didn't think The Zoologist was that bad." It wasn't bad. His father had wanted it to be better, but he wanted all his films to be better, even the ones that had won awards. His last two films, which he had acted in but had had no part in the direction or screenwriting of, had not done as well as expected. Will knew that this was one of the main reasons why there was such an air of urgency surrounding Bourbon. If it didn't do very well either, he would be very curious to see how his father reacted.

"You can say hello to him for me if you think of it," his mother says. "How long are you going to be out there? Your sister said a month."

"That's probably about right."

"I'll miss you."

"You could come visit."

She laughs. "No, not in a million years. Who's he dating now?"

"No one that I know of."

"I'm sure he's with someone."

"He might be. I haven't asked him."

"Well, never mind. Call me when you want to, Billy. Love you."

"I love you too, Mom."

They are in the middle of shooting the scene when Will gets back to the set. From where he stands on the periphery, he can see that his father's shirt and hair are drenched. He stands next to the cameraman, watching the two leads confront each other over the money Tim has gambled away. Elise and Marek are very good, Will thinks, and seem at ease in front of the camera, but his father finds fault with their interaction many times, telling Marek to look at once more guilty and defiant as he apologizes to Elise. Another time he tells her to be more physical, to push at Marek's chest, to raise her voice. He doesn't call them by their characters' names, which Will knows that some directors do. Despite the complaints that are often made against actors' public personas, his father has not, to his knowledge, been called a phony, at least not with any frequency. Many people like him because he seems, despite his considerable fame, to be a person who is not overly impressed with himself.

It is six thirty when the company wraps, a two-minute scene that took three and a half hours to film to his father's satisfaction, not including the four hours spent on setup. When they are done, his father pats Marek's shoulder. Elise looks like she wants to kiss Renn when he tells her that he can see great, shining rewards in her future. Will guesses that he means an Oscar, but it's bad luck to talk about the Oscars or the Golden Globes during a shoot.

"What about me?" says Marek.

Will's father turns to face him, opening his mouth, but before he can reply, Marek says, "I'm just giving you a hard time."

"You too," says Renn. "I'll do what I can to help you both get your due."

In the car on the way back to the hotel, his father is buoyant with the pleasure of the day's work done well. Will listens to him and the driver talk about the catering company, one that was contracted for a reasonable price. "They make the best jambalaya I've had in years," his father says, turning to look at him. "Did you try some?"

Will shakes his head. "I bought some nuts at Target. I had a few of those." He doesn't tell him about the Oreos. It seems a childish confession.

"Is everything good for Saturday?" his father asks.

Will gives him a blank look.

"The interviews for the glossies. You called Fran, right? Has she gotten back to you yet? Where's the phone I gave you?"

The phone is still in the side pocket of his cargo pants. He has not called Fran. In the excitement of watching the shoot, he has forgotten to take care of this task. When he confesses this, his father exhales loudly. In the rearview mirror, George's eyes meet his boss's for a second, but the driver keeps his face neutral. Will can feel himself sweating.

"Maybe you don't really want to be here, Billy," his father finally says. "Is that what this is about?"

"No," he says, voice cracking. "That's not it at all. I'm really sorry."

His father closes his eyes and presses his fingertips to his eyebrows. "Then what are you doing?"

It is a question Will wants to be able to answer without sounding like an irritable child. Although he has never said it directly, he suspects that his father has thought of him as one for years. *My son the leech, the slacker, the listless, the attention-deficit-disordered, the spoiled brat.* The jobs he has had since college: day trader, entrepreneur (with two friends, he founded a dog-walking business and a personal-assistant service), health-club manager, and furniture salesman, all failed to hold his interest for more than six or seven months. Because he has not needed to work to eat, he has never felt the same urgency as his coworkers about keeping a job. He has wondered how much time people spend doing things they'd really rather not do, and he knows that there are two probable answers: (a) at least half of it, or, (b) most of it. But unlike him, they can claim that they are doing something with their lives every day. They are setting goals, and in some cases, achieving them. His parents and sister have all done this, whereas his main goal each day is to resist inertia.

"I was so tired earlier," he says, not looking at his father, "that it slipped my mind. George and I went to Target, and I got sidetracked. I'm really sorry."

His father emits a small, harsh laugh. "If this is going to work, you need to do everything I tell you as soon as I tell you to do it."

"I'll call Fran right now."

"You can try," he says gruffly. "She's not going to like having to spend the evening making phone calls for me."

"I'm sorry, Dad."

"I was going to say that we should go out for dinner, but you've got work to do now. Ask Fran if you can help her contact the journalists. You can call room service for your dinner. The food at the Omni is all right."

George pulls up to the front of the hotel, and his father thrusts open the car door and doesn't wait for Will to climb out before he strides into the lobby. From the car's floor, Will grabs the bags of socks and cookies and T-shirts and follows his father, feeling like he has just shown him a report card filled with Ds and Fs.

On the elevator up to their rooms, Renn looks at him and says, "If you don't want to work for me, I won't be angry with you. If you do want to work for me, I can't have you fucking up like this."

"I'll be better from now on. I didn't sleep well last night," he says, sheepish. "Who are you going to have dinner with?"

"Myself, probably. I don't feel like making small talk tonight."

Their rooms are on the same floor but at opposite ends of the hall. "Call me if you need anything," his father says. "After I get something to eat, I'm going to look at the dailies in one of the conference rooms downstairs. I'd say you could join me, but maybe tomorrow would be better. Let me know when the interviews are set up."

When they part ways outside the elevator, his father doesn't say good-bye. "I'm sorry, Dad," Will calls after him. "It won't happen again."

Renn doesn't turn around. Instead, he raises his hand in a half-hearted wave.

Fran answers her phone on the second ring and sounds disappointed when she realizes it is the son, not the star, who has called her. It is only five in L.A., but he suspects that the work his father has for her will take a couple of hours. Even so, she doesn't want his help. "It's easier if I do it myself so there won't be any overlap in the schedule," she says briskly. "It's fine, Will. I'll get back to you as soon as everything's firmed up. Because most of these people are in New York, I might not reach them until tomorrow. I wish you or your father had e-mailed me this list earlier. I don't know why he's so averse to computers."

There is nothing more for him to do that evening, but he doesn't dial his father's room to say they could have dinner together after all, or that he wants to watch the dailies with him and the assistant director. He tries calling Danielle, but she doesn't answer. He tries his sister next, and she doesn't pick up either. She is probably working, making good use of her intelligence and energetic kindness. When they were kids, they used to play school, and because she was younger, he always made her be the student, but she sometimes had to remind him of the year of the first moon landing or the name of the man who had invented the lightbulb. The subtext to her corrections was always, "What are you doing at school each day if you're not listening to the teacher?" Daydreaming, he supposed. Thinking about his toys that were sitting idle at home, or the after-school soccer game where he wanted to be a striker for once instead of a boring defender.

He wonders where Elise is staying. It is likely that she also has a room at the Omni. He doubts that he has a chance with her, but possibly they could become friends, and eventually he might become important to her, whether or not she ever lets him have sex with her.

But a little while later, he sees that it is unlikely he will ever matter to her very much. He is on his way out of the hotel in search of dinner when ahead of him in the lobby he spots her with his father. Renn's hand lingers for a moment at her lower back as he guides her toward the doors that open onto Chartres Street, both of them dressed in black—she in a minidress, he in a short-sleeved shirt paired with khaki pants. People watch them leave, and within a step or two of the exit, Will can see that someone has stopped them on the sidewalk to ask for an autograph. His father signs what looks like a newspaper for two college students. Elise signs the same newspaper and smiles at the two boys in their oversize LSU T-shirts. Will feels his heartbeat accelerate, not sure if he should go out and try to insinuate himself into their plans, pretend to his father that he is not particularly impressed by the fact that Elise appears to have fallen for him. He could go out to the street and say that he only wants to give him back his phone, Fran having at last been contacted, and wait to see if Elise invites him along.

Despite his desire to be near her, he doesn't want to be a hanger-on. He lets them walk out of view and hesitates for several seconds near the doors before he follows them into the humid night. But once in the street, he doesn't see them. A taxi has spirited them away, or they have disappeared through a nearby door and entered a room filled with people who will remember their sighting of the two movie stars for years. If he were to join them at their table, no one would really notice him. He would feel as incidental as the salt and pepper shakers, part of the scenery and not even an important part.

He knows that he could do anything he wants to with his life. If he wanted to study oceanography or take photographs of gazelles in the Serengeti, no one would tell him that he should find a more practical career, one that would enable him to pay his bills and support the family he would surely want one day. Isn't he lucky to have so much? He should be happy, they would say. In fact, he should be ecstatic.

CHAPTER 2

FLATTERING LIGHT

Because she does not want to be unkind, even when provoked, she will never admit that she was initially attracted to him because of his father. The two men look enough alike that for the first few weeks she dated Will, it felt as if she were with the famous man rather than his undistinguished son. She knows that Will suspects this fact; he has teased her about how he is sure that she wishes the actor rather than his boring son were offering to take her to San Francisco for a long weekend, or to Rome or Rio or Montreal, wherever it is she wants to go. They can travel anywhere she would like to because he can give her many of the same things his father can. He isn't famous, but he is young and has money, although he isn't the person who earned most of it. He also has time, which his famous father generally does not.

Danielle met Will through a friend who went to high school with him in Pasadena, the city where his mother moved them after she and Will's father divorced. Renn Ivins kept the house in the Hollywood Hills and still lives in it, though he has since married and divorced a second woman, one who moved to Big Sur with her divorce settlement and alcoholism, an affliction she has publicly blamed Renn for. Despite the cheapness of the gossipy industries that surround the truly famous, Danielle finds these mean-spirited declarations fascinating and knows that many people do. Will has told her more than once that if he had fewer scruples, he could make quite a lot of money disclosing to gossip columnists details about his father's personal life. He wouldn't have to work at all if he were willing to play the double agent.

He doesn't have to work anyway, a fact she doesn't remind him of because it upsets him. He also isn't privy to many of the details of his father's private life because after thirty years of working in the California film industry, Renn Ivins is skilled at avoiding the more lurid of the spotlights. He confides in very few people, with Will's sister Anna among these confidants more often than Will is. The three times Danielle has seen Renn in the fifteen months that she and Will have been dating, he impressed her with his kindness and sense of humor and how politely he treated the servers at the restaurants where they met for dinner. In her most honest moments, she knows that the accusations Will could assail her with are true: *If he asked you out, you'd leave me for him in a second. You wouldn't have given me the time of day if I weren't his son.* Realistically, how could she not feel this way about Will's father? Long before they met, Renn Ivins was more familiar to her than many of her own family members. She has seen almost all of his movies, a number of them years before she started to date his son.

And yet, whatever her feelings for his father, she probably cares for Will as much as she has for any man since the college sweetheart she married during their senior year at UCSD, a marriage that lasted only two years. Her husband enlisted to fight in Iraq without first discussing it with her, she seeing his enlistment as a betrayal, he as an honorable and patriotic act. Joe is now stationed in Afghanistan, but the last time she saw him, at a college alumni party two years earlier, he was almost unrecognizable, not so much because of his physical appearance as because of his rigidity and quickness to perceive insult when no one was, in fact, insulting him. His face reminded her of certain landscapes she had seen in photographs, ones ravaged by fire.

She is older than Will by four years, and already tainted by domestic failure (a feeling she has trouble suppressing), whereas he has never been married or engaged. She is a tall, pretty redhead who regularly attracts the attention of other men, but she likes being with Will. Even if he doesn't yet have a career, he is reliable, smart, and not self-congratulatory in the way that the close relatives of famous people she knew in college sometimes were. His plan, before he went to New Orleans to help his father, was to take the LSAT a second time and apply to law schools. But upon his return from Louisiana, he decided not to fill out applications for next year. What happened while he was working on *Bourbon at Dusk* isn't clear to her, though her impression is that he wouldn't take orders as noncommittally as expected, being prone to bad moods and intractability where his father is concerned. If she hadn't been in Maui with two college friends when Will's father called suddenly to ask him to come to New Orleans, she would have advised him against it.

Her own career, reorganizing and streamlining work and living spaces for restless wealthy people, is profitable, and, she has found, more fulfilling than she had expected when she began to work as a life space consultant, a title she made up for her business cards. She admires simplicity, uncluttered rooms, natural light. Will has let her redesign his place, which is in a high-rise just off Sepulveda Boulevard. His neighbors are all doctors or movie people or privileged offspring like himself, living on inherited money.

He has been back from New Orleans for a little over two weeks when he tells her that she can move in with him if she still wants to. It is something they have discussed a few times, but usually without any real conviction on his part and hurt or irritated feelings on hers. When he makes this suggestion, he is rinsing a glass in the kitchen sink, his back turned. She is sitting at the table, eating some of the fresh strawberries she cut up for dessert and laced with honey. He hasn't eaten any of them. He didn't eat much of the baked chicken she made for dinner either. He has lost weight since he left to work on his father's production, and seems likely to lose more if he keeps going on the long runs he has added to his mornings without eating breakfast before or after these runs.

When she doesn't reply, he turns and looks at her. "So what do you think?"

Her mouth is full of half-chewed strawberries. She has to swallow one almost whole to keep from choking on it. "I like the idea, but I need a little time to think about it, Will," she finally says. "I thought you weren't interested in living together."

"I was always interested, but I wasn't sure."

"You are now?"

He nods. She sees that his hairline really is receding, something that bothers him so much that he has already looked into hair transplant surgery. "Yes," he says. "What do you think? You could have one of the bedrooms for your office, or we could put up a wall in the living room and make you a new office. I'm sure that I could get the condo board to approve it."

She shakes her head. "If we put up a wall, it would darken the rest of the space quite a bit."

"I wouldn't mind," he says.

"I think you probably would."

"All right. No wall. Whatever you want," he says with forced lightness, turning back to the sink.

"Let me think about it for a couple of days," she says.

"I thought you were gung-ho about living together."

"I don't know if I was gung-ho exactly, but I thought that at some point it might be nice."

He shuts off the water and turns to look at her again. "If you don't want to live with me, that's fine. I just thought you wanted to."

"Why are you so ready all of a sudden?"

"I'm not sure. I just am."

She gazes at the remaining strawberries in her bowl but doesn't feel like finishing them now. Will's phone rings, his ringtone the sound of crickets chirping. When he looks at his phone's display, he makes a sound of dismay.

"Who is it?" she says.

"My dad."

"You don't want to talk to him?" she says, realizing as soon as the words are out that it's a stupid question, the answer as obvious as a scream.

"He can wait. I'll call him back when we're done with dinner."

They are done with dinner, but she says nothing while he fills his rinsed glass with orange juice and drinks all of it in one swallow.

"Is he still in New Orleans?" she says.

"I think so."

"When's his movie supposed to wrap?"

"This week, as far as I know. Unless something gets screwed up. Don't let him hear you call it a movie. It's high art. A film. That's what he'd say, anyway."

"You don't think it'll be good?"

"No, it probably will be. It's going to be great if he doesn't get too carried away. He's due for another Oscar, this time for best director or screenplay. Maybe both." His tone is ironic, even a little sneering.

"Why are you so mad at him?" she says. "Are you still waiting to get paid for New Orleans?"

Will snorts. "He paid me. He always pays me."

"That doesn't sound so bad."

He pours himself more juice. "He thinks I'll never make any money on my own. It drives me crazy."

Do you really plan to? she could say, but doesn't. She looks down at the table, afraid he will read her mind, but he has turned away again.

His phone rings a few minutes later, and this time he picks it up without hesitating. Even before he says her name, Danielle can tell from the way his voice softens that it's his sister. She sets her dishes in the sink and goes into the living room. His offer that she move in with him has startled her. She hadn't expected it to come so soon, if at all. The last time they talked about it, a couple of months earlier, he was so evasive that she assumed it wouldn't ever happen. She loves his place, which is more spacious than her own, and closer to the neighborhoods where most of her client base is, but since returning from New Orleans, he has sometimes been so closed off that it makes her nervous to think about having to live with these unpredictable, almost hostile silences. All he would tell her about his premature return from Louisiana is that he and his father did not get along as well as they should have because Renn refused to accept any criticism, no matter how tactfully it was offered. "I have a brain too," Will had grumbled. "He's not the only one who knows how to get things done." He also said that his father wanted him to be on call 24/7, which was ridiculous because as far as Will could tell, no one else on the crew was expected to be.

From the other room, Danielle hears him say, "He's here right now? That must be why he called me. Oh, great." There is a pause before she hears him say, "I didn't feel like picking up, that's why."

She feels almost lightheaded from the realization that she will probably see Renn again very soon. The last time was the previous spring, but Will had had a cold and was such a grouch the whole time that she had to stop herself from apologizing to Renn for Will's rudeness. More than once she has wondered if he thinks she is a gold digger or an idiot, possibly both, for dating this son who is so often surly and combative with his father.

But how unnerved and giddy she feels in Renn's presence. Her girlfriends teased her while they were in Maui one night when she turned on the TV before bed and was immediately drawn into a movie from 1985 that starred Renn as a jungle explorer who spoke six languages and knew Morse code. At the time of the movie's release, he was about the same age Will is now. "Is he still as sexy?" her friend Michelle asked, tickling Danielle's side, making her squirm away with annoyed impatience. "Tell me he's not, because if he is, you're in trouble, Dani."

"He's not that sexy anymore," she lied.

Michelle smiled, showing all of her very white teeth. "You're full of shit. Men like him don't spoil with age. But no matter how much Botox we girls stick in our faces, we'll still get old."

That night after her friends had fallen asleep, Danielle's heart continued beating out its traitorous message: *Movie star. Movie star!*

Renn looks as handsome to her at fifty-two as he did at twenty-six. Maybe even more so because she knows him now, and knows that he likes her too.

When he hangs up with his sister, Will takes a couple of minutes to make his way into the living room to tell her that his father wants to meet for drinks. He's in town for a day and a half and wants to see his kids. Does she feel like coming with him? It might be boring, and his father will probably be distracted by his cell phone or strangers stopping by the table to tell him how great he is.

Even in the nicer places, he's sometimes pestered. "He picked Sylvia's so it won't be too much driving for Anna or me. How thoughtful of him," says Will, the sneer there again.

"I'll go with you," she says, careful to keep her tone neutral. "It sounds like fun."

"All right, but don't blame me if you regret it."

"Why would I?"

"I don't know. You might."

"Only if you two argue."

"I'm not planning on it."

"I wonder why he didn't invite us to his house instead. It's not any farther than Sylvia's."

"It is for Anna."

"It'd only be a couple of extra miles for her, wouldn't it?"

"Why do you think he chose Sylvia's? He wants to be seen."

She blinks, suppressing a flare of impatience. "Is he never supposed to leave the house because he'll be recognized?"

Will laughs in a harsh burst. "Who hired you to defend him? Trust me, he doesn't need it. He's got plenty of other people making excuses for him."

"What happened when you were in New Orleans? You act like you hate him now."

"I told you what happened. He acted like an asshole, and I wasn't going to stick around to put up with it any longer than I had to."

She wonders why he has agreed to meet his contemptible father at all tonight, but she wants to go and doesn't intend to say anything to make him change his mind, even if her hunch is that it won't be the most pleasant evening of her life. Will is ready for a fight, and unless Renn marshals all of his paternal restraint, he will get one.

· · ·

It is Friday night and Sylvia's is crowded, the muted sounds of a jazz band's exertions spilling out the open front door. A huddle of blond women in short, tight dresses blocks the entrance when Danielle and Will arrive, but he squeezes past them, murmuring an apology, pulling Danielle with him. The hostess looks at them with a blank expression until Will says his father's name, and then her face is transformed by a smile so sincere that Danielle feels an answering smile spread across her own face. Will doesn't return the girl's smile but his expression is softer than it was at home, when he initially resisted her suggestion that he change into an unwrinkled shirt and a clean pair of khakis. In that sour moment, Danielle could not see herself moving in with him, at least not any time soon.

Renn is already seated at a table on the far left side of the stage, one half hidden from the room's general view by a pillar decorated with a twining string of white Christmas lights. Anna is at the table too, Will's pretty younger sister who is so different from him in temperament that Danielle privately marvels over the fact they were raised in the same family. When she and Will are spotted, both Renn and his daughter stand up. Danielle can feel herself blushing when Renn hugs her. His embrace feels oddly apologetic but also proprietary, and she smells whiskey on him and a clovelike aftershave. He is warm and bearishly strong, and she can't ignore the rush of pleasure she feels when he touches her.

"It's so nice to see you both," Renn says as he settles back in his chair. "Danielle, you look as gorgeous as always."

She looks down at the table, self-conscious but thrilled. The whites of her eyes feel seared when she looks up at him again.

"Don't let her get away from you, Billy," he adds, his smiling, flirtatious gaze still on her.

"I'm not planning to," says Will, his voice a little too loud, even for the club's cacophony.

"How are you, Anna?" Danielle asks, already feeling the tension between the two men, a whole heated front having moved into the bar with them.

"I'm doing well," says Anna. "Four weeks left in the semester and then just one more before I graduate."

"Dr. Ivins," Renn says proudly. "Just like her mother."

"But she would have liked me to be a pediatrician too."

"You can help more people if you go into family medicine," says Renn.

"She could help a lot of people as a pediatrician too," says Will.

"Of course she could," says Renn, "but she should do what she feels most passionate about."

"You guys," says Anna, smiling warily. "Don't worry about me. I'm just glad I'll be graduating soon."

Renn laughs. "With the highest grade-point in the class."

"No, not at all," she says, abashed.

"But close, I'm sure," her father says. "You're too modest for your own good, sweetheart."

"What's going on in New Orleans, Dad?" Will asks, handing Danielle the beverage menu, which she finds is unpleasantly sticky. She looks at him, but his expression is as nonchalant as his tone.

"We finished shooting thirty-six hours ago," says Renn. "A day and a half ahead of schedule. I couldn't believe it. Saved us more than a hundred grand. Now we just have to put everything together so that it makes sense." He winks at Danielle.

"Is Elise back in L.A. too?" says Will.

His father drinks from his water glass, not meeting his son's eyes. "Yes, she is."

"Elise?" says Anna. "Your female lead?"

"Yes," Will and Renn say simultaneously.

Anna laughs. "Wow, in stereo."

Will gives Danielle a strange, guilty look, and in that moment, she finally understands the real source of his and his father's recent problems. It feels as if someone has come up suddenly from behind and pushed her, but she knows that she shouldn't be surprised. The beautiful, famous girls who interest the father would of course interest the son too, all the more because the son isn't likely to have them, at least not first. She teased Will about this once—had his father ever given him a hand-me-down girlfriend? She hadn't realized how her question would disconcert and embarrass him; how close, it seemed, she had cut to the bone.

Objectively, the father, despite being twice his son's age, is the more desirable man. Along with the money and the fame, it is his confidence, his stature, his sheer Renn Ivins–ness that draws people to him. He is his own thriving industry, a true celebrity, with his metal star already embedded in the famous sidewalk a few miles away. How many women have offered themselves to him over the years? How many women, the world over, believe themselves to be in love with him at that very moment? Danielle knows there have to be thousands upon thousands. Women who would compromise their marriages and self-respect for a night alone with him.

To have that kind of appeal—she can't really imagine it. What did a person do with all of that power? How could it not change you? And so often, it seemed, for the worse?

"Elise Connor?" Danielle asks, but she knows this is exactly who they mean.

"Yes," says Renn. He can't suppress his smile. "The one and only."

Will is pretending to watch the musicians onstage, tuning out his father and everyone else at the table. Danielle feels something hot and corrosive spilling into her stomach. Her girlfriends, some jealous, some well-meaning, told her to be cautious when she started dating Will. He had to know a lot of famous actresses, didn't he?

Wasn't it likely that he had dated some of them? Despite how pretty she is, how could Danielle realistically expect to compete? She might own a profitable business, one that she had started all by herself, but she wasn't famous, not even close. She was, sorry to say, an ordinary person. Will was not. At least this was what she had thought at first, but after a month or so of dating him, she knew that Will's ordinariness, as he perceived it, was in danger of permanently embittering him.

"Are you seeing her, Dad?" asks Anna, crunching a piece of ice from her water glass. Her pale green eyes are rimmed with thick lashes that Danielle has always envied and admired.

Renn takes a few seconds to reply. "I suppose I am, but please keep that between you and me." He smiles at Danielle. "And you and me."

Even in the weak light cast by their table's tiny lamp, Danielle can see that Will's face is flushed. If he weren't so upset, he would look very handsome, certainly a little mysterious, but he has spent most of his life watching his father. She suspects that he is used to being affably tolerated by his father's associates or else ignored, and although it is something that most people are forced to accept as an elemental fact of their lives, she guesses that it is harder for the family members, the lesser planets, forced to orbit the famous, greedily glowing sun in their midst.

Does she stay with Will because she wants to play some role, no matter how minor, in his father's life, or is it that Will reminds her of her ex-husband, Joe? Both he and Joe are men angry at the world, at other men who seem to have more than they do. Reading an article in a grocery-store magazine the previous week, Danielle had found herself staring at the page, unaware that the checkout line was advancing. The psychologist who had written the article argued that anger was the number-one social disease in the Western world, but hardly anyone bothered to acknowledge it. They would rather, the psychologist said, worry about quasi-abstractions like terrorist attacks or meteor strikes or alien invasions because these improbable disasters did not require the same painful self-examination that confronting one's anger did.

Noticing her expression, Will makes an effort to smile and reaches for her hand. Even though she doesn't pull away, she keeps her hand inert. She feels Renn and Anna watching them.

Anna says, "How long have you and Elise been together?"

Renn glances at his son. Danielle sees, in that half second, his contrition and his triumph. "I don't know, seven or eight weeks, maybe?"

Will stiffens next to her but says nothing.

"Are you guys serious?" Anna asks.

Her father laughs. "I don't know. Maybe. That might be nice."

Anna smiles. " 'That might be nice.' That's all you'll say?"

Renn nods. "For now, yes."

"She's twenty-four, Dad," says Will. "How could it possibly be serious? For her, if not for you?"

The waiter, a blond man in a white shirt and black tie, has materialized behind Anna, interrupting the injured silence that follows Will's question. Renn forces a smile and orders champagne cocktails for the table. Danielle is certain that Renn believes himself to be in love with Elise, and she feels an aggressive stab of jealousy. Anna looks at her from across the table, commiserating, it seems, over Will's confrontational behavior. Her solicitousness embarrasses Danielle.

When the waiter leaves, Danielle excuses herself and goes to the bathroom, unable to sit and listen to how Renn will respond to Will's questions about Elise, a woman younger than Renn's own daughter.

In the bathroom, her face is noticeably drawn and ashen; her thick red hair, pinned up high, droops dispiritedly. After a minute, Anna appears in the doorway, her face a more welcome sight than Danielle expects. Without a word, Anna walks straight to her and hugs her for the second time that night.

"I can tell you're not happy with my brother right now," she says quietly. "He knows it too. That's why he's screwing things up."

Before Danielle can stop herself, she is crying against Anna's shoulder. Anna puts a hand to the back of Danielle's head, gently holding it there. "Billy doesn't know what he wants. I worry about him more than I'd like to. Thank God he doesn't use drugs. I don't know how he avoided it when so many of the kids we grew up with did. Do."

Danielle pulls away and wipes her cheeks, embarrassed by her tears. "He drinks too much sometimes."

"I know, but not all the time, right?"

She shakes her head. "No, not that often. At least I don't think so. We're not together every night."

"He needs to start seeing his therapist again. I've been trying to get him to go."

"I think he's thinking about it."

"Work on him, Danielle. He's more likely to listen to you than anyone else."

"Before we got here, he asked me to move in with him."

"He did?" says Anna, her voice rising in surprise. "That's a big deal. He's never lived with a girlfriend before. Are you going to?"

"No, I don't think so." She is sure now that it is a bad idea. Aside from his chronic and unfocused anger, he is seriously infatuated with someone else, the kind of woman Danielle has no hope of ever being able to compete with.

"No? Did you tell him that?"

Danielle shakes her head. "Not yet."

"I'm sorry about the thing with Elise. Billy's a very sweet guy, but he can still be such a child. I know he loves you, though."

"I don't know." It is a relief to talk to Anna, but she isn't used to confiding in someone so closely related to a boyfriend. She wonders if Anna will repeat any part of their conversation to Will.

"He does. Don't give up on him yet."

She forces a smile, feeling tears surge behind her eyes again. "I won't." But as soon as she says these words, she knows they aren't true.

Renn watches her and Anna approach the table, his smile very wide. "I can't get over how pretty you two are," he says as they sit down. The champagne is on the table, and he motions for everyone to pick up their glasses. "A toast to your youth and beauty. Yours too, Billy. May you all use them wisely."

They touch glasses, Danielle glancing at Will, who manages to smile. Her eyes feel raw, as if she has been rubbing them too hard, but with Renn within whispering distance, she can almost convince herself that things are all right for as long as they stay close to him. People at other tables are looking at them, but Renn ignores this, as do Will and Anna, accustomed, certainly, to their father's effect on strangers. Danielle tries not to look, but she can't stop herself from glancing at a couple of the nearest tables. One of their neighbors is using her phone to take Renn's picture; another fumbles through her handbag, probably looking for paper and a pen. She suspects that with minimal effort, he can make lifelong fans or scornful detractors of these people.

When they leave Sylvia's an hour and two cocktails later, Anna already gone, having only had time for one drink, Renn hugs Danielle with unmistakable ardor and kisses her on the lips in full view of his son and the parking attendants. The pressure of Renn's kiss startles her, and she pulls back as if touching fire. His face is pink-cheeked and jolly when she looks up at him, embarrassed but flattered. Without a word, Will takes her elbow and pulls her briskly away, his father calling after them, laughter in his voice. "Billy, lighten up. It was just a little good-bye kiss."

"You're drunk, Dad," says Will, furious. "Leave her alone."

"No, I'm not," Renn calls, still laughing.

"Fuck off," says Will, but only loud enough for Danielle to hear. His grip on her arm is too tight. She wants to shake him off but doesn't, knowing this would only make him angrier.

And yet his anger seems a small penalty to pay for Renn's unsolicited kiss. She can still taste him, the champagne on his lips, the brine from the delicious Italian olives the waiter surprised them with, a gift from the club's manager. She was close enough to feel his enveloping heat again, to have a sense of what it would be like to be pressed even closer, if ever she were alone with him, if she were Elise Connor instead of Danielle Dixon, born in Kansas City, raised in Northridge, California. Her heart is still racing. When she turns to look back at him, he raises his hand and gives her a small wave. "Good night, Danielle," he calls. "Good night, Billy. Drive safe."

"Good night, Mr. Ivins," she says, her face very warm. It was so nice to see you, she wants to add, but doesn't have the nerve.

In the car on the way back to his place, Will is still furious. "I can't believe you let him kiss you."

"I didn't let him kiss me. I pulled away as soon as I realized what he was doing."

"It didn't look to me like you minded."

"A lot of people kiss each other good-bye. He didn't mean anything by it."

He glares at her, his hazel eyes very dark, as if fully dilated. "Of course he meant something by it. He's making it clear to me that he can still have any woman he wants."

"No, he doesn't. And he can't. I'm not interested in him."

He shakes his head. "Right."

"I'm not," she says, angry that he is needling her, wanting only one answer, one she won't ever give him. "Your assumptions are really offensive."

His jaw is rigid, but when he turns to meet her eyes, his question, the plea in his voice, surprises her. "Are you staying over tonight?"

"No."

"Your car's at my building."

"I know. I can drive home. I'm not drunk."

"Come up for a few minutes. Just to make sure you're okay."

She hesitates. "I don't like that you have a crush on someone else."

He freezes, and she wonders if he is turning red. In the dim, flattering light from the streetlamps, they are able to keep some things hidden from each other. "What are you talking about?" he says. Each word, to Danielle's ear, sounds wooden, insincere.

"Elise Connor. You and your dad are both in love with her."

He laughs a little, feigning surprise. "No, we're not."

"You don't have to lie, Will. I know she's why you left New Orleans."

He shakes his head. "No, she's not. I'm not in love with her. I hardly even know her."

Danielle doesn't reply.

"I left because he was being a pain in the ass," Will says. "He's smug and pompous and thinks that everyone should do whatever he wants every minute of the day. I told you that already. Sometimes I hate him."

"No, you don't. Don't say things like that."

"It's how I feel," he says quietly.

"What kid doesn't get mad at his parents from time to time? Your father loves you, even when you're not getting along."

He keeps his eyes on the car in front of them, one of its taillights burned out. "He thinks I'm a fuckup."

She sighs. "No, he doesn't."

"Yes, he does."

She doesn't contradict him this time. She is so tired of his bad moods and self-pity that she will start yelling if they keep talking in this airless way.

When they get to his building, Will looks so morose that she gets into the elevator with him and rides up to the fifteenth floor and sits on his couch while he turns on the TV and listlessly changes channels. She doesn't have the courage to tell him that she needs space and time, possibly for good. It is hard not to keep replaying the few seconds that Renn pulled her against his chest and kissed her, his arms firmly around her, as if he didn't intend to let her go until she had figured out that it was him, not his son, who she should be dating. As a devoted viewer of his films, he is someone with whom she has had a private relationship, one-sided but still powerful, for more than half of her life. During all of her teenage years and far into her twenties, she had never seriously imagined that she would meet him one day, let alone become his son's girlfriend.

She sits with Will in front of the TV for half an hour, then gets up to go to bed. At the other end of the apartment, a few minutes later, she hears him typing in the front door's alarm code and then his unhurried step in the hall. She will not move in with him. His routines depress her, his grievances, his inertia, his implacable bitterness.

After he gets into bed, he says, "You wish I would take Prozac and snap out of it. I know that's what you're thinking."

"That's not what I'm thinking. Not at all," she says, almost laughing at this absurd presumption.

"What are you thinking?"

"Nothing. I'm tired. Let's go to sleep."

"What if I want to move to New York?"

She stares at him. "Do you?"

"No."

"Then why did you say it?"

"I don't know. No reason." He pauses. "I'm not in love with Elise Connor. I just think that my dad should date someone closer to his age. He's thirty years older than she is. Who the hell does he think he is?"

It is a ridiculous question, something she guesses he realizes as soon as these words are agitating the air between them.

"Will," she says. "Let's not talk about this right now."

"I'm not in love with her," he insists. "I can see why you'd think so, but I'm not. She's going to dump him as soon as she meets someone else. Someone closer to her age."

Like you, she thinks.

"Let your father worry about that," she says. "You know he's going to do whatever he wants." She pauses. "If you dislike him so much, why are you so worried about what he does?"

He hesitates. "I don't know. I just am."

"You need to sleep now. So do I."

"Kiss me," he says, and she does, reluctantly, but he doesn't pressure her to do more. She has almost never refused him. Before now, she hasn't wanted to. His hand reaches for hers under the sheet and she lets him hold it for a long time, even though she has told him that she can't sleep if any part of her body is touching his. She has been like this since her marriage, when from the first night they were together, her husband slept on his side of the bed and insisted that she sleep on hers.

In the morning she can see herself making eggs and reminding Will of his dental appointment in the late afternoon. She can see him looking at her with mild amusement, or else he will be distracted, the previous night's problems and controversies returning with the force of a blow. Like her ex-husband, he is unlikely ever to be happy. At least not as he is currently living, measuring his life against his father's, a man to whom only a tiny percentage of the population can reasonably compare themselves. The kind of fame Renn has achieved, Danielle realizes, is more or less a novelty. Before the camera's invention, before movies and TV, certainly before the Internet, fame was more local, less colossal. But Will's misery, she knows, would still be powerful, no matter which century he might have been born into. His father's life is an aberration; his gifts, his privileges, all of the possibilities to which he has access, also aberrant. In that moment, an hour after midnight, when she can hear some restless soul down on the street gunning a motorcycle, she does not know how either man can stand it.

CHAPTER 3

MEANINGFUL EXPERIENCE

Sometimes I don't know what to say when I'm wrong. It doesn't happen often, but when it does, I find myself no better equipped to handle it than the last time someone pointed out an error to me. The child was allergic to wheat, not milk. The prescription should have been a hundred milligrams, not eighty-five. I married the wrong man. I married the right man at the wrong time. I shouldn't have gotten married at all. One thing I do know, something I realized a year or so after the divorce, is that I should have gone back to my maiden name. I didn't do it at the time because I wanted the same name as my children. Perhaps I also wanted to inspire curiosity or jealousy, anything that might have required me to air my many virulent grievances, to offer my story as a cautionary tale.

For three years Renn, my ex-husband, kept trying to talk to me as if we were friends, to relieve his guilty conscience and prove to himself that I was doing fine, that Anna and Billy were fine too and one day we would all forgive him, but of course we wouldn't forget him. Renn and I are almost exactly the same age. His birthday is two weeks before mine; he was born in Evanston, Illinois, and I was born a few miles up the road in Lake Bluff. We met during our junior year at USC, and when a year and a half later I was accepted into UCLA's medical school and was about to finish that first caffeine-fueled semester with high marks, we decided to get married, which we did in downtown L.A. at the city hall, one of Renn's fraternity brothers and his girlfriend our witnesses. Renn was starting to get roles by then, ones that paid. He was twenty-two and very handsome and so naturally charming that if I had been a little smarter, I would have seen how impossible it would be to keep him from attracting the kind of friends, both male and female, with money and foreign cars and sailboats and, in one case, a private plane, who would tell him not to limit himself, to experience all that he could of life because who knew? Tomorrow he might die. Or even later that same day. What did anyone really know of fate? Carpe diem, gather ye rosebuds, etc. etc.

I hated fate, I told him more than once, barely able to tolerate these new, fashionably blasé friends who couldn't stand me, the inconvenient wife, either—capable medical student or no, I was heavy baggage. Fate was a con, a fool's game. There was only life, one day after the other. Then death, of course. Things happened, and no one could predict them. By then, I had seen hematomas in three-month-old babies. I had seen two-year-olds dying of leukemia while their mothers almost managed to overdose on barbiturates in the parking lot outside the hospital. We had an earthquake or two, gas shortages, bad air, wildfires, whales beaching themselves and dying three hundred miles up the coast. We also eventually had two perfectly healthy children, miraculous creatures that I couldn't and sometimes still can't believe Renn and I created out of nothing but two fifteen-minute acts in a darkened bedroom, an act repeated millions of times over throughout the country on any given day. We were hardly original in anything we did, but for a while it all felt so fraught and urgent and specific.

Today, December twelfth, would have been our thirtieth wedding anniversary. My daughter called this morning, sweetly apologetic but unable to resist saying that she had noticed this would-be milestone too. My son has not called, nor do I expect him to. He doesn't always remember my birthday, or his sister's, or his own, from what I can tell. Am I embarrassed or irritated with myself for continuing to observe, so to speak, the anniversary of my failed marriage? Not really. It is simply a fact of my life, like the myopia I have lived with since junior high, the knobby knees, the forgetful son.

"Dad's back in New Orleans," Anna informed me, even though I hadn't asked if she knew where he was. "He had to reshoot a couple of scenes for *Bourbon at Dusk*."

"I bet he's just thrilled about that. Have you seen him recently?"

"A few weeks ago," she said. "I thought I told you that he was in town for a couple of days before he went up to Seattle to visit the guy who's doing the sound track."

"Why didn't he hire a musician in New Orleans?"

"This guy is from Louisiana, I guess, but after Katrina, he moved to Seattle. I think he still has a place down there though." She paused. "When's the last time you talked to him?"

"I don't know. Over the summer, I suppose." I could hear strangers' voices in the background and wind hurling itself against Anna's phone. She was probably on break outside the hospital where she and her classmates are doing clinicals.

"Have you talked to Billy this week?" she asked.

"I called him a couple of days ago, but he hasn't called me back yet."

"He and Danielle broke up." She sounded embarrassed, as if she had something to do with it. Since childhood, she has had the unfortunate tendency of taking deeply to heart other people's mistakes or bad luck, but I suppose it is also this impulse that influenced her decision to become a doctor.

"Oh, no. Why? Was it his decision or hers?"

"Hers. He's such a bonehead."

I was very disappointed to hear this. From the beginning, I liked Danielle; she has always seemed honest and kind and not the type of person who wanted Billy only because of his money or his connection to his father's celebrity. At twenty-six, my son is still rudderless, and he worries me much more than his sister does. Anna is one semester away from graduating with her MD, and I couldn't be more proud of her if she had won the Boston marathon or the Nobel Prize. Her decision to go into family medicine rather than specialize in pediatrics or obstetrics or something a little more glamorous than country doctorhood was a bit surprising, but I'm flattered that she has chosen the same profession as mine. Thank God, in any case, that she didn't choose her father's. For a while, I thought for sure that she or Billy would.

"What happened?" I asked, ninety percent certain that it was my son's fault.

She hesitated. "I think he has a crush on the lead actress in Dad's movie. This girl named Elise Connor. You probably know who she is. Danielle found out, and what a surprise, she was upset and broke up with him. He had just asked her to move in with him too."

I know who Elise Connor is. Of course I do. In more than one flimsy, flashy magazine that I shouldn't notice, let alone pick up, I have seen her name linked with my ex-husband's. "Mrs. Ivins III," one columnist has dared to call her. "I see stars in these stars' eyes whenever they look at each other," the so-called journalist crowed. "Are those wedding bells I hear in the distance?"

Reading words like these, I don't feel the same acid surge of jealousy that I did up until four or five years ago, but I'd be lying if I said that they didn't bother me. She is a very young girl. Renn is not a young man. He is a fool, but actors usually are, their egos so fragile and enormous. How does Elise Connor feel about his egotism? Perhaps she doesn't care, accepting it as a hazard of the trade, or else she is still blind to it. She is less than half his age, and I feel a little sorry for him about this May–December cliché. Especially because it is hardly the first time.

None of the gossip columnists ever mention me in connection with Renn anymore, in part because I'm not famous, nor are our children, and of what interest am I, except to the fans who have researched him so thoroughly that they know more about him than most of his close friends do? Those people are out there, a dishearteningly large army of fanatics. I have met some of them, before and after the divorce. How do you live with the fact, peaceably or no, that your husband is an institution, a movement, a cult with numerous irrational adherents? I never quite figured out how. That we stayed married for almost fifteen years was, I have to admit, a miracle.

"Poor Billy," I finally managed to say. "I wish he knew how to be happier." Yet who really does? I wonder. I'm not sure if it's a skill that can be cultivated or a talent a person is born with. I often think it's the latter, having seen so many people who should be happy but aren't, and so many who should be miserable but are decisively the opposite.

"I know. I told him to start seeing his therapist again, but I don't know if he will."

"I wish he'd never gone to New Orleans to work with your father."

"Well, he did."

"Yes, he did."

In October, he was with Renn for too long on the set of *Bourbon Street*, or whatever he's calling it. *A Shot of Bourbon*, maybe? *Bourbon in Winter?* Some earnestly poetic name. My son is a grown man, free to come and go as he pleases, but sometimes I wish that Renn hadn't set up those trusts for our kids after the divorce. So much money, an unconscionable amount, really. Anna has been smart with hers, and although Will hasn't been a spendthrift, not that I can tell, he hasn't been able to find a career postcollege that he wants to pursue. Renn's guilt-stricken generosity has succeeded in robbing our son of any desire he might have had to establish himself in one field or another. But Anna, I have no doubt, will excel at medicine. Her patients, her staff, her community, will adore her. Eventually she will fall in love, marry, and probably have a child or two. She will be happy and will continue to be a source of joy for her father and me until we die. Regarding these predictions, I don't think anyone will ever turn to me, pretending sympathy, and tell me that I'm wrong.

"I've been thinking about where I want to do my residency," Anna said. "I think it should be at a hospital with an underserved population. I've thought about going down to New Orleans or Biloxi, but there are so many people in L.A. that need help too."

"Yes, that's true, but if the hospital doesn't have a lot of resources, you're not going to learn as much as you would in a place that's well funded."

"Actually, I think I could learn more."

"Maybe, but I doubt it. Don't decide on anything until you talk to me first. You have the medical centers at UCLA to choose from, and they're both excellent. Or you could apply to work at Cedars-Sinai with me."

"I know, Mom."

"If you really want to work with the poor, you should do it in L.A. Your friends and family are here."

"I'd make other friends."

"I have no doubt that you would."

"I want to live somewhere else at some point. I'm not going to stay here forever."

I hesitated. "No, I suppose you won't."

She has already traveled to so many places, so many different countries. Her father and I have both made sure of that. She has never been deprived of anything, which, I realize, some would say is a different kind of deprivation. What's life without the struggle? Without the hunger to accomplish the right things, those that will bring you the respect and admiration (and envy) of your peers? But I wonder this—if you don't have to struggle, why would you? I don't think too many of us would choose to take the harder route. We simply take it because that's the only one open to us. I realize the irony here—my own children serve as examples of people who haven't had to struggle in any kind of traditional sense. The one seems to be quite happy, but the other not so much.

I don't know what to say about Billy's inertia, which isn't a recent development—it has been with him since early adolescence. Since before Renn and I divorced, I suppose. Billy saw the divorce coming too. It's clear to me, having worked as a pediatrician for so many years, that most children are very perceptive, more so than their parents are. But I don't think the problems Renn and I had caused Billy's inertia. For one, Renn was often only home for two- and three-week stints, and even when he was with us, he came and went constantly. Scheduling a family dinner was akin to arranging for an audience with the pope, something I said once to Renn, which he thought was funny, even though I hadn't intended it to be. Our children didn't see us fighting very often because toward the end, they didn't see us together very much at all.

After Anna and I said good-bye, I called Billy. He didn't answer.

I tried him a second time an hour later. My call went into voice mail again. Now, at five thirty, when I'm done with appointments for the day (twenty-six patients, all crammed into seven hours, along with several phone calls), I take the 10 to the 405 and make it to Billy's place faster than I expect to during rush hour. I want to take him out for dinner. We haven't had a face-to-face conversation in several weeks, in part because he didn't come over for Thanksgiving this year. He told me that he had been invited to Danielle's mother's house and said that I could go with them, but I was hurt that he hadn't first asked me if I wanted them to come to my house before he agreed to go to Danielle's mother's. I told him that I had already bought a turkey and ordered two pumpkin pies. He apologized perfunctorily but didn't budge, and part of this intransigence, I realize now, was likely caused by his desire to appease Danielle, but then she broke up with him anyway. Anna and I celebrated without him, and she brought along Jill, whose parents were traveling in Europe, but it was still a subdued, almost somber, occasion without Billy, even though he isn't known for cracking jokes or playing the family clown. Anna and Billy's father was in Rome or maybe it was New York, both cities where he keeps apartments, but Anna couldn't take any days off from the hospital to spend the holiday with him, and Billy doesn't spend as much time with Renn as he used to. I hope this will change, but I'm not sure how or when it will.

The building where my son lives is all gleaming steel and mirrored glass, and it reminds me of a monstrous robot. Sometimes, to get a rise out of me, he calls his home Robotland. "If I live here long enough, maybe I'll turn into one too," he once said.

"That's not funny," I said, but laughed anyway.

The doorman, a young guy named Carlo ("Not Carlos," he said with a shy smile when he introduced himself to me last year) who is maybe twenty-one but already has two daughters whose pictures he has bashfully shown me more than once, calls upstairs when I get to the lobby because my plan is to ambush my son. If I called Billy again from my cell and told him that I'm downstairs, he wouldn't answer and he'd know not to answer the doorman's page either.

It still takes him several rings to respond to Carlo's call. "Good evening, Mr. Ivins," Carlo says when Billy finally picks up. "You have a visitor. Would you like me to send her up?"

I can't take a normal breath while my son responds.

"Your mother," says Carlo, nonchalant. "Is it all right for me to send her up?" He is a professional, graceful and charming, despite his young age.

Carlo says thank you and hangs up. He gives me a look of apology; his unlined face, almost hairless too, is very kind. His wife, I hope, adores him. "Mr. Ivins asked if you'd give him ten minutes."

"All right," I say gloomily. A son should not keep his mother waiting in the lobby. It both worries and annoys me—what is it that he wants to hide? If he needs a shower, I could sit in his living room and wait for him there. If empty beer or wine bottles are all over the place, or take-out containers, or cigarette butts, I could probably do a better job cleaning up than he would. If he has a woman up there who is not Danielle, so be it. He could at least introduce us. I know he wasn't expecting me, but I don't drop in on him unannounced very often.

Despite how pleasant Carlo is, I don't feel like making any more small talk. I go outside into the traffic noise and late-afternoon sun and make a phone call to a patient's father who left a message at my office earlier in the day. One of the reasons I love my profession, despite its occasional sorrows and nuisances, is that I like knowing things. I like being an expert on something in our crowded, chaotic world.

This man's child has asthma, one of several dozen cases that I have diagnosed in the last year. The air quality here is as bad as advertised and is particularly hard on new and old pairs of lungs. When this father asks what more he and his wife can do, I repeat the prescription from their recent office visit—the inhaler as needed, a healthy diet, enough sleep, moderate exercise. The child should, as much as possible, be allowed a normal life, with games and friends and horseplay, and parents can also consider moving somewhere with better air quality, which they won't or can't often do.

It is almost fifteen minutes before I can end the call and take the elevator up to Billy's apartment. Carlo smiles as I walk by. He is on the phone and buzzes me through the glass door that leads to the elevator bank. There are three elevators for this twenty-story building, and a freight elevator that goes down to the garage, one filled with Mercedes and Jaguars and BMWs. My son drives an Audi; Anna a Prius, though her first car was a white Corvette, one her father gave her when she turned sixteen. I asked Renn if he was kidding. Offended, he said, Why the hell do you think that? Anna is not a Corvette type of girl at all, I told him, but out of politeness mixed with embarrassed pride she drove this car for a year before trading it for a Sebring convertible, which lasted until the Prius. On Billy's sixteenth birthday, he was given a 1968 powder-blue Mustang. It really was beautiful, but I didn't tell Renn that I thought so. Billy drove it until he wrecked it during his sophomore year of college. Or rather, until his roommate wrecked it by driving into a row of parked cars while trying to send a text message or change the radio station or I'm not sure what—Billy never would give me a straight answer.

When I knock on his door, the hallway light tastefully muted, the walls vanilla-colored with their big abstract paintings by artists I don't know, it takes Billy several long seconds to answer. To my relief, he is dressed neatly—clean blue jeans and a red Polo shirt—but there are dark circles under his eyes and he needs a haircut, and if I'm being honest, he doesn't look very happy to see me. He seems barely capable of forcing a smile, and I feel both heartsick and angry.

"Come in, Mom. Sorry to make you wait," he mumbles. "I was on the phone." He looks thin, too thin, and in the foyer right by the door, I notice four pairs of running shoes lined up along the wall, all new. Billy ran track in high school, but he wasn't one of the team's stars. In college he didn't play any sports, except intramural soccer and pickup basketball.

His place is tidy, more or less, though it looks like the cleaning lady is due for a visit soon—from the light of a nearby lamp, I can see dust on the window ledges in the living room where I sit on one end of the sofa and Billy on the other. The sofa is brown leather and not particularly comfortable, but it looks stylish and expensive, which it is. All of his furniture is from a Danish design showroom, one where he worked for a few months as a salesperson before growing bored. Sofas aren't my thing, he claimed. What is your thing? I wanted to know. I'll tell you when I find it, was his response, his look both defiant and sad.

"So Anna told you?" he says quietly.

I study his face for a second or two. He really does look exhausted. He must not be sleeping very well. I could write him a prescription for Valium, two or three milligrams, nothing too serious, but I am not in the habit of offering my children or friends drugs, even if some of the latter have asked for them over the years. Los Angeles is a city filled with highly and creatively medicated people. Though I suppose most cities are. I suppose this is how city dwellers keep pace or set the pace or set the traps that catch the biggest monsters.

I decide not to take his gloomy mood head-on. "Told me about—?"

"Danielle. We broke up last weekend."

"She did mention it, and I was very sorry to hear this."

"Yeah, well, I guess it was bound to happen sooner or later."

"Why do you say that?"

He shakes his head. "Not many relationships work out. Why should this one?"

"Billy, that's not a good attitude."

"You should talk," he says.

I stare at him. "Why? Because your father and I got a divorce? We were together for fifteen years, remember."

"Barely."

"We were together until the divorce."

He turns his head away, and in this mulish slant, I can see Renn in him very clearly, his old attitude of surly silence, his conviction that he had been wronged, despite the fact that he was the one who was always going off somewhere interesting while I stayed home with our children and my patients and hospital protocols and myriad resentments. Renn was making so much money by the time both of our kids were out of diapers that some of my friends thought that I should have been able to live with his absences, because weren't we set for life? I didn't have to work if I didn't want to, right? Renn had paid off my med school loans by writing two separate checks, and what, realistically, did I have to complain about? What a gorgeous home we had, what healthy, pretty children, what nice clothes/cars/crystal/linens/curtains/pool furniture. Not to mention, I had a movie-star husband. And after a few years, didn't all married couples lose interest in each other sexually anyway? Just why was I in such a rotten mood all the time?

"Okay. You were together," he says, still not looking at me.

"Let me take you to dinner," I say, suddenly very tired and feeling as if I might start crying. An oppressive malaise hovers around us like smoke. It doesn't help that almost no lights are on. His unhappiness makes me feel both lonely and worried for him. No mother, no matter her children's ages, ever stops fearing that they will somehow come to harm.

He shakes his head. "No thanks. I already ate."

It's only six thirty, and I'm certain that he's lying. "Come out with me anyway. There's a Thai place a few blocks from here that I like."

He doesn't reply.

I hesitate, but then I say it. "Come on. Today's a special occasion."

He regards me, only slightly interested. "What is it?"

"Your father and I have now been divorced for as long as we were married," I say. "It was thirty years ago today that we said 'I do.'" I know that I'm being ridiculous, that Billy will find this fact and the occasion I have made of it ironic and possibly perverse, but nothing's right with him tonight.

"Wow. Alert the media."

"Oh, Billy."

"What? Congratulations to you and Dad. Many happy returns."

"Can we talk a little about what happened with you and Danielle?"

He shakes his head. "No. I'd rather not."

"Maybe you'll feel better if you do."

"I feel fine."

"Let's go to dinner," I say. When I stand up, the sofa groans in a voice that sounds almost human.

Billy exhales. "Mom, I don't want to go out."

"Should we order in?"

"I told you that I already ate."

"It doesn't look like it. How much weight have you lost since I saw you at Halloween?"

"I don't know. A couple of pounds maybe."

"Are you doing a lot of running? I saw several pairs of shoes on my way in."

"I'm training for a marathon."

I look at him, wondering if he really means this, if he will see this project through to some favorable outcome. "Good, but you need to eat if you're going for long runs."

"Jesus. You sound like Danielle."

I don't say anything. I know that I should leave him alone, that my visit hasn't done anything but upset him. But I go ahead and make it worse. "I'm going to order you a subscription to *Gourmet* and *Bon Appétit*," I say. "Why don't you learn how to cook? You have the time."

He stares at me, and then he laughs. "Why don't I learn how to cook? Why don't I learn how to fly too while I'm at it? And why don't I learn how to drag race? When I'm done with that, I'll find the cure for cancer and bring you to the White House with me when the president throws a banquet in my honor."

I can feel my face burning. "I'm not sure about those other things, but cooking can sometimes be a meaningful experience."

"How do you know? You don't cook."

"Yes, I do. A lot more than I used to."

"Then why didn't you go home after work and cook yourself an anniversary dinner instead of coming over here?"

"All right," I say. "I'll leave. You can starve yourself some more if you don't want to have dinner with me. Try running a marathon on an empty stomach and see how that goes."

"God, Mom, don't be so fucking melodramatic." He says these words with such derision that I almost slap him, something I haven't done in at least ten years. He knows I'm angry too. He gives me a look that I remember well from his adolescence, one somewhere between condescension and defiance. *How pathetic you are*, his eyes would say. *How above all of this I am. You and Dad are the ones acting like children, not me.*

At the door, we make only glancing eye contact and don't embrace. Before I have taken more than a step into the corridor, he shuts the door firmly behind me.

By the time I get into the elevator, furious and chagrined, all of the old resentments that used to plague me have resurfaced. Most of them, I eventually realized, were directed more toward Renn than at our children, no matter how badly Anna and Billy were frustrating or infuriating me. For at least a year after Renn left, I hated him. It was a corrosive, implacable hatred, the kind that leads tyrants to burn down enemies' villages, to maim and destroy. I said some very stupid things about him in front of our children, things that I'm pretty sure they remember. One of the ironies of the whole ugly show, however, was that by the time he left me to marry Melinda Byers, a woman whose life, as far as I can tell, has amounted to very little, I didn't want to be married to him anymore, but I also knew that not being married to him was likely to feel worse.

In the empty elevator, I let out a small scream. Then I let out a second that leads to a third, and when the door opens on the first floor, the three people waiting to step on all give me strange looks. I lower my eyes and walk past them quickly, my face a garish red by now, I'm sure. In the lobby, Carlo is listening to a radio that he abruptly turns down when I push open the glass door, but I hear enough to know that the song is an old one by the Rolling Stones, Jagger's lascivious wail recognizable in the few notes that reach me before Carlo lowers the volume.

"You don't have to turn it down," I say, though I can't bear to meet his eyes, knowing he will see how upset I am. When he starts talking, I keep moving toward the front doors. "I have to go," I say softly, embarrassed. "Sorry to be in such a rush, Carlo. Have a good night."

"Don't apologize. You're a doctor," he calls after me, as if delighted by this fact. "I know you're busy!"

When I think about it later, after I eat a peanut butter sandwich at home for dinner and drink two glasses of white wine so fast I get the hiccups, I realize that I don't remember the drive back from Billy's very well. Did I listen to the radio? I don't think I did. Was there a lot of traffic between his place and mine? There must have been, but this I don't really remember either. I do know that my phone didn't ring, but I kept hoping that it would. I wanted my son to call and apologize. I wanted him to tell me what happened with Danielle, and if it's true that he has a crush on Elise Connor, and whether or not his father really is serious about this girl. I could call Renn myself and ask him, but I don't. Even if he is likely to pick up my call and would tell me whatever I want to know. I don't think he's ever considered me an enemy, though he must have known that I once considered him to be the worst of my life.

One thing that helped me get past most of my jealousy and rage over our divorce is that his marriage to Melinda (whom he met on the set—but she was a caterer, not a costar) also failed. This does not make me look particularly noble, I know, but being left for another woman isn't something most wives can forget. Our marriage began to exhaust me once people started to recognize him everywhere we went, after he became famous enough that paparazzi sometimes lurked outside the gate at the end of our driveway, but I was not ready to give up. Still, it was clear that a marriage that lasts does not have the rest of the world pressing in on it; it does not have fanatics or floozies feverishly hoping to catch a glimpse of one of the principals, to touch his hand or whatever other part of him they can reach. A marriage that lasts does not feature one of the principals being paid to simulate sex on camera with someone young and very attractive, which is impossible for the other principal to get used to because this movie sex looks real and therefore it must feel real to the couple being filmed. A marriage that lasts does not have the aura of a siege, of a boat being rocked so hard I felt almost permanently ill. I knew I would lose him; I think I knew this very early on, but it wasn't something I let myself say to anyone, and I tried never to say it to myself either.

After my sandwich, after the news and an unsuccessful attempt to read a book by a surgeon who is also a skillful writer, I call my son. He doesn't answer. I call him ten minutes later and still no response. After another twenty minutes, I call again and this time he picks up.

"What now," he says.

For a half second, I think about hanging up, but it is such a desperately childish move that I manage to quell the impulse. In any case, I don't hang up on people anymore. I don't want him to be mad at me for the rest of the night either. He was angry enough with me while growing up, even though his father was the one who left. "I'm sorry that I stopped by unexpectedly today," I say.

I can hear him exhale. "You don't have to apologize, Mom."

"I didn't mean to put you on the spot about Danielle."

"It's understandable that you'd want to know what happened."

I don't answer, waiting for him to say more.

"What did you call for, Lucy?" he says.

I bristle. I don't like it when he uses my first name because it sometimes sounds like he's spitting it out. "To apologize," I say.

"Okay, thanks. Apology accepted."

"Maybe you could apologize to me too."

He laughs in a short, caustic burst. "Are you serious?"

I'm botching this now as badly as I botched the visit. It's almost as if I'm observing someone who looks exactly like me, and I want to shake her and tell her to stop. But I'm also so angry that my head is aching, something I've been ignoring since leaving his place three hours earlier. "Never mind. Forget I said that."

"I have to go now," he says, flatly. "I have someone on the other line."

Before I have a chance to respond, he hangs up. In the few seconds of silence before the beeping begins, I pretend he's still there. "I know you're unhappy," I say, "but that doesn't mean you have the right to treat other people like trash."

It has always been a little disorienting that my personal and professional lives are defined by serious disparities. At the hospital or in the clinic where I take appointments, I am the brisk, competent Dr. Ivins who almost always commands other people's respect. Outside of work, of course, it's very different—I am only another driver on the car-choked freeways, another impatient person in line at the grocery store; I am someone's mother, tolerable to my children most of the time but still a cross to bear. I am also a famous man's ex-wife, the one he left for someone younger and less educated. I have a bad temper; I have fears and grave insecurities. I want always to be right, to have the last word, to be respected and obeyed without question. Some days it takes all of my self-discipline to force myself out of the house. Some days I am almost speechless from regret or loneliness or anger over nothing that I can clearly articulate. Some days I eat nothing but cookies for breakfast and potato chips for lunch. Too often, I get more satisfaction than I should from other people's disappointments. It is hard to dispute the evidence that we are a race defined to a significant degree by our pettiness, by how vicious our desire is to keep track, to compare, to win.

My phone doesn't ring for the rest of the night, and although there are people I could call, I don't. Thirty years ago, my children hadn't yet been born, nor did I know for sure that I would become a mother. Renn and I were twenty-two, in love, talented in our different ways. A movie star had just become our president. We assumed that we were bound for greatness too, and one of us, I guess, really was. Our children, we assumed—still assume—might also be bound for greatness. It is possible that Billy's unhappiness will end tomorrow. That he will find something to do with his life that fills him with joyful suspense. I'm still going to order him those cooking magazines. He will probably throw them away, but maybe he won't. Maybe he'll look through one of them and decide that he wants to open a restaurant or wait tables or chop vegetables for a while, maybe long enough for it to become a career. If he wants to run marathons, he can. If he wants to brood and resent me and the rest of the world, I can put up with this for a little while longer, but after a point, it will have to stop, or else these feelings will define his life, and the thought of this bothers me greatly.

Because his life is extraordinary. He has already had so many experiences most of us will never have. He has met some of the most interesting people in the world, and on more than one occasion he has shaken the hands of the leaders of foreign countries, those who invited his father to dine in their mansions while he was in their countries promoting his movies. Billy has seen the Nile, the Alps, the Taj Mahal, the Great Wall of China, the Himalayas, most of the major cities in the U.S. and many elsewhere too. For a while I was jealous of all that his father could offer him and Anna—such remarkable experiences that I would never have been able to produce for them, let alone participate in. I have assumed since they were very small children that their lives would both be better, more momentous, than my own. I don't know if all parents want this for their children. Many seem to. I'm not sure if I'm one of them, though. I want my own life to be as momentous as theirs, maybe even more so. I don't think this is wrong—I am simply being honest. If we work hard enough, we should all be able to achieve lasting contentment. Billy's bitterness and lingering inertia in the face of his astounding good fortune aren't really surprising. But they are disappointing. Even when he acts graceless and unkind, however, I don't wish him ill. What kind of mother would wish that on her child?

CHAPTER 4

THE FINEST MEDICAL ATTENTION

Anna has two close friends, Celestine and Jill, women she has known since childhood, the three of them from families with live-in housekeepers and feuding parents and assorted, neglected pets. They have gone through periods of intense closeness as well as bouts of jealous competition, which, in one case, resulted in Jill not speaking to Celestine for almost a year because Celestine began dating Jill's ex-boyfriend two days after he had broken up with her.

It is Celestine's and Jill's lives that often have the air of a siege, not Anna's, at least as she perceives their confessions and self-mocking admissions. Both of her friends are prone to spending too much money on clothes they might wear only once, to dating more than one man at a time, and to having sex with their bosses, or even, in one case, a boss's wife. They confide in Anna often, despite how busy she has been with medical school over the past four years, how tired but often exhilarated she feels when she's at the hospital, following around the attending physicians she and the other fourth-year students have been assigned to. Dr. Glass, one of the attendings for her internal medicine rotations, is her favorite. She guesses that he is in his mid-forties, though he looks younger, his face turning especially boyish when he smiles. His credentials make it clear, however, that he has been out of medical school for close to twenty years.

She began working with him in the spring of her third year, when clinical rotations began, and now, a year later, with her coursework finally finished and a full-time summer residency under way, she is with him for nine or ten hours at a time, five days a week, unless he alternates with the other attendings she has been assigned to for the internal medicine rotation, Dr. Fitch and Dr. Kaczmerski, who are older and often humorless. Dr. Fitch also has a wandering eye and on some days, bad breath; Dr. Kaczmerski snaps when he is impatient and favors the male interns.

"The hospital is full of the busiest, most important people in the world," Anna has joked to Jill and Celestine. "Nowhere else on the planet is anyone's work as important."

"If you start acting like your bosses," Jill said, "we'll have to kill you."

Anna laughed. "You can't kill me. I'm too important. You'd have to call it an assassination."

But Dr. Glass is not, as Anna has told her friends, a stuffed shirt. He is thoughtful and handsome, and his temper doesn't fray easily. "I have a long temper," he said soon after they started working together. "But that doesn't mean I never get mad. I just prefer to handle problems without a flare-up. My expectations are that you will also be on your best behavior and do the most rigorous work you have done so far in medical science."

Two weeks into her summer rotation, Anna realizes that she thinks about him more often than anyone else in or outside of the hospital, and twice she has had dreams about him, both leaving her with a sexual ache that lasted for an entire day. When she is choosing a carton of strawberries at Von's or deciding which blouse to wear or else lying restless in bed despite how exhausted her body is, she finds that her mind is running a series of impressions and images that all feature Dr. Glass. She sees his curly black hair, which he had cut very short the week her summer rotation began, his newly shorn head alarming her for days. The curls had suited him, and their removal had struck her as too aggressive, as if instead he had cut off an ear or a finger. More than once she has pictured the clipped curls being swept from a salon floor and dumped without ceremony into a trashcan, his hair forced to commingle with strangers' clippings, this anonymous intimacy oddly troubling to Anna. There is silver visible on his head now, these strands spikier than the dark brown ones. Many times she has wondered what he would do if she reached up to touch one of these bristling hairs. She thinks that he likes her too, not necessarily in the same way that she likes him, but he seems to keep his gaze on her longer than on any of her classmates. And every morning when she presents herself to him, his face changes a little, as if someone has opened the blinds in a room dark with night.

But he isn't free. He has a wife and two sons, both of them teenagers, one a soccer player, the other a talented pianist. He rarely talks about his personal life, but with all the time she and the other students in her rotation spend with him, they do sometimes speak about their lives outside of the hospital. He has only mentioned his wife once, to say that she had asked him to pick up a dozen quail's eggs for a dinner party, and did anyone know where he might find a store that sold them? Jim Lewin knew, because, in part, he knew everything. Anna did not know where to buy quail's eggs and couldn't imagine what Dr. Glass's wife planned to do with them. She went home that night and looked them up on the web and found two stores that sold them, both within an eight-mile drive of the medical center. She sent an e-mail to Dr. Glass with the store names and addresses, but he didn't respond, not even to thank her, until an entire week had passed. In the days preceding his belated thank-you, she hadn't dared to ask if he had received her message.

The quail eggs had come up in the spring of Anna's fourth year during a six-week internal medicine rotation—six whole weeks with Dr. Glass Monday through Thursday and Dr. Fitch on Friday and Saturday. Dr. Kaczmerski hadn't yet been assigned to her group. After this rotation, she spent four weeks in ob-gyn, her attending Dr. Hlvacek, who was from Bratislava, but at twenty-one had moved to Boston to study medicine at Tufts—fiercely homesick and barely proficient in English, she had confided to Anna with a sheepish smile. Her English was now nearly flawless, and she was also beautiful, but not, it seemed, overly preoccupied with the power this beauty imparted her. Anna often caught herself wondering if Dr. Glass had a crush on Dr. Hlvacek, as most of the male doctors whose paths they crossed seemed to. When they discussed Anna's performance on the last day of her obstetrics rotation, Dr. Hlvacek had startled her by saying, "What is the expression? A double threat, brains and beauty? Whatever it is, you will be just fine, Dr. Ivins. I am sure of this." For days afterward, Anna had replayed Dr. Hlvacek's words in her head, not certain if she was more happy to be called pretty than intelligent, though she knew which one she should value more.

Her family and friends are impressed that Anna is studying to become a doctor, but on the phone, when her father called her after the

Cannes festival, where *Bourbon at Dusk* had done well but the Palme d'Or had gone to *Ten Pretty Girls*, an Israeli film about a child prostitution ring, he asked if she was sure that she wanted to make a career out of giving people bad news. She couldn't tell if he was kidding, knowing that he has bragged many times to his friends and acquaintances about her chosen career.

"Most of the bad news is given by specialists," she told him. "Potentially serious problems get farmed out."

"But won't you get tired of doing immunizations and physicals?"

"I don't think so. They'll be a relief because I'll have to do other things like lancing boils and stitching split lips." She laughed. "No, seriously, what I want is to have real relationships with my patients, like a lot of doctors used to before the insurance companies took over and made everything so bureaucratic."

"Those insurance companies are your bread and butter," he said. "Or they would be if it weren't for, well, if it weren't for me."

If Dr. Glass knows who her father is, he isn't interested, or else he refuses to show it. She can't see him asking her the usual questions: What was it like to grow up with a movie star as your father? Why didn't you go into acting too? Or did you and it didn't work out? Which of his movies is your favorite? Is he a decent guy? For real? Come on, you can tell me.

She does know that Dr. Glass likes movies, that he sees them when he has time, though he has said that he stays away from films about doctors because they often contain errors, or else some important element in them has been altered in order to keep a mainstream audience happy. "Contrary to what Hollywood might tell us, there are no perfect doctors," Anna remembers him saying the day he appeared at work with his very short new haircut. "Just like there are no perfect people. You'll make mistakes; everyone does. Thankfully, most of them can be corrected. Your duty, however, is not to make the same mistake twice."

"What if we do make the same mistake twice?" asked Jim Lewin, who, despite having the highest grade-point average in the class, had confounded many of his professors and classmates by declaring, like Anna and a dozen or so others, a family medicine concentration rather than a specialization like oncology or neurology.

"You could lose your malpractice insurance," said Dr. Glass. "Because you're likely to get sued, if you haven't been already. Small mistakes. Those are the kind you want to make."

"I don't want to make any, big or small," said Jim.

"Of course you don't. No one does. That's the spirit, Dr. Lewin." Dr. Glass looked at Anna and smiled. "What about you, Dr. Ivins? Are you planning to make any mistakes?"

She hesitated. "No, but I probably will. I keep wanting to knock on wood, but I'd feel embarrassed if anyone saw me."

Dr. Glass shook his head, still smiling. "You're superstitious. Almost every new doctor is. A lot of older doctors are too."

She felt her face redden. "I wish that I weren't."

"It's perfectly normal. We know how fast things can change for any one of us. Aneurysms, heart attacks, strokes—they happen to healthy people too."

"We have such a hard job," said Jim, his brown-eyed gaze unnerving in its directness. His upper lip was sweating, something that happened whenever he was excited, which seemed to be most of the time. For the first two years of medical school he had had a crush on Anna but had never found the nerve to ask her out. She is glad that he didn't because she would have said no and felt bad about it. She does not find him attractive, despite his pleasant face and lean, tall body. If he weren't so earnest and so intent on knowing all of the answers, she is sure that he would do better with the available women in their class.

Dr. Glass regarded him. "Yes, we do, and not everyone can handle it. You'll know a lot more about yourself by the end of the summer."

The first time her path crosses his outside of the hospital is pure coincidence. She is walking past a sandwich shop in Marina del Rey after visiting Jill at her new apartment, her friend having moved from North Hollywood where she had lived since college because, she said, only half joking, that she had used up all of the interesting straight men there. Her new place has a view of the Pacific and is so pleasant and spacious that for a few minutes Anna thought about looking at a unit for sale on another floor, but the effort required to move when she is already so busy makes the idea too daunting. Dr. Glass is sitting by himself at an outdoor table, eating a salad and reading a book, one whose title she can't see. She isn't sure if she should bother him and timidly turns her face away, but he looks up at the same moment and calls her name. Her heart begins to beat so forcefully that she wonders if he will see it pounding beneath the thin fabric of her blouse. With her denim miniskirt and hair in two long ponytails, she knows that she doesn't look professional. She suspects that she might even look silly, hardly a woman to take seriously, let alone to entrust anyone's life to. At the hospital she always gathers her light brown hair, which is the same color as her father's and as thick, into a bun.

"I didn't know you lived in the Marina," says Dr. Glass, motioning for her to sit down. He is wearing a pale green cotton shirt, a color that suits him. His hair is starting to grow out too, and with his dark stubble and wire-rimmed glasses, he looks especially hand-some.

"I don't, but I have a friend who just moved here. She wanted to be close to the beach, and she doesn't mind the crowds." She sits in the chair across from him, careful to pull her skirt down as far as it will go, but it stays well above her knees, one of which has a blue-green bruise the size of a quarter.

"But you do?"

Anna nods. "I like it quiet when I'm home. There are too many cars here anyway. It took me fifteen minutes to find a parking spot."

"There are too many cars everywhere."

She smiles. "That's true."

"Where do you live, if not here?" he asks, dabbing at his mouth with a napkin. His salad is only half eaten, and she realizes later that he didn't eat any more of it while they were talking. She wonders if he worried about looking graceless, as she does when she eats, es-pecially on first dates.

"Silver Lake."

"Do you own your own place?"

"Yes. For a few years now."

"Any roommates?"

She shakes her head. "I rent out the first floor to someone be-cause it's a big house, but she's a tenant, not a friend."

He smiles and shakes his head. "Sorry for all of the questions. I'm not usually so nosy."

"You can ask me anything you'd like to," she says, then looks down, embarrassed by her brashness. It is as if she has never before talked to a man she finds attractive. She doesn't quite understand why Dr. Glass affects her as he does, especially in view of her many inter-actions with her father's glamorous friends—some of them among the most accomplished, and the most handsome, actors in the world.

"You're going to be an excellent doctor, Anna," says Dr. Glass.

"Do you really think so?" she asks, blushing. "I'm trying to learn everything I can, but it still feels like I'll never know enough."

"You're already very good, and I don't say that about everyone."

"Jim's better than I am," she says, then cringes inwardly.

He shakes his head. "He's different, not better."

"He notices everything."

"That won't always be the case. But he is very bright. There are plenty of more experienced doctors out there who aren't as sharp as you two."

She wonders if he will remember this conversation later and wish that he hadn't been so frank. She has no idea if he is flirting or simply being indiscreet. She glances at the hand that rests next to his water glass and sees his platinum wedding band, an intricate ivy pattern etched onto it. "I should let you get back to your lunch," she says.

"No, no, please stay as long as you'd like to. You're not interrupting me. It's nice to see you outside of the hospital." He pauses. "I know it was a while ago, but I want to thank you again for sending that e-mail about the quail's eggs. I felt bad about not replying sooner. I didn't end up needing them. All my wife talked about for a week were those ridiculous eggs, and then at the last minute, she changed her mind."

She looks at him, surprised. "Really? If you need them in the future, at least you'll know where to go now."

"I don't think we will. No more dinner parties, at least not for a while, if I have my way. They're always much more disappointing and expensive than my wife thinks they'll be."

"I've only hosted one. It was small, but it was still a lot of work."

"I'd rather just go to a restaurant." He smiles, motioning to his plate. "I guess that's obvious."

"I should let you finish your salad," she says and stands up, wondering if he will see the bruise on her knee. The sudden wild thought arrives: Will he think that she got it during sex? She doesn't remember how it happened, but it wasn't from sex. She hasn't slept with anyone in four months, since an ex-boyfriend visited from Tucson. Because they were both single, she let him stay with her while he was in town for a conference. During medical school, it has been hard to find time to date, and aside from her classmates, many of whom are already attached, she meets so few men she would consider dating. Her mother and brother, both unhappily single, wonder why she doesn't complain more about not having a boyfriend; what she doesn't tell them is that she misses having a sex life but not the effort of keeping a relationship from going flat and finding the time and space for a boyfriend in her already crowded life.

Dr. Glass is the first man in a while to whom she has had an immediate visceral response, but the ethics of their situation are undebatable: a professional relationship, nothing else. Even a platonic friendship outside of the hospital would be frowned upon, at least while she is still his intern.

"You were the only one in your group who suggested that the zoster virus Grace Whiting is suffering from might be a sign that her breast cancer is out of remission. Not everyone remembers this possibility."

She smiles, her eyes on the table. The pleasure of his praise is almost unbearable. And her competitiveness shames her; she hadn't realized before today just how much it bothered her that Jim Lewin is considered more of a star student than she is. "I hope I'm wrong, for Mrs. Whiting's sake," she murmurs.

"I do too, but what's most important is that you thought of it. I ordered some tests, and we'll know more in a couple of days."

She glances toward the street where a group of shirtless boys in swim trunks are walking noisily by. She would like very much to stay with Dr. Glass for a while longer, but she can't believe that he truly wants her company. There is also the chance that his wife and sons will ambush them, and that he will act like it is the most ordinary thing in the world for him to be sitting at a restaurant with one of his young interns, a woman who also happens to have a crush on him, something he must sense. Something his wife would also be likely to sense. Oh, and by the way, did Mrs. Glass know that the intern's father is Renn Ivins, the movie star? though Anna and Dr. Glass have never discussed this. She does not want her father's shadow to intrude on this private area of her life, this guilty but sexy possibility, at least not until she gets to know Dr. Glass better, if she will be given the chance.

And it seems likely that she will be. When she has made up her mind not to linger any longer, he smiles and says in a light tone, "I'm here at this time on most Sundays. You have an open invitation to join me whenever you're in the neighborhood." He extends his hand and she grasps it, realizing that this is the first time they have made a point of touching each other, aside from the day they met when they also shook hands. Her palm keeps tingling as she walks to her car, and she nearly forgets where she parked it. It is as if she is in ninth grade again and has just received the first love letter of her life.

On the drive home, she thinks of calling Jill and Celestine, but she knows that they would both tell her to accept his invitation and whatever it implies. *Go next Sunday and the Sunday after that. He wants you. Of course he does! Why else would he ask you? If you won't go, I'll go in your place. Especially if he's as cute as you say.* Both of her friends have always been a step ahead of her, both having lost their virginity at fifteen, almost three years before Anna did, both pressuring her to loosen up and do it too—what was she waiting for? It was the best thing ever! Obviously she had no clue, otherwise she wouldn't be sitting around with her legs crossed morning and night. But Anna knew, even then, that neither of them were necessarily happier after sleeping with boys who went on to snicker with other boys about what they had done, Jill angrily defiant about the rumors until she learned to ignore them. Celestine, however, had trouble ignoring them; it was easier to humiliate her, her Catholic mother having indoctrinated her from a very young age with the directive that nice girls don't. Jill's response to this had long been: Nice girls do but don't admit it.

By the time Anna walks through her front door, she has already imagined him leaving his wife for her, introducing her to his surly sons, whom she will quickly win over because her father is a movie star. She can see herself giving up her earlier intention to do a residency in some dangerous and impoverished area of the L.A. sprawl because she does not want to risk being killed or assaulted if she has him to come home to at night. She remembers something her mother once said about Anna's father during the divorce proceedings, that the brain shrinks to the size of a walnut when sex is in the equation, which, incidentally, is about the size of quite a few animal brains. "Your father can't think properly because he's forfeited most of his brain cells. He wants to keep them from getting in the way of his dick." At the time, Anna was angry with her mother but also unsure if she really understood the insult. She had just turned eleven, and when she later repeated their mother's words to her brother, he had looked at her and said, "She's right, but so what? Men are supposed to think with their dicks." He was twelve, and it wasn't until several years later that she realized how cynical his response was. She didn't believe that she shared his cynicism, but having been raised by the same parents who had conferred to them many of the same genes, she wasn't sure how this could be possible. It wasn't until medical school that she finally understood how his moodiness, his air of aggrievement and difficulty in yielding to any potentially joyful impulse, were not qualities that she also possessed, ones simply waiting for the proper conditions to express themselves.

The week following their encounter is her last under Dr. Glass's tutelage until September, and during the five days that he mentors her and her classmates from seven thirty to five, he says nothing about their encounter in Marina del Rey. He treats her no differently than usual, and she feels alternately disappointed and relieved. He is married, she reminds herself. But in the next moment she can't believe that his invitation was innocent. All week she goes back and forth with her silent, fruitless attempts to determine the definitive reason for his behavior on Sunday. But like baffling symptoms that refuse to yield to a diagnosis, his motives are indiscernible. It is also possible that he didn't know what he was up to that day either.

Some of the patients she sees during the last week with Dr. Glass before she moves to an ICU rotation—*just before,* she will come to think of this time of self-recrimination and agonizing anticipation— have embarrassing, messy afflictions. One of them, a Slovenian man in his late fifties, is suffering from what tests will soon reveal to be advanced colon cancer, and Anna and her classmates must examine him, despite the fact his ailing body exudes an odor worse than anything she has come across in her life. She has to try very hard not to gag when she stands close to him, and one of her classmates actually does gag—not Jim Lewin, but Anna thinks she sees tears of pained restraint in his eyes when he gently palpates the man's abdomen, trying not to cause him more anxiety or suffering.

The man of Sunday's flirtation seems very remote when they are examining the sickest patients, and Anna views him in the same light that she often perceives her father when watching one of his films—at a distance, almost as a doppelganger, someone who looks intensely familiar but is unapproachable. She thinks that he couldn't possibly have been serious about the invitation to see him again in Marina del Rey, and in her disappointment over this realization, she understands that she has already made up her mind to meet him.

"Grace Whiting's cancer is still in remission," Dr. Glass tells her after she sits down across from him at the same table as the previous week, self-conscious in her pale pink sundress and a strand of small, flawless pearls, a gift from her mother on her twenty-first birthday. She feels overdressed, which she knew would probably happen, but the dress is her favorite and she has only worn it once before today. Everyone else is in shorts and T-shirts, or short skirts like the one she wore last week, but Dr. Glass is wearing a cornflower blue linen shirt and pressed khaki pants. It seems that he too has made an effort.

"I'm so glad to hear that," she says. "I've been wondering what happened with the tests you ordered last week." In fact, Grace Whiting had slipped her mind, neither she nor Dr. Glass mentioning her case during the past week. Like her father, it seems that she too is susceptible to the walnut-brain phenomenon.

"Her T-cell count was normal and her lymph nodes were clear. I think she'll be fine. Her immune system is probably still a little worn down from the chemo last winter. The trick is not to let her get addicted to the painkillers we prescribed." He gives her a sheepish smile. "I need to stop teaching, don't I. We're off the clock."

"It's okay," she says, though she already knows the things he has just told her. "I'm so happy that you think she'll be fine." She sips from her iced tea, which is weak and too warm, but she doesn't want to complain at the register and ask for a new one.

"Were you visiting your friend again today?"

"Yes," she lies. "But I remembered on my way to the car that you said you'd probably be here." Her palms are sweating, and her underarms, though it is a perfect day—seventy-two degrees and a blinding blue sky.

"Next week if you're free, why don't you let me take you to lunch? We don't have to meet here. If you like seafood, there's a nice little place a couple of blocks away. Or we could meet somewhere closer to you. I like Silver Lake. It has a couple of bookstores that I used to go to before I had kids and still had time to read."

"You were reading last week when I saw you here." She cannot quite believe that he has just asked her on a date. She feels her heartbeat accelerate. *Tachycardia*, she thinks, the technical term for her condition there without prompting.

"That's true. I was. Do you like Bellow too? I don't like his later books as much as his early ones. *Ravelstein* wasn't as good as I'd hoped. He never could beat *Augie March*, which he wrote when he was still in his thirties. I think he must have known he'd never do better, though *Humboldt's Gift* is very good and Mr. *Sammler's Planet* is too, but it isn't really much of a story. Bellow probably thought of himself as a philosopher as much as a novelist."

"I've only read *Seize the Day* and *Herzog*."

Dr. Glass nods. "That's more than most people. Did you like them?"

"I did, but it's been a few years. I don't know how well I remember them."

He regards her, a small smile on his lips, ones she has thought countless times about kissing in the past week. "So, Dr. Ivins, how about lunch next week? We can talk some more about books. No work chitchat, I promise."

"I don't mind talking about work," she says, nervousness like a weight in her stomach. "I think lunch would be nice. If you really do want to come to Silver Lake, there's a good Indian place near my house. Or I could come out here again."

"I'll come to you. Sunday's the one day a week that I'm usually a free man. My sons are out with their friends, and my wife goes to see her parents."

She wonders if he has done this before. If he is serially unfaithful—each year a new intern? Is it something his wife knows about but chooses to ignore because she thinks she is lucky to have married a doctor, one whose earnings have made a certain type of lifestyle possible, one that offers other benefits if not marital fidelity? Or is she a doctor too and busy working with her own interns, having her own affairs? Anna has no idea what Mrs. Glass does, if anything, for a career.

What does she really know of marriage anyway, other than her parents' flawed one, where so often in the years leading up to the divorce she witnessed her mother's abject fury, her sorrow and fierce sense of personal affront? And then her father's subsequent marriage: even more disastrous, his second wife a more or less well-meaning and kind person but so cowed by Anna's father's whims and will that after a while, Anna realized that they had probably been doomed to divorce from day one. She knows there must be unorthodox marriages that work, arrangements, tacit or no, where one or both parties are permitted to take lovers. The trick, she suspects, is discretion, no flaunting, no sloppily covered tracks. *Don't ask and I won't tell*—this has to be how it's done.

Nonetheless, the fact that she is considering any of this, she who has only slept with four men in her life, and never a man who had another girlfriend, let alone a wife, is both humbling and a little shocking. When Jill and Celestine call to tell her about their affairs or one-night stands, she advises them to have fun but not to get too serious. What she used to say was not to get involved at all, not to sleep with anyone who had some other woman at home or on speed-dial, because her friends weren't at all likely to get what they wanted. How many times had they seen it before? The pathetic single girl in tears when the man she witlessly has fallen in love with won't leave his wife for her? It's a scenario from countless movies and every single soap opera. Infidelity, along with alcoholism and drug abuse, is ubiquitous, the most prevalent open secret of most Western societies, and it seems almost always to end with something broken.

But Anna's father, Jill and Celestine have reminded her, is the sort of man who really could have almost any woman he wants, and he left his wife for the other woman, didn't he? "True," Anna has conceded, "But look what happened. A second divorce and an ex-wife, who, up until a couple of years ago, still called and yelled at him when she was drunk."

"Is one o'clock good for you?" Dr. Glass asks her now. "Or is noon better?"

"Either would work. I think I'm off all day."

Before she leaves, he says, "If you don't want to have lunch with me, please don't think that you have to. I only thought that it might be nice. I could invite your classmates too if you'd like me to."

She tries to keep her face from falling. "Whatever you'd like," she says. "It's really up to you."

"Okay," he says, his smile as boyish as any she has seen before. "Then it'll just be you and me. We'll have fun, I promise."

She wishes that the memory of her mother's unhappiness during her prolonged and bitter divorce were enough to keep her from seeing Dr. Glass again, but it isn't. After a mostly restless night when she resorts to taking two of the Ambien in her medicine cabinet and still can't sleep for stretches of more than an hour and a half, she calls Jill and tells her what she thinks she is about to do. "Why can't I stop myself, knowing what my mother went through?" she asks.

"You're a human being, Anna, not a saint," says Jill. "It was only a matter of time anyway. How could you not be boning one of the doctors you work with? You're gorgeous, and they're all old goats who must be drooling every time you walk by."

"Dr. Glass isn't an old goat," says Anna, wishing she had called Celestine instead.

"No, but he has a dick, doesn't he?"

"You're so crass. He's not like that."

"How do you know? If you gave them even the slightest encouragement, you'd have so many guys chasing after you that you'd need a bodyguard. I'm sure Dr. Glass is thinking about you when he yanks it in the shower every morning."

"Stop it," cries Anna, but the image of Dr. Glass masturbating is now in her head and she can't send it back. "Tell me that I shouldn't go out with him because he's married and has two kids."

"He has to answer to them. You don't. Do whatever you want. Let him worry about his family."

"That's a convenient way to look at it."

"You knew I'd tell you to go out with him. Why else did you call me? Did you already call Celestine and ask her what she thinks?"

"No."

"She'd say the same thing. We're both whores." Her sudden burst of laughter is loud and self-mocking.

"No, you're not," says Anna.

"Yes, we are. You know it too. You don't have to lie. I'm over it."

"Do you think I'm a whore?"

"No," Jill says quietly. "I think you're just being honest with yourself. You're attracted to him. He's attracted to you. You're single, and clearly he's not getting everything he needs at home. You can't always be good, especially growing up with a father like yours. If he were my dad, I'd have a big crush on him and be totally fine with it. How could I not? He's still so hot."

"No, you wouldn't. That's disgusting, Jill. I don't have a crush on my father. I never have."

"Don't get your undies in a bunch. I'm just kidding," says Jill, but Anna knows she isn't. Both Celestine and Jill have had crushes on her father since junior high. Anna also wonders if one or both of them have had sex with him. She hopes it is only her jealous sixth sense, adding weight and meaning to the glances her two friends have exchanged with her father over the fifteen years she has known them; even so, she has almost no doubt that they would leap into bed with him if he so much as hinted that he'd be willing.

The fact that Jill has joked more than once that Anna must be attracted to him too is something she finds more irritating than perverse because in her private heart, she is unsure if, while watching his films and occasionally seeing him work on the set, her feelings have always been innocent. How not, from time to time, to see him as the man countless others desire? This is, after all, how he has managed to make a life as an actor. He has long been a sex symbol—several magazines over the years having baldly declared this fact on their covers, Anna rolling her eyes over this news even as she quietly wondered if she would grow up to marry a man like him. She does not want to think that Dr. Glass is this man, but he and her father are not very far apart in age, and he has power over her too; in some ways, even more than her father does. When this thought arrives, she hastily turns it away, but its traces remain, like light seeping from behind a closed door.

"Go out with Dr. Heart-of-Glass, Anna. I have a hunch that he'll give you the finest medical attention you'll find anywhere. Just go and have fun. If you fall in love with him, then you can worry."

I might already be in love with him, she almost says.

"I was thinking that I might want to go out with that Jim guy you were telling me about last week. Do you think he'd like me?"

"I'm sure he would, but I don't know if you'd like him."

"Will you give him my phone number or e-mail? I really want to meet him."

"He'd probably drive you crazy," says Anna. "And I don't want him hating me if things with you don't work out. I'd still have to see him all the time."

"I'll be nice to him."

"No, you won't."

"Yes, I will. At least for the first date." She pauses. "Dr. Glass might fall in love with you too. Don't rule that out."

Her friend's words make her breath seize. "I don't think he will," she says softly.

"Well, darling, you could be wrong."

All week during her ICU rotation with two doctors who are related in some obscure way—the spouse of a cousin? the aunt of a nephew's wife? Anna thinks of her impending date with Dr. Glass and tries to convince herself to call and tell him that her plans have changed or that she simply thinks they had better not. She could say that she really would like to get to know him better, but she knows her feelings for him are inappropriate, and surely he understands that she does not wish to compromise their professional relationship or intrude on his personal life?

But she doesn't do it, doesn't want to do it; it has been so long since she has felt as excited about a man, and despite her fatigue each night after the long hours at the hospital, she has gone out to buy a new skirt and blouse, along with a black silk bra and matching thong, these two items alone costing her a hundred and fifty dollars. The night before their date, she hardly sleeps, but in the morning finds that she doesn't look tired, her anticipation having released floods of endorphins, hormones that keep her awake and almost fresh-faced, her cheeks pink, as if she has been out walking in the sun.

When she arrives at the restaurant at one o'clock, Dr. Glass is already there. He stands up from the table and takes her hand, not letting it go until he has pulled back her chair and motioned for her to sit down. She is so nervous that she has trouble looking at him, but his eyes seem to be steadily on her. "I have to think that you're a woman of the world, Anna," he says while they eat vegetable samosas and drink tepid tea.

She smiles, startled. "Why do you think that?"

"Well, in part because of who your father is."

"You know who he is?"

"Of course. I think most people do."

She looks down at the table, trying not to let him see her discomfort. She does not want to talk about her father. She does not want him to be present for any part of what she is probably going to do with Dr. Glass—Tom—which he has asked her to call him outside of the hospital. "My mother's really the one who raised my brother, Billy, and me," she says. "My father was gone a lot while we were growing up, and he and my mother got divorced when I was eleven."

"But you still must have seen him when he was in town."

"Yes, I did." It isn't strictly true that her mother did most of the parenting. She and Billy were with their father relatively often because they sometimes went where he was working during their school holidays, and when he was in L.A., they stayed with him on the weekends, Melinda, his second wife, babysitting them until they were old enough to take care of themselves, which was about the same time that he divorced her.

"Why didn't you want to go into acting too?"

"I guess I didn't have the guts."

"You need more guts to be a doctor, I think."

She laughs softly. "Yes, that's probably true."

"It is, Anna. Don't doubt it."

"My mother's a doctor."

He nods. "I remember you saying that during your first week with me."

"I did?"

"Yes."

"Do you mean my first week last year or my first week this year?"

"Last year."

She looks at him, as pleased by this admission as anything he has previously said to her.

He hesitates. "One thing I feel I should say is that I don't make a habit of asking my interns out."

"I didn't think you did."

He regards her. "Have you ever dated one of your professors or attendings before?"

"No."

"They were too shy to ask you, I'm sure."

"I doubt it. But that's fine, because I wasn't interested in any of them." She glances at his hand and sees that he is wearing his wedding ring. She wonders if he ever takes it off or if he has left it there to remind her that he belongs to someone else.

"But you are interested in me?" he murmurs.

She feels a nervous laugh bubbling in her throat. "Yes, but I know that I shouldn't be."

"Why not? Because I'm married?"

"That's part of it."

"Because we work together?"

"Yes."

"I won't name any names, but attending physicians go out with interns all the time. As long as everyone's discreet, it's not a problem. Some of my colleagues have married their former interns." He pauses. "You don't have to worry about my wife. She and I give each other a lot of breathing room."

It seems likely that two or more of these statements are a lie, but Anna doesn't challenge him. Her heart is beating so hard that she can feel it pulsing in her throat. She barely tastes the food they have ordered, and the sounds of other diners' conversations filter into her ears but hardly register. She will never be able to tell her mother about Dr. Glass. It would be smart not to tell anyone about him, but she has already told Jill, and the day after their conversation, Celestine. One of the pleasures of behaving badly, she is beginning to realize, is how good it feels to have dirty secrets, and how hard it is to keep them to herself.

After their waiter brings the check, Dr. Glass looks at her (Tom, Anna reminds herself) and says, "If you don't want to go back to your place today, we don't have to. But if you do want to, I think that'd be nice."

Is this how it's done? she wonders, surprised by how naive she feels, knowing what she does about the rarefied plane her father inhabits, about the things that the people he works with sometimes do, how some of them have lovers in cities all over the world, how some have been treated for sex addiction, which has always seemed to her a surreal ailment to be "cured" of—how can one suppress the libido for the long term? It has never seemed possible to her. Instead, some people seem eventually to lose interest in sex, their hormone levels shifting, their habits and desires becoming uninteresting or possibly unpleasant.

"I'm not like my father," she blurts. "I've never had an affair before."

Dr. Glass stares at her, laughing a little in surprise. "I would never confuse you with your father, Anna. Please don't think that. Working with you this past year, I think I have a pretty good sense of who you are."

She looks at him. "You do?"

"For one," he says, "you've never once mentioned your father or his fame."

"It's not something that I usually do."

"I know." He takes her hand from where it rests next to her plate and presses it to his lips. "I think you're very lovely. I've never met anyone like you. You have so many things going for you, but you don't ever seem to need to remind anyone of this."

She has to look away from his earnest gaze. He is saying everything she wants to hear, but he doesn't have to. She wants him, unequivocally, and within ten minutes they are at her house, the blinds closed, the radio clicked on so that they won't have to hear her downstairs tenant walking around or talking on the phone with her windows wide open. Anna's clothes are in a heap on the floor next to the bed, his draped over a chair. Even as she shivers with nervous desire for him, she can't shut off her analytical mind. He put his shirt and pants over the chair so that they won't wrinkle, she thinks. He doesn't want his wife to wonder what he's been doing, because of course she will be suspicious.

But then her mind does recede, or at least soften its cynical inquiry. Once his hands are on her breasts, his lips kissing the warm hollow of her neck, murmuring, "You're so beautiful, Anna," once the whole hot length of him is pressed against her shivering body, she knows that he is worth it, that whatever will happen, whatever expectations she will eventually have to forfeit, it is worth it to spend this hour with him, maybe two if he has the time to linger. She doesn't know, can't yet know, what he will be able to offer her. One of them will make most of the demands, she realizes, and it will probably become a pattern—the one asking, the other sometimes granting but often not. He will arrive at an appointed hour to undress himself and part her legs before getting into his car again and driving away until the next time she unlocks her door, behind which she has waited for him in something lacy and expensive. But right now, there is this first time, and it will always be the first time. She knows that she will remember it long after other details of this summer have faded. She will remember how he stepped out of his shoes and left them side by side next to her dresser, how he folded his pants over the chair before taking her into his arms and falling with her onto the cool, oceanic expanse of her bed.

CHAPTER 5

STOLEN GODS

At age twenty-eight, instead of being a promising young screenwriter who has just bought a custom-tailored tux for the Oscars, I'm a freelance propmaster whose biggest claim to fame so far is that Renn Ivins remembers my name when our paths cross during a shoot. This wouldn't bother me so much if I thought that my screenplays were MFBS (masturbatory-fantasy bullshit), but they aren't. They're original, morally complex stories like Truffaut's and Kieślowski's, but I'm in Hollywood, not in France or Poland or even New York. Needless to say, no one gives a shit.

It could be that I don't fit in here the way I should, despite going to UCLA and spending the last ten years of my life in southern California. Countless people, I'm pretty sure, live large portions of their lives within pissing distance of the 101, the 110, and the 405, but don't ever really feel like they fit in. It depends in part on what you expect from your life—if you want to be rich and famous, this probably isn't the best place to start, paradoxical as that must sound. You would probably be better off writing screenplays and making short films in Omaha or Minneapolis for a while and approaching Hollywood from an oblique angle instead of head-on like I did.

At eighteen, I showed up for freshman year at a big, sun-dried university in a place that wasn't anything like the town between Ann Arbor and Detroit where I grew up. I brought along huge expectations with my extra-long twin-set sheet and new gym socks, and a long-distance relationship that, no surprise, went off the rails a few weeks before Thanksgiving. I liked many of the differences between here and home, but it wasn't like the best film studios had their doors wide open, their sexy receptionists waiting to take me upstairs to see the executives with all the biggest stars on speed dial.

I thought college would be different from high school, filled with charismatic, friendly weirdos, but after a year or so of living in student squalor at UCLA, I realized that the rest of the world, Hollywood in particular, is no different from the tenth grade. It's probably much worse, because the people in charge have real power. They decide who makes what films, and how, and these are the films that the rest of the world flocks to see. The studio executives, the directors and producers and marketing millionaires, many of them no more evolved than newly pubescent twelve-year-olds, are responsible for the images America beams out to the billions on the planet who aren't Americans. That movie about the two idiots who can't remember where they parked their car because they were too high the night before? This is the cinematic ambassador we deliver to the rest of the world, ninety minutes of Grade-D eye candy that forever corrupts the gray matter of twelve-year-olds in Tokyo or confirms the low opinion that the teashop owner in New Delhi has had of Americans ever since a group of fat, belligerent tourists from Hartford staggered into his shop and complained that his teacups were dirty.

I was in the drama club in high school, and instead of trying out for the plays, I stuck to the stage crew. I learned how to work hard, move quickly, and let the actors and director take the credit for a good production. Even at fifteen, I understood that all clubs have their ritual hazings, especially ones where members of both sexes find themselves in close, competitive relationships, an underpaid teacher barely in charge of the whole hormonal gang. A Hollywood movie set isn't much different. I get most of my paying work for Sony, and it comes in more or less regularly, but it's not like I'm flying to Maui every other month to spend time at my second home. There aren't many union or guild jobs anymore for people who aren't in front of the camera; like everywhere else, the movie industry is trying to make as much money as possible by spending as little as it can on production.

Before the mostly regular Sony gigs, I worked as an assistant in set decoration at Paramount after spending six years at UCLA, the last two in the graduate screenwriting program. I moved to props within a year and thought that I'd only have to do this kind of work a little while longer before I'd have saved some money and found a backer so that I could start my own production company, Binocular Spectacular. Needless to say, it hasn't happened yet. The truth is, without a friend in a high place, you often have to start on the lowest rung in the film industry, which is porn. You work as an editorial assistant to some coke-sniffing greaseball director out in the Valley, and you learn how to use the editing software and you pretend you don't mind and maybe if you're lucky, you move up to some B-level but more legit studio, and then from there, you keep going. If you're lucky.

There's no way around it. This town is superstitious about everything, especially good luck. If you have it, they love you. If you don't, or don't outwardly appear to, no one will give you the time of day or night. They don't want to be tainted by you or your ugly luck.

The job I've been doing at Sony, however, isn't without its rewards. I get to work closely with the actors, making sure the briefcase opens the way it's supposed to, that the wristwatch the Eisenhower-era lawyer wears is the right one. Before I became propmaster, I sometimes had to run miscellaneous errands that other production people were supposed to do but managed to squirrel out of, like finding the star her favorite shampoo, which could only be purchased at salons in Palm Springs and Miami, or I had to race across town to pick up a prescription for the constipated cinematographer who didn't want anyone else to know about his affliction.

The two movies I've liked working on the most during the time I've been at Sony have starred Renn Ivins. His son and I were under-grads together at UCLA for two years. When he was a freshman and I was a junior, we took a class together, a film studies course in which the professor kept trying to convince us that Godard was much more brilliant than Truffaut, which made me furious. The professor gave me a C because I questioned his arguments on a few occasions, but it seemed to me that each time I called him on some-thing, he had no real basis for his claims. Ivins's son didn't ever say anything in class, and the couple of times I tried to talk to him, he was polite but it was clear that he didn't really want to have any-thing to do with me. He played a game on his phone a lot under the desk and wrote in a notebook that had a picture of a black horse on its cover, the kind of notebook a girl would carry in the fourth grade, but maybe he thought he was being ironic.

I wondered about him, wondered what it was like to have Renn Ivins for a father, someone who has managed to make more of the right films than the wrong ones, though The Writing on the Wall from eight or nine years ago was a disaster, an ambitious one, I guess, but it ended up being a joke because Ivins had no business trying to play a transsexual opera singer. He must have thought that he hadn't taken enough risks with his career, but seeing him in scene after scene with those ridiculous blond wigs and that frosted lipstick seriously made me wonder what kind of drugs he'd been taking when he read the script and talked to his agent about it. Didn't he know that after *Tootsie*, all that needed to happen with the gender-swap thing had already happened?

Not long after he played the tranny, he made *The Zoologist*, one of the best movies I've ever seen, and all was forgiven. He directed and had a small role in it, and *Zoologist* is different from all the other movies he's been associated with. The title character is a forty-nine-year-old woman who lives by herself in an old Texas ranch house with a huge number of stuffed animals, the toy kind, not the taxidermied. They all have names and she spends a lot of her time making clothes and writing little plays for them that she then stages. It's an amazing film, one I wish I'd written, and maybe at some point I would have if a person named Pamela Liston hadn't written it first.

I know a lot about Ivins, and though he knows next to nothing about me, he does remember my name when our paths cross at Sony. I know that he likes to eat maraschino cherries right from the jar when he's out of sorts, probably because he's worried about his business manager embezzling millions from him, or some con artist in Germany is going from city to city impersonating him and getting laid every time he turns around. I had to go out once during a blinding downpour and buy a jar of cherries for him. I know that he doesn't like to gamble, even though he likes Vegas. He took part in a celebrity poker tournament last year because the prize was a half-million-dollar donation to the winner's favorite charity. Ivins's was an AIDS hospice in Pasadena where a friend of his from college died in the early 1990s. He won the tournament too, though I'm not sure how, because if he really doesn't like gambling, how was he good enough to beat the other guys who do like to gamble and do it often? He might be lying about not liking it, or else he used to like it but doesn't anymore. I blog about him sometimes and read other blogs about him, and I have some of his old costumes, items he left on the set and I collected. If I hadn't, these things would have moldered away in the studio's huge wardrobe storage area: three white T-shirts and a pair of running socks, a couple of pairs of khaki shorts, a pair of Moroccan leather sandals, and three hats—a derby, a straw Panama, and a wool fedora. I also have a pair of gold cuff links that he wore in *Pacific Coast*, a wristwatch (a stainless steel Seiko, not a Rolex), a pair of reading glasses (+2.0 magnification), and a tattered paperback copy of *The Stranger* (which he told a film critic at the *New York Times* is his favorite book, but I'm not sure if he's actually read it. I've never seen him reading anything but a script). I've managed to obtain other clothes and trinkets of his, but I sold them on a sort of black-market website. I don't sell anything on eBay because someone from Sony would probably catch me. Other things of his that I've picked up—an empty cherry jar, a half-used bar of Irish Spring (two stray hairs included), an old razor, a blank checking deposit slip, a few yellow pencils with teeth marks near the erasers, a stray wooden button, receipts from Starbucks, salt packets from the Habit and In-N-Out Burger, several sticks of Doublemint gum, silver foil intact.

Perhaps the best find of anything that I've ever collected: his cell phone numbers. They were written on a little yellow slip of paper that he'd wedged into the frame around one of his dressing-room mirrors. I suppose it might be hard to keep the two different numbers straight, but if he can remember all of those lines, I don't really get it. I knew they were his because I called them to make sure. When he answered, I said nothing and hung up. He sounded like he'd been sleeping, and even if he hadn't been, I knew that I was being a jerk, not saying anything, not even "Sorry, wrong number."

If I ever did call and talk to him, if I ever said who I am and asked for his tolerance and patience and he agreed to talk to me for a little while, I have the interview questions ready. I'd like to make a documentary about him. One of the reasons I'm so interested in him is because he's the kind of actor other actors respect, and he doesn't ever really seem to fuck things up, aside from the tranny movie (which John Waters was supposed to direct, but the rumor is, he wanted to cast Keanu Reeves in the lead, not Renn Ivins). I'm not sure how Ivins keeps doing it, how so much of what he touches seems to blossom or at least not to wilt. My documentary project probably won't ever happen, but if I did have a chance to ask him my questions, I have a pretty good idea how he'd respond to most of them.

THE IMAGINARY IVINS INTERVIEW

Jim M.: Of which role are you most proud?

Renn Ivins: I like something about all of the roles I've played, but if I had to choose, it'd probably be *Javier's Sons*. We shot most of it in Peru and I got to see Machu Picchu for the first time. It's really an amazing place, and to think they built it before the discovery of electricity or the invention of the steam engine.

I also felt even more respect for human rights workers after making this film. They're extraordinarily brave people, living and working in strange, hostile places, and fighting for abstractions like justice, peace, and equality, things that most of us take for granted in America.

JM: What was your least favorite role?

RI (*laughs*): Oh, I've liked every film I've made.

JM: That's a diplomat's answer. What's the real answer?

RI: If you really have to know, I'd say that it was *Broken English*. Not because I didn't like the cast or the director, but a lot of things didn't turn out the way they were supposed to with that film. We were going to shoot it in Toronto, which is where quite a few films are made now because Canada doesn't charge as much as a lot of places do for permits and other things you need to make a film. But we ended up having to shoot most of it in Cleveland, which was fine, overall, but I'm still not really sure why. Also, one of the stunt people, a young woman named Paisley Braun, died while driving a car off a bridge, which is supposed to be a pretty routine stunt. You can imagine that someone dying is enough to make any shoot tougher than usual.

JM: Yeah, I can see how that'd be true. I heard somewhere that you didn't like making *Cloudburst*, that it's a movie you wish you'd never been associated with. But I love it, and the reviews were really good, weren't they?

RI: I don't know who told you that I didn't like making *Cloudburst*. I liked everything about it. Who's spreading these rumors? Where did you hear that?

JM: I read it online somewhere. I don't remember where.

RI: Whoever wrote that is full of shit.

JM: Now that you've achieved a level of success that most people can only fantasize about, what's next?

RI: I don't know if I'm really that successful. It doesn't—

JM (*laughing*): Of course you are. Unless you're doing an independent project, you usually make a minimum of nine or ten million a picture. You don't think that's success?

RI: Financially, sure. But there are other things that matter more. I'd like to take a year or two off and travel for leisure, rather than only for work. I've traveled all over the world already, but I don't usually have much time to relax and sightsee when I'm overseas. I'd also like to write more screenplays. I really loved writing *Bourbon at Dusk*, and even though the whole process was pretty arduous—I nearly gave up on it about five times—it was immensely rewarding. More than acting is. Maybe even more than directing.

JM: If you don't mind me asking, I'm wondering if you've always been a ladies' man, even before you became famous.

RI (*hesitates*): That's your question?

JM: I think a lot of guys want to know how you do it, but they don't have the guts to ask.

RI: How I do what?

JM: How you handle all of the sexual attention.

RI: Those are different questions.

JM (*pausing*): You're right. I guess what I really want to know is, how hard is it being faithful if you have so many women throwing themselves at you all hours of the day?

RI: I'm certainly not a ladies' man, and I don't know if I have that many women throwing themselves at me. Certainly not at all hours of the day.

JM: Come on. Of course you do.

RI: Some days I do have to, you know, tactfully decline the offer of a date or two, but in general, it's not like women are lining up around the block to give me blow jobs.

JM: I'm sure you've had your share.

RI: You sound like my ex-wives.

JM: They both said that?

RI: Yes. On many, many occasions. If I had a dollar for every time . . . you know the saying.

JM: Your second ex-wife, Melinda Byers—

RI: I remember her name. Thanks.

JM: Your second ex-wife has a book coming out next month, a tell-all about the four and a half years she was married to you. What do you think about this? Didn't you have her sign some kind of prenup so she wouldn't be able to reveal any of the secrets of your marriage?

RI: Secrets of my marriage? What qualify as secrets of my marriage? Do you mean like how often we had sex? Or how much she stole from me to give to her ex-husband, who used the money to buy heroin? Isn't that all common knowledge by now?

JM: I guess it's a given that you wouldn't be too thrilled about Ms. Byers becoming an author.

RI: She's not an author. She's an opportunist.

JM: And a scumbag.

RI: Those are your words, not mine. Make sure that's clear.

JM: I'm sorry that you have to put up with these kind of things.

RI: The price of fame. Needless to say, most people can't afford it.

JM: I heard she's calling her book *This Isn't Gold*.

RI: Not a bad title, I guess.

JM: Does she mean it as in "all that glitters"?

RI: I suppose she does. I haven't read it.

JM: Will you?

RI: Not unless I'm kidnapped and threatened with beheading if I don't.

JM: What about your first wife? Are you two on good terms? Is she going to write a tell-all memoir too?

RI: Whatever Lucy's faults might be, she doesn't kiss and tell.

JM: What are her faults?

RI: I don't really want to talk about her. Water under the bridge.

JM: Of course it is. But it would still be interesting to hear what you think of her.

RI: I almost never talk about my exes, but I will say that she's a decent person, very smart, and I know that my work schedule was pretty hard on her while we were together, especially during the last seven or eight years. She also has a short temper. She's impatient and holds grudges much too long, and while we were married, she was prone to believing the worst. She still is, I think.

JM: You left her for Melinda. I suppose in that case, she was right to assume the worst.

RI: I'd really rather not talk about this. As I said, it's water under the bridge.

JM: How would you describe your relationship with your children?

RI: We're good friends. I love them, and I'm pretty sure that they love me.

JM: I read somewhere that your daughter is about to finish med school. You must be really proud of her. What does your son do for a living? I looked him up online, but there wasn't much information about what he's doing right now.

RI: He's thinking about going to law school. I think he's doing some online trading too.

JM: I've always wondered how he reacted when you made *Parachute Point* and played Wickley Ryerson's father, who I think was probably the same age as Will at the time. Was your son jealous when he saw it and he had to watch you doing all of the fun things fathers sometimes do with their sons, like when you took Wickley to the park to fly a kite or when you taught him to swim the front crawl or gave him advice about how to talk to girls? Did he think you meant it when your character said "I love you" to Wickley's character?

RI (*long pause*): I think Will has always been pretty good at separating fantasy from reality.

JM: You hesitated before answering. What's the real story?

RI: That is the real story. Will and I have a complex, constantly evolving relationship. Believe it or not, we're not very much alike. And that's just fine. He should be his own person.

JM: Just a couple of more questions. What's Renn short for?

RI: Renaldo, but I've gone by Renn since I was about thirteen.

JM: Why not just one "n"?

RI: I don't know. I like two.

JM: Okay, now for one more: what's the story with you and Elise Connor?

RI (*hesitates*): We're close friends. She did a stunning job in *Bourbon at Dusk*. I think she'll be remembered when the awards season starts.

JM: I've heard that you two are a couple and that it's serious.

RI: She's important to me.

JM: She's a lot younger than you are.

RI: Yes, I'm aware of that. What's your point?

JM: No point. I suppose I'm just stating the obvious.

RI: That's not necessary.

As you can see, I've given him a few quills. He's not without his defenses—to get to where he is, you have to be tough, but I think he keeps the darker side of his personality, which I know is there, pretty well under wraps most of the time. I've only seen him have one real temper tantrum, and that was when a sound guy kept hitting the top of his head with a boom mic. I think the sound guy might have been stoned, or else he was just sleep-deprived. Some of the crew couldn't stifle their laughter when they saw Renn getting bonked again and again, and the guffaws, no surprise, made him angrier. The sound guy was told to leave the set, but they let him come back the next day. He was union, so that was part of it, I'm sure. Renn has sometimes gotten a little grouchy about the catering, and he also complains if there's even the smallest chance he'll look fat onscreen—this is one thing he's pretty adamant about with the wardrobe people, unless the role requires him to look paunchy, but I can't think of more than one or two movies where this was the case. I don't think he takes roles where he's required to look bad, unless there's a huge transformation somewhere in the script where he ends up looking like himself again by the middle or end.

He's going to be releasing *Bourbon at Dusk* soon, a film that he directed and co-wrote. I've heard it could win a little (or a lot) of everything—Golden Globes, Oscars, BAFTAs, SAGs. It was only a finalist at Cannes, but that is still a solid accomplishment. After his big trip to France, however, he has had to come back down to earth very fast because he agreed to do a cameo in the film I'm working on right now, *More Liar's Poker*, which isn't about poker, instead, two rival hitmen organizations that are hired to kill each other. Ivins is playing a retired hitman who is like a hitman guru. It's a nothing movie (which is a sequel to, yes, *Liar's Poker*), but he's got one of the few slightly less dull roles because the director is his friend, as is one of the two stars, Wells Bradford, which is a fake name, but his real one, Hubert Smids, isn't exactly marquee material.

Ivins is only in one scene, but it's an important one—five minutes, which is long in movie time. Many scenes only last a couple of minutes, and quite a few are shorter, which means that the crew work their asses off with all of the setups and teardowns for these two-bit scenes, though some can be unforgettable when you see them in finished form, spliced into exactly the right place. They're like the one card that causes the house to collapse if it's pulled out.

In his scene, which is with Wells Bradford and some guy named Billy Pistol or Billy Pirate who is at least a few years younger than I am—I'd be lying if I said that this doesn't make me bitter (though it's not like I could ever be an actor—I get too nervous if too many people are looking at me)—Renn is wearing a glued-on goatee and a black silk shirt with gray pants and these very cool Ray-Bans I want so badly that I'll have to find a way to get them on the Loss/Damage report when we wrap.

For four hours, between errands and phone calls to track down two Depression-era ebony walking sticks, I keep checking to see if they're done with the scene. When they finally are, I know that I'll have to wait some more before I have a chance at those sunglasses. Ivins heads straight for his dressing room, which isn't far from the sound stage where we filmed his scene. I hang around in the hall outside, making more calls about ebony canes, until Ivins comes out about fifteen minutes later and nods at me and I nod back and smile as if the person on the other end of the line is testing my tolerance for stupidity. I don't hear the click of the lock when he shuts the door of his dressing room.

After he disappears down the hall, I try the door and it opens. I slip inside, already sweating, and close the door behind me without turning on the light. I have trouble finding the sunglasses. What look like manila folders and unopened mail are scattered across a small table and the sofa next to it, and there are also several pairs of shoes in a pile by the door. I trip over one of the shoes, almost falling, and it isn't until I start to look for a case rather than the glasses themselves that I find them. I grab the case, along with a couple of cheap pens, and these three things are in my hands when the door opens. The lights come on, and my heart almost stops dead. Despite all the studio property I've removed from the set over the past couple of years, I've never been caught. Even before I turn around, I know it's him. It occurs to me then that he left the door unlocked because he was planning to come back, and he must have trusted me, the peon out in the hall, to keep an eye on the place for him.

Framed by the doorway, he looks very tall and burly, menacing too, but it's probably because of the fake goatee that he hasn't yet ripped from his face. He says nothing, only sighs when he sees me drop the pens and sunglasses on the table I've just taken them from. I can't meet his eyes, my shame worse than the afternoon fifteen years ago when my friend Cal's mother caught me shoplifting a Snickers bar from a gas station near our school.

"Is there something I can help you with in here, John?" Renn Ivins asks in a calm, weary voice.

"Actually, it's Jim," I say, realizing too late that this probably isn't the best time to correct him.

"Jim," he says flatly. "Was there something in particular you were looking for?"

"No, I was just checking to see if you had enough bottled water in your fridge." The words come so easily that it's as if someone else is speaking for me.

"And my sunglasses were helping you accomplish that task?"

I force myself to hold his gaze. "I was just going to try them on."

"Everyone likes those Ray-Bans," he says. "They were a birthday present from my son. I'd let you borrow them, but I wear them every day. We're burning through the ozone layer pretty fast, and you know what that means, don't you?"

"I think so."

He ignores this. "Wrinkles," he says, laughing in a hard burst. "Eye damage too. The sun has one mission: seek and destroy."

"I was just going to try them on," I repeat lamely. "I'm sorry."

"As long as you weren't going to steal them, Jim. Some of my things here seem to grow legs and walk off. I know it's best not to get too attached to your possessions, but I can't help but feel fond of a few of them. I'm sure you understand."

I nod, wanting very badly to leave but not sure how to manage it. Ivins is still in the doorway, and he has started to pry up the edges of his goatee, which makes him look both comical and sinister. "Tell me, do I need any water?" he asks. "Or is my fridge well stocked?"

Along with *yes* or *no*, I can only think of one other reply, *not really*, which means that I probably have a thirty-three percent chance of choosing the correct answer. I have no idea if Ivins knows what's in the fridge; his face gives nothing away. I wonder if he recognizes that we're playing our own game of liar's poker.

My throat feels very dry. "You could use a few more bottles," I manage to say.

He gives me a long, unblinking look. "Really? Why don't you double-check?"

A horrifying urge to laugh seizes my chest. I take the few steps over to the fridge and am now even farther from the door. The refrigerator is almost empty. Inside are only two bottles of water, one very shiny Granny Smith, a few pieces of string cheese, and a bottle of O'Doul's. O'Doul's? Despite the fact that I'm in no position to judge him or anyone else, I can't help but wonder. Does he really drink that swill? Or does he keep one on hand for his friends who are in AA? Would they even be allowed to drink O'Doul's?

"Gotcha," he says. He's standing only a couple of feet behind me now. "You looked pretty nervous for a minute or two. I bet you weren't too sure what you'd find in there."

I turn around but can't meet his eyes. "I'll go get you some water," I mumble. My stomach feels like it's living in my shoes now. I shut the refrigerator and move toward the door. I have never in my life wanted so badly to leave a room.

"Hold on a second, Jim," Ivins says.

It stings like a slap, but I force myself to look right into his tired, suntanned face.

"I'll let you off this time," he says, his eyes malice-hardened. "But I don't want to catch you in here again." He peels off his goatee and rubs his reddened chin for a few seconds. "There's a reason you're the person you are and I'm the person I am, no?"

"Yes, I guess so," I say.

He finally steps aside and lets me go. I hear him shut the door behind me, the lock clicking into place.

He must know that I won't have the guts to bring him the water. I wish that I could prove him wrong, but I can't. *You're the person you are and I'm the person I am.* I find one of the caterers and ask her to bring Ivins eight bottles of Evian, which she does without complaint, her pretty face blank, but I know she doesn't mind.

Admittedly, he did me a favor. He could have had security throw me out, and I would promptly have been fired, possibly arrested. He could also have made it impossible for me to be hired anywhere else. Maybe he still will, but I don't think so. It's over now though—my side business, our friendly acquaintance, if that's what it was. Yet as far as I know I'm still employed at the studio. I still have a decent place to live, a coach house that I rent in Topanga Canyon, a two-bedroom with a small garage that sits behind a bigger, nicer house. I have a car given to me by my parents when I graduated from UCLA. It's a Honda, only six years old, and hasn't needed any major repairs. Larissa, my girlfriend, who is a full-time preschool teacher and a part-time spinning instructor, seems genuinely to care about me and stays over three or four nights a week, if I don't have to work too late. She doesn't know about my side business, and I haven't ever had the urge to tell her. She still thinks one of my screenplays will sell and be produced and I'll win an Oscar or at least a Golden Globe and then I will finally be able to take her to Spain and France, the two countries she has most wanted to visit since high school. I don't see us going there any time soon, even if I have a second bank account into which I've now deposited a couple of thousand dollars, most of it money from the things I've taken from Renn Ivins and a few of the other actors I've worked with. My plan has been to use it to get Binocular Spectacular started so I can film one of my screenplays if no one else will. Sometimes, to get ahead, to step out of the rapids that are rushing you toward nowhere but death, you have to do a thing or two that wouldn't make your parents or the president or your therapist proud.

I learned in high school that character is fate, but I can't remember who said it. At the time, I thought, Sure, whatever. Now, no surprise, it's a little more complicated. *You're the person you are.* I don't like it at all that Renn said this. It might be the worst thing anyone has ever said to me. Especially because he must think he's right.

A few months ago, probably to guilt her into visiting, Larissa's mother sent her a copy of the newspaper from the small Wisconsin town where her family still lives. Larissa spent half an hour reading it, and before she tossed it in the recycling bin, she pointed out something on the last page. It was the town's police blotter, laughably benign with its reports of bounced checks and littering citations and high-schoolers blowing off stop signs. There was also a small section that should have said "Stolen Goods," but someone hadn't proofread very carefully and the heading was printed as "Stolen Gods."

"I wonder what gods were stolen last week?" Larissa said, chuckling. "What will their owners do without them? Will their goldfish start barking? Will their rosebushes grow legs and run off?"

I rolled my eyes but couldn't help laughing. "You're strange."

"I hope whoever stole those gods knows what he's gotten himself into," she said. "Their phone bill alone will probably be enough to put him in the poorhouse. How much does it cost to call Mount Olympus or wherever it is they live?"

"And the grocery bill. Nectar's expensive."

"If you ever want to steal a god," she said, looking at me intently, "make sure you consider the possible consequences. At least when you buy something, you get a receipt and can return it."

She saved that section and taped it onto my refrigerator, a small gray square from Beaver Creek's weekly newspaper that's supposed to remind me to laugh, not to take myself too seriously. I'm pretty sure that she doesn't know about the goods I've stolen because I've been careful about where I hide everything. I might only be a second or two away from getting caught every time that I take a hat or a shoehorn or a pair of cuff links from the set, but at home, it's not hard to keep this business to myself. If I didn't take these props, I wouldn't be able to pay all of my bills each month—rent and student loans the worst of it. Hardly anyone tells you in film school that you're not likely to make any money after you graduate, not for a long fucking time, if ever. Or if people do tell you this, you ignore them. It's like getting married—you've heard how many couples end up filing for divorce, but you go ahead and get married anyway, thinking your marriage will be different. Maybe it will. But more likely it won't.

In any case, there are worse things than stealing a couple of hats and cuff links to get by. And it's not like I'm some slob who goes home and stares at the TV every night until it's time to go to bed. When I'm not too tired and Larissa and I aren't going out, I sit down at my desk and write for a couple of hours, and after several years of doing this, I have eight unsold screenplays. This has become one of those jokes you once thought were hilarious, but after telling it so many times, it's turned rancid.

The three screenplays I like most are *Winter Equinox* (I realize there's no such thing), *Old Growth Forest*, and *So Close to Home*. *So Close to Home* is the most autobiographical of any film I've written so far, and it's probably also the one I'm most ambivalent about. The protagonist lives in a tiny apartment in one of the most complicated cities in the world, and he works with famous people who live in beautiful houses that a few of them earned enough money to buy before their eighteenth birthdays. Some of these people worry that they aren't nearly as talented or as interesting as they're supposed to be, and they go on to make unnecessary trouble for themselves and those closest to them. What they want in their secret hearts is simplicity—less clutter and more substance, both objects and people—but they're not sure how to achieve either of these things. They're often lonely and undereducated, superstitious, grudge-bearing, worried, and envious about how much publicity (which to them, equals love) their friends and competitors are getting for their latest projects. Even though they are actors, skilled at creating a facade, they cannot keep these feelings from glaring through from time to time.

Most days they speed from one freeway to the next, from one lunch meeting or fitting or screening to the next, feeling like they're missing something, that this thing, whatever it is, will always be missing.

I don't have any solutions to their problems, but I love these characters. They are children inhabiting beautiful adult bodies. They are victims of their own appetites, but I suppose this is true of everyone. They will stuff themselves with junk before dinner or sleep with their friends' wives or drive their cars over cliffs because they own ones they don't know how to drive or else they are desperately lonely. Their nightmares are other people's daydreams. At least, that's how I've chosen to write it.

CHAPTER 6

UNPACKED SUITCASES

1.

*W*hen they met, one of the things she liked about him right away was that he let her finish her own sentences, even if she had to pause for a second or two to find the right words. She had worked with other directors who talked for or over her, putting words in her mouth, trying to convince her that she felt or wanted something that she didn't. She hadn't completed her senior year of college, and three years later she remained self-conscious about this omission, despite her successes in the "real world," which was supposed to be where success counted most. Twelve credits stood between her and her diploma because she had permitted her acting career to preempt other responsibilities, but no one she knew considered this a foolish choice, except maybe her parents. If her decision to leave school hadn't turned out so well, she could always have returned to Austin to finish her degree—if she didn't get herself pregnant or become a drug addict or shack up with some deadbeat boyfriend who made her sell T-shirts (or herself) on

Venice Beach—which were the sorts of things that she suspected her parents had initially feared.

Another thing about Renn that Elise had liked immediately was that he hadn't tried too hard to impress her, not in the way she had become accustomed to men and boys doing over the past five or six years, ever since, as her sister Belle, three years older and ironically, much plainer, had declared, Elise had become "aggressively beautiful." There were, she had to admit, few shortages or deficits in her life, except maybe for free time and privacy, a fact that, she had a feeling, would wear on her more in the future than it did right now. Her fame was still a novelty to her, and on some mornings she awoke and felt, unaccountably, like laughing: the knowledge that she had made it as an actress, that her fame and sudden affluence were not a mirage, dawning on her with the same pleasurable warmth that she felt when newly in love.

They had been filming in New Orleans for a little over two weeks when she and Renn became lovers. She had never before gone to bed with a man more than a couple of years her senior. She also hadn't gone to bed with nearly as many men as some of her friends had either, despite the number of willing and sometimes pushy suitors she encountered. It was occasionally difficult to deflect with grace the passes a few of her admirers made, but she understood that she shouldn't complain. If no one were coming on to her, she would likely miss the attention and wonder if something was wrong with her. Her mother had also set her straight on this topic, her words spoken softly but tinged with what sounded to Elise like scorn: "If you plan to be a movie star, you'd better be able to live with the good and bad attention you're asking for. Just do your father and me a favor and don't accept any roles that require you to take off your clothes. That way you'll have fewer perverts stalking you."

Perverts. The word had always sounded comical to Elise, even more so when her mother said it, because it was not the kind of word she was in the habit of using. Her mother spoke with a pronounced southern accent, being a native Texan, but her father did not because he had been raised in Ft. Wayne, Indiana. (Elise had been told that she also spoke with a twang, but it was not as obvious as her mother's. Still, it needed to be effaced for most of the roles she would play, if not all.) Mrs. Connor used words like critter and britches as naturally as a character out of a John Wayne movie. When Elise told Renn about some of the southern peculiarities in her mother's speech, he had laughed. "Does she say it as in 'too big for your britches'?" he asked.

Elise smiled. "She sure does. What else? Too tiny for your britches? Too pretty?"

"I bet she said that about me, if you told her about us."

"You are too big for your britches. And too pretty," she said, looking down the length of his unclothed body, one that had surprised her by being more muscular than she had expected. He was almost thirty years older than she was, and although he looked good in his clothes, she hadn't been sure what would be lurking beneath them. They were in his room at the Omni Hotel; it was their second week together, and she was thinking that she might be falling in love with him. She wasn't sure what he felt for her though, aside from lust, and it made her nervous. Was he considering their relationship a fling, destined to end as soon as they wrapped Bourbon at Dusk? He had talked about introducing her to his friends, and to his son and daughter (both older than she was), but maybe he had no intention of doing so. The age difference should have made her feel as if she had the sexual edge, but she felt as if the opposite were true—he might think her too immature and unworldly and already be very close to tiring of her.

"You don't have to say that," he said quietly, but his smile was so sincere and uncomplicated that she could see how much he liked hearing it. He was as keen for flattery as any of the other men (eight? or maybe it was nine—why was it that she couldn't recall exactly?) she had been with by then.

"I know I don't."

"If you keep giving me compliments like that, I might have to marry you." He laughed but then abruptly stopped smiling.

She couldn't tell if he was serious. He's an actor, she reminded herself. I really have to make a point of remembering this.

"We'll have to see about that," she said, burying her face in his neck, breathing in the scent of the lemony soap he had used in the shower before she had come to his room.

"I want a small wedding to go with my big cock," he said solemnly.

She shrieked and pulled back, thrilled by his crudeness.

"It has to be small," he said. "Otherwise my cock will get jealous if it's not the biggest thing in the room."

"You're terrible," she said, laughing.

"Yes, I am, so you'd better get used to it." He squeezed her sides until she shrieked again.

"Shhh," he said. "What will the neighbors think?"

2.

To Elise's and everyone else's minor amazement, Renn and his assistant director were able to stay on the production schedule for Bourbon that they had devised with their producers, but inevitably, at the end of the fourth week, events began to conspire against them. Renn's personal assistant had to take a leave of absence due to a family emergency, and the cinematographer contracted a virulent strain of food poisoning from a plate of crawfish that laid him up for three days. On top of that, the costume designer's assistant quit because his boyfriend broke up with him over the phone, and two hours later he had fled home to Long Beach in tears to try to convince the boyfriend to change his mind. There were twenty-four days left on the schedule and about forty-five more pages of the script left to shoot, and if any retakes were necessary, they would have to be done before the company left New Orleans. Building sets on a soundstage in L.A. would be prohibitively expensive, and Renn intended for everything to be shot on location anyway. This was very important, in his view, to maintaining the authentic atmosphere of the picture.

When he told Elise that he had asked his son, Billy, to fly in from L.A. and work as his personal assistant for the remaining weeks of the production, she had hidden her curiosity from Renn. Since moving to California, she had interacted with enough men around his age who pretended to an amiable camaraderie with some of the younger men they worked with, but on at least two occasions, she had sensed an undercurrent of vicious competition between the older and younger man, in one case, a father and son. She had been a psychology major at UT-Austin, and even before college had believed that her hunches about people were often correct. Most of the time, even among the wealthy and powerful people she now interacted with each day, little happened to prove her impressions too far off.

Billy arrived on *Bourbon*'s set on a windless, thickly humid Thursday afternoon. He was visibly exhausted, unsure of himself, very cute. She could tell that he was surprised and flattered when she told him that he looked a lot like his father. After the introductions, Renn was anxious to get the next shot under way and hadn't kept Billy on the set long enough to have a real conversation with her or anyone else. She later learned that Renn had given Billy a time-consuming PR task (which Billy promptly forgot about, and hearing this later, she felt sorry for him, considering how tired he looked) and an off-site errand for him to do with George's assistance, Renn's driver, a taciturn, slow-to-smile man who gave Elise the creeps, but Renn had told her that he trusted George more than anyone else he had worked with over the past twenty years.

It wasn't until a couple of days later that she and Billy had a chance to talk for more than a few seconds. Renn was conferring with her costar, Marek Gilson, about a crucial solo scene, and the crew was setting up the next shot. The heat was still oppressive, and she was resting in her trailer and thinking about returning a call from her sister, but she wasn't looking forward to doing it because she thought that Belle wanted money but would not be able to ask for it directly, something that drove Elise crazy. Through the window she saw Billy walking by and got up to open the door and call out to him. In the glimpse she caught of his face before he could rearrange his features into nonchalance, she thought she spotted nervous excitement, and possibly joy. Her heart sped up a little, responding to his flattering happiness.

"Come in and put your feet up for a minute," she said. "You can help me go over the lines for my next scene." She had already memorized them but thought he might refuse, fearing his father's wrath, if she didn't have a good reason to invite him in.

He hesitated, smiling up at her. "Are you sure? I don't want to bother you."

"Don't be silly. You wouldn't be bothering me at all. But are you in a hurry?"

He shook his head and ascended the three metal stairs that led to her trailer's door. She debated for a second about leaving the door open, not wanting to fuel any rumors that she was having an affair with both the father and the son, but the thought emboldened and irritated her. She shut the door, almost slamming it. If she wanted to have a conversation with the director's son, innocent or otherwise, that was her business. They were adults, for Christ's sake. "Yes, sweetheart, but people know you now, *a lot* of people, and they're going to be watching you," she could hear her mother querulously counseling her.

After Billy had come inside and sat down, she looked at him intently and said, "You really do look a lot like your dad. I hope you don't mind me saying that."

He shook his head. He was perspiring, the underarms of his green Lacoste shirt darkened by sweat, his hair dampened too. "I know you mean it as a compliment. I could do worse than look like my dad."

"That's for sure." She paused. "Do you want some water? I have some in the fridge."

"That'd be great," he said, his eyes flitting to her face before he glanced at the window.

"You're sure I'm not keeping you from something? I don't want to make your boss mad."

Billy opened the water bottle and took a drink. He started coughing almost immediately, his face reddening as his eyes filled with tears. "Oh God," he choked out. "How embarrassing."

"Keep coughing," she said. "That's the only way you'll get the water out of the wrong pipe."

When the fit ended, he had tears running down his cheeks and his face was a furious red. Handing him a tissue, she felt a rush of tenderness for him, something almost maternal. Here's a guy, she thought, who needs to be looked after. "Do you have a girlfriend?" she asked, his weakness giving her courage.

He blinked, surprised. "Yes, I guess I do."

She smiled. "You guess?"

"Yes, I do. Sorry. I don't know why I said that."

"What's her name?"

"Danielle."

"I hope she appreciates you," she said, earnest.

He nodded slowly. "She says she wants to move in with me."

Elise regarded him, intrigued. "Do you want her to?"

"I think so, but I'm not sure."

"Do you have a picture of her?" she asked, suppressing a sudden urge to wink, something she never did, except at small, shy children.

He hesitated before taking his phone from his back pocket, and after a few seconds of pressing and repressing two or three buttons he found a picture and handed her the phone. The display showed a startlingly pretty redhead in a black tank top, Billy in a Dodgers hat looking handsome and proud and suntanned next to her, his arm around his girlfriend's pale, gleaming shoulders. "That was taken a few months ago," he said, blushing. "We were in San Francisco for her birthday."

"She's so gorgeous," said Elise, feeling a tremor of jealousy in spite of herself. Didn't she have her hands full enough with Renn? Yet it was terribly fun to flirt with Billy, and she savored this perilous impulse, as if on a dare she were thrusting her finger through a flame. "She looks very sweet too. I can see why you're with her."

"She is sweet. Most of the time, anyway." He paused, putting the phone back in his pocket. "What's it like working with Marek Gilson?"

She reached for his water bottle and took a drink. "He's very good," she said. "His heart really seems to be in it, but I think everyone in the cast is crazy about this film." She liked Marek well enough but wasn't nuts about his recreational name-dropping, which seemed a little absurd to her because he had already made it, and in her opinion he had little to prove, though there was also the chance that he was trying to remind her of her place, making it clear that he knew more people than she did, that he was the film's real star whereas she was still at the stage where she needed to prove her worth. Before she had started acting, she had always assumed that male and female actors did not feel competitive with each other, that there was only same-sex rivalry, if there had to be any rivalry at all. Now she realized how naive this assumption had been.

"My dad loves this film. His screenplay is really good."

"You should tell him that," she said.

Billy looked at her. "Why do you say that?"

"I don't know. I just think he'd be happy to hear it. I would be."

"I think I already told him that I liked it."

There was something unstudied about him that she liked, something softer and less demanding than the swagger or smugness of the grown children of the other seasoned movie people she knew. She wondered if it was his mother's influence, or else Renn had tried not to spoil his son and daughter too much. Elise was a little afraid to meet his daughter, whose med-school pedigree intimidated her.

"It's so hot today," she said, lifting her hair off her sweaty neck.

He nodded, then looked away. "I'd better go," he said.

"Really? Already?"

"Yes, I'd better," he said. He didn't say good-bye but gave her a small wave before he opened the door to her trailer and disappeared. He hadn't taken his bottle of water, which she noticed was still in her hand.

That night, after a bubble bath and a room-service dinner in Renn's room, she discovered that the rumor mill was as robust on the *Bourbon* set as anywhere else. "I told Billy not to bother you," he said. "Especially when you're resting."

"He wasn't bothering me. I invited him up. I wanted him to tell me all your secrets."

"I don't think he knows them."

She laughed. "Really? He must know a few."

"Not if I can help it," said Renn.

She couldn't tell if he was being ironic. Her amateur powers of psychoanalysis seemed to be eroding under his influence. She said nothing.

"Why did you invite him into your trailer?"

Well, she thought, suppressing a smile. He's jealous.

"I wanted him to help me go over some lines for my next scene." She wasn't sure why she persisted with this lie.

"You shouldn't have left your assistant back in California, Elise. She might have come in handy here." He smiled as he said this, but she could tell that he was annoyed.

"I feel more comfortable being on my own than having Gwynn with me all the time. I don't really like being someone's boss."

"All right, but you can always ask one of the production assistants here to help you. Or I'll do it if I'm not busy."

She laughed. "You're always busy."

"I suppose that's true."

She hoped that she hadn't gotten Billy into trouble. The PR task, at least, had been straightened out to Renn's satisfaction, and *Bourbon* was likely to receive as much prerelease buzz as he hoped for, maybe more. The first movie he had directed, *The Zoologist*, had done very well critically, and although the box office receipts were modest, it had still earned a little more than expected. She had watched it before she auditioned for *Bourbon at Dusk*; some of it had been over her head, and there wasn't a lot of dialogue, but she had been able to tell Renn that she had loved how he had progressively softened the light on the female lead, one of only five characters in the film with a speaking role. By the end, she was almost out of focus, something that had reminded Elise of how Laura had been portrayed in a film version of *The Glass Menagerie* that she had seen in high school. Renn had been impressed, telling her that Tennessee Williams was his favorite playwright. She didn't know if she had a favorite playwright, but she told Renn that he was hers too.

"Billy was a perfect gentleman," she said.

"I'm pretty sure that I can trust him," said Renn, giving her a foxy smile. "But the jury's still out on you."

3.

There was a moment a week later when Elise thought that Billy might kiss her. They were alone in the elevator at the Omni, riding up to their rooms, and she was telling him a silly story about how her childhood pets had all been named after flowers, even the males. At the end of the story, the elevator doors about to open, he gave her a look that she recognized as the kind that sometimes accompanied a romantic confession: "I'd really like to make love to you right now," or "You're the most beautiful woman I've ever seen." It wasn't that these words had ever been spoken to her in this situation, not exactly, but she had heard them in movies and had always hoped that she would someday find herself in an elevator or on a rainy boardwalk with a handsome man who would reveal that he wanted to kiss her and then he would do it. It would feel right too, and they would somehow make it to the nearest bed without much difficulty, and maybe, a year or two later, she would marry him. (They would also be millionaires but not really have to work, and aside from two perfect children, she would rarely desire anything else.)

After she and Billy had stepped off the elevator and were standing uncertainly in front of the closing doors, he didn't kiss her, but he touched her arm and said something that she knew she would remember for a long time. It was a confession, a startling one that she would keep to herself until she started seeing a therapist several months later who suggested that she ask herself if maybe it was the son she really wanted, not the father. The therapist would also say that Elise was probably not ready to commit to anyone for the long term and might not be ready to do so for several years.

"If it weren't for my dad," Billy said quietly, "I'd be doing everything I could to convince you to go out with me."

She didn't know what to say, but when she opened her mouth to speak, he held up his hand. "Please forget I said that," he said, blushing. "I never say things like that."

"I'm very flattered," she said softly.

"You are?"

"Of course I am, Billy."

He faltered, his smile apologetic. "Would you mind calling me Will?"

"Oh," she said, embarrassed. "Sure. I'm sorry."

"No, it's fine. I just prefer Will." He pulled a folded piece of yellow paper from the back pocket of his shorts and handed it to her. "This is for you. I hope you won't show it to anyone."

She stared at him. "What is it?"

"It's something I wrote last night. I'm not a writer, so it's not very good."

She could feel her stomach leap. "Hey," she said. "You should never apologize for a gift. That's something my grandfather taught me. He'd even refuse a gift if someone apologized for it. My grandmother hated it when he did this, but people stopped apologizing, or else maybe they just bought him better presents." Her cell phone started to ring then, the ringtone the one she had assigned to Renn, but she didn't reach into her purse to answer it.

"You'd better get that. I'll see you later," said Billy.

"Billy. Will, I mean. Wait."

He looked at her.

She held up the note. "Thank you."

He nodded, then turned and left her with the paper gripped in her damp fingers. Her room was in the opposite direction, around the corner and at the far end of the hall, only three doors down from Renn, something she wondered if he had requested when their hotel rooms had been reserved. She couldn't wait to read Will's note, but when she was slipping her key card into her door, Renn opened his door and she hastily stashed the note in her purse, annoyed but not showing it. He was wearing his robe and a smile, the robe meaning that he wanted to have sex before dinner. After dinner, if there was no night shoot scheduled, his habit was to watch the dailies. If they waited until after the dailies to have sex, he was sometimes too tired, or else he didn't last long and she would have to finish for herself. But when he was awake and had the energy, he was the best lover she had ever had.

4.

Six days later, Will went back to L.A. He left without saying goodbye, and although she had a pretty good idea why he left the set early, she was surprised that he hadn't tried to speak to her one more time before going home. She didn't have his phone number, and she wasn't sure where he lived, only that his place was close to the Getty. The night he gave her the note, she hadn't been able to read it until almost midnight; Renn had asked her to watch the dailies with him, and she said yes because he didn't always ask. Taking her clothes off and slipping into bed with him before dinner, she was reminded that he was the most exciting man she had met in a long time, much more exciting than the French teacher she had had a crush on during her junior year at UT-Austin, a young professor whom all the female students and a few of the male students had been smitten with because he was from Paris and not yet thirty, but most of all because he resembled Olivier Martinez, the sexiest film star anywhere, aside from Renn maybe, that Elise could think of. As if she had scripted it, M. Tanguy became her lover a few weeks after the semester ended. She had run into him at the grocery store, where he was buying mangoes and Camembert. He had chuckled over the cliché: "I love French cheese," he said, grinning adorably. "It is true that you cannot take the France out of the Frenchman." That he had not spoken in French made her wonder if he was nervous seeing her too. Without directly meeting her eyes, he had asked her to share the cheese with him, and they dated until early August, when he went home to Paris for three weeks. After his return, he told Elise that he had gotten back together with an old girlfriend and that he could not keeping seeing her. Now, from time to time, she wondered if he had seen any of her movies, if he regretted breaking up with her so unceremoniously. It had taken her all of the fall term to get over him, even after she had been flown to Hollywood and had auditioned for a role in a Vince Vaughn comedy that subsequently she was chosen for, and from then on, her life was very different.

Will's note was half poem, half love letter; it made her smile until her cheeks hurt, her eyes tearing up, in part because she had a feeling that she would have gone down the hall to thank him, and maybe also to kiss him, if she hadn't already been involved with his father, who was asleep on the other side of the locked bathroom door.

Dear Elise,

I'm not sure if I'll give you this. It seems
too much of a risk, for so many reasons.
      I think of you
                    as a woman
who must receive notes like this one
almost every day.
      Still,
              I cannot keep
these thoughts to myself anymore.
When I close my eyes
              I see you
as spun from gold and silk
            and a dove's soft wings.
I can only guess what it is like
            to touch you—
you would be softer than warm rain
              falling
from a midnight sky.
            Yours would be the one
breath to bring me back to life
          if I were trapped
in a room with no windows,
        the light fading outside,
the walls too close. It is impossible
for me to stop thinking about you.

—New Orleans, October 26

At first, she did not want to recover from the feeling the poem gave her. It was as if she were lying on her back, floating in the Pacific, nothing at all on her calendar for the next few weeks. This never happened anymore, both the blissful beach-going and the open schedule.

When she climbed into Renn's bed after reading the poem several times, she could feel Will's presence down the hall. She imagined him lying in his bed too, wondering if she had liked his note, if she might also have a crush on him. She didn't know if she did, but his poem affected her more than any other gift had in a while, even the elegant platinum bracelet Renn had given her two days earlier. He had had it sent overnight from Tiffany's, a detail he had only shared with her after she had pried it out of him. As far as she could tell, it was not his habit to brag about how much money he spent. The fact that he had ordered her such a beautiful and tasteful gift while under the many pressures of Bourbon's production had impressed her. Or had he made Will order it? She really hoped not, especially now. Yet whoever had ordered it, the bracelet seemed proof that Renn was wooing her, that their involvement was probably more than a fling to him.

At one thirty in the morning, sleep still not close enough, she wished that Will had never come to New Orleans. She had been perfectly happy before his arrival, when all she had wanted was to concentrate on her new relationship with Renn and on acting as capably as she could in her role as Lily, the film's heroine. What could Will possibly be expecting her to say to him? "You're irresistible"? "I'm dumping your dad, and as soon as this movie wraps, let's elope"? Maybe he only wanted her because he couldn't have her, and certainly not without a big scene where someone was likely to get hurt badly.

Finally, at 2:00 a.m., she got up and took one of Renn's sleeping pills, and all the next day she felt alternately sluggish and anxious, wondering when she would see Will, and why he affected her as he did. He was very sweet and good-looking, but his poem and its schoolboy earnestness affected her more than his looks. And the fact that he had bluntly told her he desired her, knowing as he did that she was seeing his father—it was this impulse, its rebelliousness, and above all, its murky, masculine competitiveness—that attracted her most.

Will didn't appear where she was until five that afternoon. He couldn't meet her eyes because he was with his father, and when he turned and left the set, she glanced timidly at his retreating back, his shoulders slumping as if in resignation or defeat. There seemed no way that anything could happen between them. But she didn't think she wanted anything to happen, either. Most plainly, she wasn't free, and he was also seeing someone else—a woman whom Elise could even imagine herself liking if they were to meet. Will had no business cheating, nor did she. And his father, as calculating as it might be to think such a thing, would undoubtedly be able to do more for her, *was*, in fact, already doing so much for her.

5.

Even in early adolescence she had not believed that she could settle for the kind of life that it seemed most adults she knew had settled for. While her friends were already discussing how many children they would have, what kind of houses and cars they wanted, and where they would work and live and take their vacations, she was thinking that she might do something else, that maybe she could be famous and not have to live in a brick ranch house with three small bedrooms and plumbing problems because tree roots had grown into the pipes. She did not want to marry her high-school sweet-heart, who was likely to become fat and lazy by the time he reached thirty. She had read too many *Cosmopolitan* articles and Dear Abby columns about infidelity and marital discord before her seventeenth birthday that it was probable that marriage's supposed enchantments had been spoiled for her for life.

As for her nebulous desire to be famous, her mother had enrolled her and her sister in tap dance and ballet classes starting when they were four, and although Elise had done well in both, she had not been the best student in the class. Her sister Belle had been a little better than Elise was, but what interested Belle most about the classes were the costumes—the special shoes and leotards and especially the tutus they got to wear for the ballet recitals. Belle was her mother's daughter: infatuated with pink and ruffles, and learning to sew, and matching her hair ribbons to her shoes and girl-sized purses. Elise was her father's daughter: athletic, impatient with clothes that needed to be ironed and hung in the closet, bookish and boyish-looking until she reached puberty and suddenly she had breasts, as well as shapely arms and legs that extended far beyond hemlines. By fifteen, she was two inches shy of six feet and growing into the face she would have when a film director visiting Austin for the South by Southwest Music Festival in the spring of Elise's junior year at UT spotted her in a club and gave her his card and asked her to call him because she might be the girl he was looking for to play the daughter of a character Diane Keaton had all but committed to playing in this director's next picture. Elise had the look—she was that memorable.

A week later, she did call him and he remembered her, but instead of flying her to Hollywood, he asked her to send headshots, ones she had a friend take because she couldn't afford to hire a professional photographer, and when she sent them off to the director, he didn't acknowledge their receipt for two months, and by that time, she was dating the French professor, but the director didn't forget her, and it was he who called in early October and asked if she might be interested in auditioning for a comic role in a film about two brothers who were driving the corpse of their eccentric uncle cross-country in order to complete a secret burial ritual, one his will had specified. She thought it sounded like a very stupid movie but she agreed to audition, and then it turned out to be a Vince Vaughn picture and she knew that she would take the role if they thought she was good enough. She had been in the drama club in high school and had acted in three plays in college, but had only had small roles because the acting students always won the leads. It was clear to her that the director wanted her mostly because he liked the way she looked, but there were plenty of others who had started out this way too.

The dead-uncle movie ended up being a big hit, and she was offered roles that were much better, but paid much less. Even so, her agent said, "Take a couple of them and raise your stock, because the people who make the better studio movies will see that you can actually act."

When her parents saw that she was succeeding, they were relieved but worried that she had been forced to do things that compromised her self-respect, which she hadn't, not really, though the director she'd met in Austin had made it clear while they were filming *Uncle Fenstad's Last Request* that he would be game for an affair if she were interested. She was not at all attracted to him, and he was newly married. By flirting outrageously but pretending a religious aversion to adultery, she was able to sidestep his offer without crushing his ego. This performance, she realized a year or so later, had been much better than the one memorialized on celluloid for *Uncle Fenstad*.

Her sister's reaction to her success was more complicated than their parents'; Belle was jealous and felt excluded but was also intensely curious and, like their mother, full of grim warnings. "They're eventually going to want you to show your tits," she said. "They'll make you, I bet."

"Not if I have it written in my contract that I won't show them."

"You can do that?" said Belle, disbelieving.

"Yes. A lot of women do."

"But you're just starting out, so you're probably going to have to do things you don't want to."

"Maybe, but I'm not going to worry about that until I have to."

"Well, I'd worry about it now. You should be prepared."

Since graduating from the University of North Texas two years before Elise left for Hollywood, Belle had been living in Dallas with their parents and was employed as a social worker at a county medical clinic where she counseled immigrants and other disenfranchised poor. Elise admired her but suspected that her sister had already had a bit of a martyr complex before taking the clinic job, which was underpaid, exhausting, and full of miserable cases that Elise tried not to imagine, at least not with any frequency. She and Belle had been very close as girls, but when Elise was growing into her long-limbed body, Belle grew awkward in hers, and she gained more weight from late-night pizzas and candy bars at college than anyone had expected. That most of the boys who called the house, starting when Elise was in ninth grade and Belle in twelfth, were asking for the younger, not the older sister had been one of the first wedges to come between them.

Another wedge: after *Uncle Fenstad*, Elise donated fifteen thousand dollars to Belle's clinic, hoping this would help restore her to Belle's good graces, but her largesse had the opposite effect—Belle resented that she didn't earn anywhere near enough money to be able to make the donation herself. Their mother also seemed unnaturally accepting of Belle's self-pitying tendencies and general unhappiness—

"Belle has such a good heart. I just don't understand why there isn't some decent young man out there who will see how wonderful she is and adore her as much as she deserves to be adored." It was disorienting and upsetting to feel her mother's and sister's growing hostility in regard to her own good fortune. When Elise made the mistake of saying to her mother during an argument that she and Belle were resentful of her for doing so well on her own, her mother grew very chilly: "I can't believe you would say such an ungracious thing about your sister and me. Shame on you, Elise. We have always wished for nothing but happiness for you."

As the phone calls home grew more stilted after Elise moved from Austin to California, she made them less often. Her father was the one constant; he sounded the same as always—cheerful but missing her, supportive but cautious. He also visited her more frequently than either her mother or sister did, Belle saying that she had trouble getting time off from work, which Elise knew was mostly true. Her mother worked too; she was part owner of a flower and garden shop, and the other owner was often at home, attending to a disabled son. Her mother also said that she did not like L.A.; she found its endless freeway systems ugly and frightening, and the people unfriendly and self-obsessed.

"But they're like that everywhere, Mom," Elise said. "Dallas isn't exactly the altruism capital of the world either."

"I know that," Mrs. Connor said tartly, "but people are worse where you are."

About these strained family ties, Renn had given Elise what she thought was good advice: "Just wait it out. This is all as new for them as it is for you." Later he added, "It can be rough when the people you're close to become successful, especially if things stay the same for you."

6.

It wasn't a Freudian slip, at least she didn't think it was, but she had acted careless in a way that she usually never did: she left Will's poem on the desk in her room, only half covered by a folder of hotel stationery. She kept going back to read it and didn't always take an extra few seconds to put it away. Most of the time she went to Renn's room anyway, because it was bigger than hers. But four nights after Will had given her the poem, Renn stopped by unexpectedly while she was still getting dressed for dinner. Before she had any idea what he was doing, Renn had read the poem and set it back on the desk.

"My son wrote that, didn't he," he said. "I had no idea he was a poet."

She was in the bathroom, applying mascara. Hearing his words, she froze.

He stood in the doorway now, looking at her, his expression carefully nonchalant. "I don't want you to bother lying about it, Elise. I recognize the handwriting. If you're interested in him, you can tell me. If he's the one you prefer, okay, but I don't want you seeing both of us."

He was smiling, but she could see that he was upset. I'm going to screw this up, she thought, feeling guilty, even though she knew that she had done nothing wrong. It didn't seem like she had, in any case.

"He's not the one I prefer," she said, putting the mascara wand back in its tube. She went to Renn and hugged him. "Not at all. You're the one I want."

Renn let her embrace him for a second but then pulled back to look into her face. "What does he think he's doing, writing poems for you? He knows we're together."

She hesitated. "Have you told him that we are?"

"He knows."

"If you didn't tell him, maybe he didn't."

"But you told him after he gave you the poem?"

"Yes." She paused. "Wait. Maybe he said that he knew you and I were dating, but he still wanted to give me the poem."

Renn's face colored. "Did he."

Fuck, she thought. I'm so fucking stupid.

"He might not have. I can't remember," she said.

"Try."

She could feel herself start to sweat. "I really don't remember, Renn. I know he said that he wasn't much of a writer but he was going to give me the poem anyway. That must have been what he said."

"He's not in a very good place right now, Elise. He's never had a real job, and he's almost twenty-seven. I think he's suffering from depression, but I doubt he'd acknowledge it if anyone asked him. The kid has been spoiled his whole life, and I can admit that some of this is his mother's and my fault, but some of it is his. His sister is about to finish medical school at the top of her class, and the two of them couldn't be more different if one of them had been raised by wolves, the other by nuns."

"I'm not interested in him," she said. "Really, I'm not."

"You're your own woman, and I won't tell you what you should or shouldn't do, but if you're going to be with me, there can't be any others."

"There aren't," she said. "That's the truth."

He studied her for a long moment before pulling her to his chest. "Good, because I won't share you. I'm not capable of it."

"I'm not either," she said.

"You're the only woman I'm seeing, Elise. If you weren't, I wouldn't have any right to tell you not to see someone else."

She hoped he would never find out that she had gone to Will's room two nights earlier to thank him for the poem and had allowed herself to be invited in, the door closed behind her. They had talked for a minute, Will blushing, she nervous and a little giddy, and then she had let him kiss her. She had let him put his arms around her and she had put hers around him, her body pressed against his, and she had felt his hardness while they kissed, and then she had pulled away, guilty with her desire for him, and ashamed of herself for giving in to her curiosity and lust when she was the girlfriend of Renn Ivins, a handsome and very talented actor-director-screenwriter whom she knew she should consider herself lucky to work with, let alone share a bed with.

Will had said nothing after she pulled away, even though she meekly apologized before leaving him in his bachelor's room with its bedside lamp illuminating the rumpled bed, the sheets and comforter twisted violently, as if by a fever victim.

7.

One thing she had been warned about but had found herself unprepared for was how it seemed that almost everyone she knew now felt entitled to gifts of money from her. Loans she would have been more amenable to, but the few people who pretended they were asking for loans made it seem as if it were a joke—she had enough money, didn't she? Why couldn't she just give it to them? Ha ha. Only kidding.

They also wanted auditions or some sort of industry job or introductions to other famous people, whether she knew them or not. They wanted invitations to A-list parties (or B- and C-list—any Hollywood party would do), and life-size cardboard cutouts of characters in films that had been released years earlier. They wanted to borrow the clothes she had worn for a role, which were the studio's, not hers. They wanted to stay at her house for a couple of weeks while they looked for a place of their own, or else they just wanted to live with her, period, and be a part of her entourage, because surely she had one. Didn't all famous people have entourages? Even worse was that people she had barely said three words to in high school or college were somehow finding her private e-mail address or phone number or else they were leaving messages at the studio asking her to help them break in to the business. She was also being asked to donate to every imaginable charity, to put in guest appearances at fund-raisers and hospital galas and company picnics and grocery store and car-dealership grand openings and the quinceñera for her landscaper's daughter. When she complained about these requests to her agent, he told her to let her personal assistant or her publicist talk to the demand-makers; she should never talk to them herself. When she complained to Renn, he laughed and said, "You'll need to get used to these kinds of requests as fast as you can. The more successful you are, the worse it gets."

In airports, at the post office and the gas station and Starbucks, she was asked for her autograph. She was told how beautiful she was—*even more so in person than on the silver screen!* (a claim she didn't really believe)—how talented, how destined she was for everything a person could hope for: Oscars, Golden Globes, the perfect husband, the perfect children, the perfect house and house pets and gardener and poolmen and Grammys. (*Oh wait, Ms. Connor, those are for singers, aren't they?*)

Because now, quite suddenly, she had something that tyrants and revolutionaries had waged wars over for thousands of years: power—both financial and sexual. It was not an illusion either; she could ask for any material object or personal service that she desired, pay for it, and have it delivered, overnight or later that same day. Any straight man she wanted, she could probably also have. Her power alarmed her, and on one morning when the sun shone furiously behind her heavy silk shantung curtains (new and expensively hand-sewn) at the house she had bought in Laurel Canyon less than a year earlier, she had been seriously resistant to getting out of bed. This was after *Bourbon at Dusk* had wrapped, while Renn spent four nearly sleepless weeks editing the film, fortifying himself with caffeine and something stronger from his doctor, she suspected—during which she was alone with him precisely five times, one of them on New Year's Eve, and only for three hours. He couldn't afford any real breaks until he was done editing the dozens of scenes they had shot into a presentable enough format to submit to the Cannes Festival's screening committee by their mid-February deadline.

She had gone home to Dallas for Christmas because she knew that Renn planned to see Will and Anna and then go right back to editing. Elise wasn't sure if she would be invited and assumed not, considering Will's love poem, which Renn had not brought up again, but it was still there between them like a small electric force field. Nonetheless, he had wanted her to stay in L.A. so that they could be together when he wasn't working. She had planned to visit her parents for four days but left on the morning of the third day because she and her mother had argued so often, and her sister had recently been dumped by a guy she had gone to high school with, who, a few minutes before breaking up with her, had asked for Elise's e-mail address, something that it seemed Mrs. Connor blamed Elise for more than Belle's ex.

Coming home from Texas, she had felt depressed and sad and resentful of the unfair treatment her mother and sister had inflicted on her. Renn told her that it would pass, and although he sounded sympathetic and told her to come straight from the airport to his place, she said that she would see him in the morning if he could spare an hour or two because she knew that he worked best at night and she didn't want to distract him. In fact, she wanted to go home and mope. She did not feel like talking to anyone, especially after having to be nice to the few dozen strangers who had stopped her at both airports to ask for her autograph. She could only hold a smile for so long before it started to feel like her face would freeze into a permanent grimace.

At home, she put her suitcase in the guest bedroom closest to the master bedroom. She had left two other larger suitcases in there already, neither of them unpacked. Her days were so busy, or else she felt too tired to put away the clothes she had taken to New Orleans, despite being home for more than a month now. Her next project, You Knew Me When, would start in late February, and most of it would be filmed in southern California, with one two-week shoot in Argentina scheduled for early April, but she didn't know when she would bother to unpack the New Orleans suitcases, and now she had the Dallas one too. It seemed easier to buy new suitcases, which could be purchased online in about three minutes, and she also grew tired of her clothes so quickly these days that she preferred to shop for new ones rather than unpack the old ones and keep wearing them. She had told no one that she was doing this; she knew it was shameful, the opposite of her parents' admirable thriftiness. Her thought was that eventually she would donate her old clothes to charity or give some of them to Belle if she lost enough weight and wanted to take them.

She could have had her housekeeper unpack the suitcases for her; Marita had offered several times, but Elise wasn't yet used to the idea of someone else organizing and maintaining her wardrobe. Gwynn, her personal assistant, who was ten years older, very efficient, and not particularly talkative, which was fine with Elise, could have been asked to unpack the suitcases too, but she had not told Gwynn about them, fearing her disapproval, or worse, the confused, vaguely scornful look that would pass across her face while Elise tried to explain herself.

8.

A week before Elise left for Argentina, two things happened: Belle tried to kill herself—halfheartedly, as it turned out, but it nonetheless deeply frightened Elise and her parents. The second thing was that Will wrote to her; it was the first time she had heard from him since he'd left New Orleans.

Elise was only given a day and a half off from *You Knew Me When* to fly home to Dallas to visit her sister in the hospital, and although she tried to get another day off, the producers said, No way in hell. Her sister looked pale and puffy and embarrassed when Elise arrived in her hospital room, their parents sitting nearby, faces drawn and very weary.

Elise didn't know what to say, other than "Why would you do this to yourself? To our parents? What the fuck were you thinking?" She kept her mouth closed.

Belle cried when Elise leaned down to the bed to hug her, and Elise started crying too. "I'm sorry," Belle said weakly into her sister's hair.

Elise could feel Belle's tears on her neck and wondered for a witless second if she was responsible for Belle's misery. If she hadn't gone to that club and met the director . . . if she hadn't called him back . . . if *Uncle Fenstad* hadn't done so well . . . but these were ridiculous thoughts. Even so, they persisted. If only Belle were a brother, then the sibling rivalry would be of a different shade, if it existed at all. From what she had been told, Renn's brother Phil handled Renn's success capably. Sisters, however, especially ones close in age, rarely seemed to be devoted allies, something Elise had figured out in high school.

Her mother was too stricken with grief and worry to start an argument about anything, and when she flew back to L.A. the next day, Elise felt a little more secure in her relationships with her mother and sister than she had in a while. Belle had told her that she hadn't actually wanted to kill herself, but she had been so angry at her exboyfriend, having seen him out with another girl the night before, that she supposed she had wanted to show him what a bastard he was.

Elise wondered if Belle had lost her virginity to the bastard, but she didn't ask. Belle claimed to have lost it her freshman year in college, but Elise had never been sure, especially because her sister had gotten so chubby, and as far as Elise knew, Belle had not had a boyfriend in Denton during her four college years.

Before she went to the airport, Elise offered her sister a gift. "If you'd like to go to a spa and relax for a couple of weeks, I'll send you to one I like in Scottsdale. There's a great one in Cabo San Lucas too, if you don't mind going to Mexico."

"I'm not sure," her sister said wanly. "I'll let you know."

"I think it'd be really good for you."

"I look so bad in a swimsuit," said Belle.

"Don't be silly. It's a spa. You can wear a robe the whole time you're there if you want to. You can sit on the veranda and read romance novels and not do a thing except get a massage and eat fresh fruit all day."

"I'll have to think about it," was all Belle would say.

Before Will called her, he sent an e-mail asking if she minded if he called, and if she didn't, could he have her number? He had gotten her e-mail address from his sister, who had most likely gotten it from their father, but Will didn't know for sure. He included his own phone number in the e-mail, saying that if she wanted to, she could always call him. But she didn't call, nor did she know what to say in response to his e-mail, so she stalled. Before she had a chance to think of a tactful reply, he called her. Hearing his voice, her stomach and heart both leaped. It was as if he were in the same room, about to kiss her again.

"Can I see you?" he said, no hello, no awkward pleasantries.

"How did you get my number?"

"I've had it since New Orleans." He hesitated. "My dad gave it to me when I first got there. He gave me all of the main cast members' cell numbers."

". . . Will, I don't think it'd be a good idea for us to see each other."

"Does that mean you don't want to see me, or you don't think you should?"

"I don't think I should."

"Why not?"

"You know why. Because I'm with your father."

"But maybe you could be with me instead if you wanted to."

She sighed. "No."

"Could you translate that?"

"No," she repeated.

He was silent. Then he said, his voice breaking, "I can't stop thinking about you, Elise. I don't know what to do about it because I've tried to date other people since Danielle and I broke up, but I haven't been interested in anyone else."

She felt her throat constrict. She wanted to see him, but would not let herself tell him. It would be a mistake, for so many reasons. "I'm sorry, but I can't be with you. I just can't."

"Break up with him. I think you might want to be with me instead."

"I haven't heard from you in over five months, and now you're calling to tell me to break up with your father?"

"You know it's been five months?"

"Yes, of course I do." She paused. "I have to hang up now, Will."

He was silent.

"Will," she said, plaintive and impatient. "I have to hang up. Please say good-bye."

He still didn't speak, and after a few more seconds, she hung up on him, sick as it made her feel. It was only five days since she had gotten back from Dallas, and although her sister was home again and had taken a leave of absence from work, Elise continued to feel off-kilter and anxious, and *You Knew Me When* was no longer as much of a joy as it had been before. She had had trouble sleeping since Belle's hospitalization, and Will's e-mail hadn't helped. And now this phone call where he had put her on the spot, and to her alarm, she had felt a strange elation when he'd said, "I think you might want to be with me instead." But why did she? He had no job and no clear idea of what he wanted to do professionally, and he also seemed to resent his father's success, just as her sister and mother resented hers. Her life had been going along fine without him. She was in a relationship with a man she desired and respected; she was acting in good films and making a lot of money. *Bourbon* was going to premier at Cannes, and she would get to go there with Renn and it would be her first visit to the south of France and everything would be perfect if she could learn to focus on what was good for her rather than trying to sabotage her life by letting in the chaos she seemed lately to be so attracted to.

Will's number was in her phone now, and his e-mail was on her computer. He was offering her something that she knew she shouldn't want because it could not compete with what she already had. But he was competing anyway, and she had to admire his bravado, taking on a man like his father who did not, as far as she could tell, ever lose.

CHAPTER 7

NOTES FOR
THIS ISN'T GOLD

A MEMOIR BY MELINDA BYERS

EARLY ON

He told me when we met that he had been fat as a child, and it wasn't until he turned sixteen that he lost the extra thirty pounds he'd been carrying around since age eleven. I wasn't sure if I should believe him because at the time I was working as a caterer, and I thought he might be making up this story in order to persuade me to bring him low-fat snacks that weren't on the menu the studio had decided on. It turned out that he wasn't lying, because eventually I saw the pictures that proved he really had been a fat kid. He looked so different in these photos from his current healthy and handsome self that his transformation seemed almost miraculous. "What finally made you lose the weight?" I asked.

"My brother's girlfriend," he said.

"Was she an aerobics instructor or something?"

His smile was sly. "No, I had a crush on her and wanted to steal her from him."

I think I laughed, but I can't remember for sure. I do know that I was a little taken aback. "Did you?"

"No, but I certainly tried."

He loved to eat, still does, I'm sure, and I know how to cook, so it was, for a little while, a match made in the kitchen, if not in heaven. That day in July when he appeared at the table where I was setting out fruit cups and brownies, he was the sexiest man I had ever met. He was thirty-eight and I was twenty-nine, recently separated from a husband who was very earnest about ruining his life by shooting up whenever he could get the drugs his body had become dependent on, which was every day by the time I left him. If you had told me when Toby and I separated that my next husband would be a movie star, I would have laughed in your face. Even though I catered movie sets all the time, the only guys who talked to me were the crew and a few of the actors with bit parts, probably because they assumed I'd be an easy lay, which wasn't true because (a) I was married, and (b) I'm not a slut. But I was, I guess you could say, kind of a babe. I had big breasts (real) and long legs and thick black hair that has since gone gray and now I have to dye it. I still have the boobs and the legs though. Renn was a fan of all three. He was also, for a while, the ideal man, a wild dream that seemed to have come true. Not surprisingly, I assumed that he'd be the love of my life.

It should be clear from the start how much I cared for him because some of the things I have to say on these pages won't flatter him. Nonetheless, I feel like I have to write this book because a lot of people think that marrying a movie star is the next best thing to being a movie star. Well, guess what, it's not. It's very hard. Basically impossible, as it turns out, and I'm pretty sure that Renn's first wife would agree with me, considering how things worked out for her too. I have never suffered so much as I did during the four and a half years of my marriage to Renn. I never once felt that I had him for real. I assumed that he would go back to his wife and kids, or that one of his beautiful, famous costars would steal him from me. It happens all the time. If it didn't, part of the economy would collapse because a whole slew of gossip rags and bloggers would be out of business. The fact that it doesn't happen even more often is a mystery to me. If you spend three months, six or seven days a week, behaving with someone the same way that you behave with your lawfully wedded husband or wife because the script calls for it, you are bound to get attached. The line between what's real and what's not is easy to blur, and on a movie set, it sometimes feels like how my college dorm felt on Friday nights—there's the sense that just about anything goes, and with everyone's parents so far away and oblivious to what their children are up to, sometimes crazy things do happen.

RENN & CO.

Where is Andrea, Renn's brother's coveted girlfriend, now? She's married, with three grown daughters, and lives in Youngstown, Ohio, where she's been an elementary school teacher for the past twenty-four years. (I know this because Renn's brother [Phil] told me. He got in touch with her recently through Facebook. Renn's brother's Facebook friends: 217. Renn's Facebook followers: 1,089,476. Not as many as younger actors, but still a pretty good number for an actor in his fifties. He [or, more likely, his publicist] maintains a fan page instead of a regular account because I suppose it would be too hard to keep up with so many individual "friends," and he would also probably have to deal with a lot of messages and posts from fans gone rabid. I used to have these nightmares where strange women would come up to me and throw acid in my face when I was out with Renn because they were so jealous. It never happened, but more than a few times we almost had to run away [literally] from someone who wouldn't leave us alone.)

I once asked Renn if Andrea ever contacted him after he became famous, and he said that she had. I asked if anything had happened between them. It took him a few seconds to reply, but he said no, no, he was already married to Lucy by then.

Where is Renn's brother now? In Niles, Illinois, which is a Chicago suburb not far from where they grew up. Phil is also a teacher, though he teaches high school students, not grade-schoolers. He works at Niles North, which is close to a fancy shopping mall where a month before we were married, Renn bought me three thousand dollars' worth of clothes at the Marshall Field's department store— four dresses, three pairs of shoes, two summer sweaters, one pair of tailored linen slacks. We were visiting Phil and his family because Phil's son was graduating from high school and he wanted Uncle Renn to come and make him look good in front of all of his unconvincingly jaded classmates. Renn was nice about obliging because he liked playing the role of the coolest uncle in the world, as Phil's son called him in front of all of his teachers and the entire graduating class during his salutatorian speech. Tyler didn't mention his father in the speech, but Phil was smiling when I glanced at him. I suppose he had gotten used to the fact he couldn't compete with his brother, at least not anymore.

The irony is, after Tyler's speech, Renn said to me under his breath, "I wish my own son felt even half as lucky to have me as a father."

Self-pity? Yes, I suppose so. Even if you make twenty-five million dollars or more a year, you're not necessarily going to be happy. What I'll say about Renn's son, Billy, is that he wasn't a bad kid. He was twelve when Renn and I got together, and his sister, Anna, was a year younger. (I thought she was a sweet girl when I knew her, and she probably still is, but she didn't return my phone calls while I was working on this book.) Anyway, if you're twelve and your parents are getting divorced, you're going to be mad at them and at the world. Billy was no exception, but he didn't take out his anger on the family cat and dog (Squirt and Tuba) or hit his sister or steal cigarettes from the convenience store near his middle school. I always thought that he would become an actor too, but in high school he only tried out for a couple of plays and was cast in small roles that he apparently thought weren't worth his time. In college he majored in economics, but I don't think he's put this degree to use. He's good at math though, something his father isn't, which is one reason why he's been robbed by two different business managers in the course of five years (though both of them were caught—one by Lucy, the other by Renn's investment broker—and forced to return the money).

A SHORT DETOUR: A FEW NOTES ABOUT ME, YOUR GUIDE ON THIS HOLLYWOOD WALK OF FAME

I was born in Cary, North Carolina, and for the first ten years of my life, I wanted to be a nurse because one of my mother's sisters, Aunt Judy, was a nurse. She is one of my favorite people and can play the harmonica and the piano and tried to teach me both, but I couldn't sit still for long enough to get beyond the practice scales. After that, I wanted to be a teacher, and then a radio broadcaster, either as a deejay or as a producer. After college, though, I couldn't get a job in radio to save my life or anyone else's, despite the increasingly short skirts I wore to interviews when I knew the interviewer would be a man. The jobs almost always went to a male candidate, a couple of whom were fired within a month, and then they'd bring me back to interview again and not offer me the job a second time. Eventually, out of fury and desperation, I took a job at an overpriced, mediocre restaurant in Century City as a prep cook before I decided to learn how to cook for real, which required more loans, for culinary school this time, and several angry promises to my father that I would pay him back, which I did, but not all I owed him until I married Renn.

Movies have always been a part of my life, as they are a part of most people's lives, and because I lived in Los Angeles from the age of eighteen on, they became even more important to me because I would often see movie stars doing the same things that average people did—sitting in traffic jams, eating breakfast at a diner, even, in one case, checking out library books (it was Debra Winger who I saw doing this, or else she had an identical twin). When I started catering for movie studios, I was even more intimately connected to them, but I felt as if there were an invisible wall between me and the actors and more famous directors, one through which I would never be allowed to pass. It's not like I cried myself to sleep every night thinking about how small my life was compared to the people who were getting top billing (or even middle) in the credits in each production that I catered, but I did feel this sense of isolation and hopelessness at times—my husband's drug use certainly didn't help matters—and when Renn noticed me and started coming by the catering van a couple of times a day to talk to me about the places I had traveled (not very many) and the books I had read, I probably would have forfeited ten years of my life to be his mistress, not to mention his wife. Girls from small towns in North Carolina (or anywhere else, for that matter) do not usually end up the wives of famous men. We are taught, tacitly or no, to stay out of trouble, to think kind thoughts and behave with tact and forbearance, to get a good education, and to be sure that we can provide for ourselves if necessary. We are not supposed to talk back or expect too much from life or put on airs. If we do those things, we will surely be putting ourselves in harm's way. You reap what you sow—this is probably the mantra of all small southern towns, if not northern ones too.

I have reaped what I have sown, and this, I suppose, is my cautionary tale.

Q & A

Over the years, a few people have asked me what one thing Renn did while we were together that upset me more than anything else. If you're going to ask a question like that, you probably aren't too worried about causing pain because you're forcing someone to revisit a moment in her life that likely she has tried to forget. Yet if you catch her at the right time, she might actually enjoy this chance to say something unkind about the person who treated her badly.

What was the one thing? Well, there wasn't just one. Marriages fall apart because eventually there is a critical mass of wrongdoing and petty selfishness that suffocates all of the affection and desire that presumably once existed between the couple. Renn almost never bothered to call me or have someone call on his behalf when he was delayed in meetings or on the set. I can't remember how many times I cooked us what I hoped would be a dazzling meal but then was forced to eat alone or throw it in the garbage because by the time he came through the door, grouchy and not at all interested in talking to me after his long day at work, the food was cold and congealed and generally unappetizing. And this was when he was in town. For half the time we were married, at *least* half, he was far away, often on the other side of the planet. I was invited to go with him to a few of his faraway shoots and stay for a week or two, but usually that was when his kids were also invited and he needed me there to look after them.

Some other things he did that won't win him any trophies:

1. He sometimes went to parties hosted by his movie friends and didn't invite me along.

2. He wouldn't even discuss having a child with me. "Out of the question," he said. "Who's going to raise the kid? I'm gone a lot and you certainly can't do it by yourself. You can barely get yourself dressed in the morning." (An exaggeration. I had bad days once in a while, but they didn't happen that often.)

3. He hadn't had a prenup with Lucy, but he did have one with me. He must have known that he would eventually want to dump me too. It wasn't that the agreement was stingy, but I should have known that if he could foresee the possibility of divorce, he could probably also foresee himself going through with it.

4. He cheated on me. He slept with at least two of his costars, the first when they were off filming in Bordeaux, the second in Lima. These were the two affairs that he admitted to. I'm sure there were more, but I didn't have proof. The reason I found out about these two tramps was because the one from the Bordeaux shoot called and told me. She was trying to steal Renn for herself, I'm sure, not do me any favors, which is what she had the nerve to claim: "You should know that he's not a good guy. If he'll run around on you, you really don't need that. What self-respecting woman does?" I told her to go to hell. I told her that it wasn't any of her goddamn business what happened in our marriage because I was the one wearing the ring on my finger, not her.

The tramp from the Lima shoot didn't call, but she did send a letter to Renn that I intercepted. She was such an idiot; she should have sent it to the studio, not his home address, but I guess she thought that I'd be too lazy to collect our mail each day, let alone open it. I can only imagine the stories Renn told her about me, the two of them bonding over my alleged bouts of depression and how my gray moods must have taken a toll on poor Renn who deserved a strong woman, even if he wasn't ever home to spend time with her or to talk to her for more than five minutes every few days when he was out of town.

5. He tried to keep his kids from me after he filed for divorce. It was sad for Billy, Anna, and me because we liked each other, for real, and the fact that Renn didn't want me seeing them anymore, let alone talking to them on the phone, was probably more hurtful than when I had to deal with the two tramps gloating over how he'd fucked them.

6. He often laughed at me when I mispronounced a word or if I didn't know things like Kathmandu is the capital of Nepal or that Bora Bora is an island in French Polynesia, not a city in Malaysia. But how many people do know these facts? I graduated cum laude from USC with a degree in communications. I'm not stupid, but there are so many things to know about the world, and God forbid I didn't know all of the exact same things that Renn knew. Does he know how to make beurre blanc? Does he know that cheesecloth is an important tool when you're making fruit preserves or Greek yogurt? I'm sure he doesn't. He was so condescending so many times that it's a wonder I didn't dump him before he had a chance to dump me.

7. He left me for another woman. Poetic justice, some will say, considering how he and I got together. Sure, I understand. But that doesn't mean I didn't suffer. He didn't marry her though, probably because she moved to Prague to pursue a career as a sculptor, which seemed pretentious and ridiculous to me at the time, and still does, frankly. She had the money to do it though and not get anxious if her work was awful and didn't sell, because her father owned a rifle factory in Virginia. Renn met her when he was making a film about the Civil War in the same town where her father's factory is. After he divorced me, it was only a few months before she moved to Europe and told him that she was going to dump him if he didn't buy

a place in Prague and spend at least a few months of the year there with her. I have to say that I kind of admire her guts, or maybe it was just an air of entitlement. She was only twenty-four at the time and almost model-beautiful and probably had lots of men after her, though I doubt any of them were both famous and rich the way Renn was.

Other questions people (therapists, mainly) have asked:

What one thing did Renn do that made you happier than anything else?

That's a hard question too. I guess you could say it's that he noticed me, when there were so many other women (and men) who wanted him to notice them too. He also made it possible for me to quit my job, which I liked well enough while I was doing it, but if you don't have to work, it's pretty tempting not to. I started to drink more than I should have though, having so much free time on my hands and no kids to take care of, other than my step-children once in a while. But they didn't need me to take care of them, both of them independent and bright enough to keep themselves busy. I once blamed Renn for my excesses with alcohol, and this got around in an embarrassingly public way, but I don't drink anymore and haven't in about a year and a half.

What did you learn about yourself while you were married to him?

One thing I learned is that I don't do well with uncertainty. This is something my current therapist helped me to figure out. I realize now that most people don't do very well with uncertainty because the biggest events in our lives, namely, our births and deaths, are out of our control, so in between these two points, we try as hard as we can, almost to the point of insanity (and beyond, in some cases), to control what we can. I'm not a fatalist, but I do think that there are quite a few things that we can't control, like what time the mail will be delivered or how many dings we'll get on the car in the parking lot, or why we like raspberries more than strawberries. Actually, many things probably are beyond our control, even the people we'll fall in love with, but I suppose that if a movie star comes calling, you're more likely to fall in love with him than the guy bagging your groceries. I suppose what I mean is, I could have been smarter, I could have recognized the odds against long-term happiness when I fell for a movie star. The bagger is probably a safer bet, even if he doesn't earn much of a living, because for one, he doesn't have anywhere near the same number of sexual options that a movie star does.

There was never a day or night when I felt truly at ease being Renn Ivins's wife. I think I must have known from day one that it wouldn't last, in part because he left someone else for me, which I did feel bad about (I'm not the sort of competitive freak show who thrives on stealing other women's guys), even though I didn't ever offer to return him to her. If I were a different kind of woman, all along I might have been able to say to myself, "Just have fun and enjoy the ride while it lasts," but I'm not that kind of woman. I wish I were, but I'm not.

What have you learned about yourself since the divorce?

I knew myself pretty well by the time Renn and I divorced, but I wasn't particularly thrilled with what I learned during our marriage, namely that I was often very jealous, insecure, needy, angry, vindictive, afraid. I knew that people everywhere were plagued by these same feelings, but it didn't matter because I was the one feeling them. That's like saying, "Don't be afraid of death because we all die." No kidding, but that doesn't really make it any better, does it?

What did Renn spend his money on?

1. He spent it on cars. When we were married, he had a Porsche Spyder like the one James Dean died in, a Jaguar, a silver Mercedes convertible, a Lexus, and a Chevy half-ton pickup for when he felt like pretending he knew how to do home-improvement projects like repairing the cedar deck that led from the sliding glass door off the kitchen to the pool. I think he still has most of those cars, or newer models, along with a Smart car (a gift from the manufacturer—I doubt he ever drives it, but his housekeeper apparently does) and a hybrid Ford Escape. He keeps half of these cars in a separate garage that he rents one town over from his house in the Hollywood Hills.

2. He spent it on his kids. He put something like six or seven million dollars × 2 into trusts for his son and daughter, which they couldn't access until they turned twenty-one, and I think the most they can take out during any one year is two or three hundred thousand, unless Renn gives them permission to take out more. That's still a lot of money, and with these trusts earning interest and dividends on the bonds and stocks or whatever Renn set up with his broker, Anna and Billy are set for life.

3. He spent it on his first wife. She gets a lot of money from him every year because she has never remarried. Something like two or three million, probably, on top of the twenty million in property and liquid assets that she got at the time of their divorce. She doesn't need it either, being a doctor who probably earns at least half a million on her own annually.

4. He spent it on food. He goes to the French Laundry up in Napa Valley as often as he can, which is about three or four times a year. He goes to Chez Panisse almost as often, which, like the visit to the French Laundry, requires a flight up to San Francisco and a limo driver or else he rents a car and drives himself and whichever woman

is accompanying him. He also has an excellent chef named Spike Light (really) who, since our divorce, cooks his meals whenever he's in L.A. and not dining out. He took this chef with him from time to time when he was doing shoots in Mexico or other places not too far away, but eventually he had to stop because the chef is married and his wife got angry when he left town for more than a few days, not trusting him to keep it zipped up or who knows what.

5. He spent it on staying (or at least looking) young—personal trainers, nutritionists, collagen injections, facials, Botox, dietary supplements, very expensive hair and skin products, hair and eyebrow stylists, massage therapists, private yoga and Feldenkrais classes, acupuncturists, aromatherapists, fashion consultants, karate and capoeira instructors, mud spas, mineral baths, protein powders, spirulina, manicures, and yes, pedicures.

6. He spent it on real estate. He owns vacation homes in Palm Springs and on Sanibel Island in Florida. He also owns a huge house in L.A. (where I lived with him after Lucy moved out with their two kids), a three-bedroom condo in New York City (with a twenty-eight-hundred-dollar monthly assessment, which he pays whether he's there or not), and a two-bedroom apartment in Rome.

7. He spent it on clothes. He likes Armani, as clichéd as it is for a movie star to like this designer. He also likes Ralph Lauren for casual clothes, and someone named Manfred G, who is a designer in New York who "creates" silk neckties and socks, charging something like five hundred dollars for his boring, monochromatic ties and two hundred for a pair of silk-and-wool socks.

8. He didn't spend it on drugs, nor did he spend it on strippers, as far as I know. He did give some of his money to charity every year, and he was generous with friends and family. I think he has probably "loaned" his brother Phil at least a million dollars by now. Renn put his nephew Tyler through college, and gave him money for a car,

clothes, books, and spring-break trips, all of the same things he gave to Billy and Anna.

9. He spent it on reserving a seat on a Space Shuttle trip to the moon. (Just kidding.)

10. He spent it on an astrologer. (Not kidding—at least once a month, either in person or over the phone, depending on where he was working. It cost five hundred an hour or something exorbitant like this. Renn might not be a drunk or a druggie like my first ex-husband, but he certainly has his expensive addictions.)

MISCELLANEOUS BITS, BUTS, & MAYBES*

Some things Renn said:

1. On 9/11, which is about the same time our marriage collapsed: "How could this not have happened to us? We barge around the world with our guns loaded and our dicks in our hands and expect people to offer us their virginal daughters and oil reserves, but not everyone wants to do what we tell them to."

He also said, after the bombs started to fall on Afghanistan: "If I were a younger man, I'd go to Kabul and teach drama classes for a year."

I told him that they needed volunteers to rebuild their hospitals and sewer lines and restore their power grid more than they needed someone to teach Shakespeare or David Mamet or whoever he would have taught. He was offended by this and told me that I was a philistine, a word I had to look up later. But I still thought my comment made sense—before opening their copies of *Romeo and Juliet*, the Afghanis would need functioning toilets and lights to read by, wouldn't they?

I also didn't see why he had to be a young man to teach in Afghanistan. He could go at forty-three as easily as someone who was twenty-three. It's not like I wanted him to go, but by that time, I was so tired of his lame excuses for not doing the things he bragged he might do that I wouldn't let him coast by with this whopper.

2. "I understand why people want to be vegetarians, but who do they think they're fooling? We're carnivores, and most of us have the pointy canines to prove it."

He said this during a discussion he was having with his daughter about her decision to become a vegetarian during her freshman year of high school. She didn't stick for very long with her no-meat diet, and when she returned to her old ways, Renn gave her a twenty-pound box of Omaha steaks, which she wouldn't accept, furious with what she perceived as his gloating. "I told you that I'm only eating chicken and fish, not red meat. Ever," she fumed. I'm sure she meant it, but I'm also pretty sure she did go back to eating red meat again. By that time Renn and I were divorced, so I don't know what he did when he found out that she was eating steak again. In case it's not clear, he likes to tease people, but he's not a big fan of being teased himself.

3. "I'm an ass man *and* a tits man. Why should I have to choose between the two?" Indeed. The usual laws of supply and demand do not apply to movie stars.

4. "The reason I'm hired for the best roles is because I am the best. I don't think there's anything wrong with saying this, because it's true."

He said these modest words after *Parachute Point* debuted (his crappiest movie, worse than *The Writing on the Wall*, if you ask me. *Parachute* is totally cheesy, and the boy who played his son was smarmy with a capital S) when being interviewed by a movie critic for the *L.A. Times*. I'm not sure why Renn thought he could get away with saying something as self-aggrandizing as this and not be made fun of or lose some of his fans and industry allies, not to mention his friends. His publicist had to perform God knows how many unholy acts to convince the journalist not to publish this quote.

5. "I love Monet. I don't care what those assholes think. If they could paint like he could, they wouldn't be such stuck-up pricks about his water lilies or cathedrals or dying wife."

At a fund-raiser for the Getty where he donated a big wad of cash to their endowment, he was almost apoplectic when he saw a couple of museum officials rolling their eyes after he said that his favorite artist was Monet. "Isn't it possible that they were rolling their eyes over something else?" I asked him, trying to make him feel better. His reply: "I know you can be pretty fucking dense sometimes, but I think this one wins the grand prize."

6. "I'm not a bully. Bullies beat people up and can't control their tempers. I've never been like that in my life."

He knew that he was being pretty selective in his definition of bully. I told him that he was forgetting about the people who are emotionally and verbally abusive, which, needless to say, I thought described him pretty well. He said that all married people argue sometimes, and it wasn't my job to rate everything he said by some asinine bully scale that I'd gotten from watching *Oprah* or listening to *Loveline* or whatever sorry-ass bullshit I squandered my time on when he wasn't home. (Oprah, by the way, adores him, and by then he had been on her show at least four or five times.)

7. "If one more person stops me and says how my movies got them to quit drinking or gambling or fucking their brother's wife, I'm seriously going to kill them."

We were at the Grove when he said this, late for a birthday party for Martin Landau, I think it was, and were trying to find a suitable gift. Renn liked shopping, but if he wasn't in the mood to talk to fans, he knew better than to go to the mall thirty minutes before we were supposed to be at a surprise party ten miles away.

*Most of the above was excised from the published version.

The books on his nightstand:

1. *Zen and the Art of Motorcycle Maintenance.* What California guy or wannabe hippie of a certain age and social class doesn't pretend to like this book?

2. *Women* by Charles Bukowski. I didn't read this novel until a few years after we were divorced. It helped me to see why Renn treated me the way that he sometimes did. With this being one of his favorite books . . . well, read it for yourself and see if you too aren't worried about a guy who thinks this is the best thing since clean water.

3. *The Stranger* (both a French and an English version). He knew passages of this book by heart, and for some reason, he identified with Meursault, Camus's strange murderer/anti-hero, who hoped at the novel's end that he would be greeted by cries of hatred from the people who had come to witness his execution. I didn't get this, and Renn thought that I was ignorant for not understanding what Camus was doing.

"He's finally starting to feel something at the end," he said. "After being indifferent to everything before now."

"But why cries of hatred? That's terrible," I said. "You actually identify with him?"

"Yes, I do. It doesn't matter if they're cries of love or hatred," he snapped. "The point is, he feels something after a long time of feeling nothing. He's lucky. It's a story of redemption, ultimately."

I didn't think so, and still don't. Needless to say, I don't have to discuss it with him any longer.

4. *Romeo and Juliet.* One of his dreams when we were together was to make a modern-day version of this beloved (but tiresomely everywhere) play in Paris with Jean-Pierre Jeunet, with Juliet as a lonely cashier at a Parisian movie house and Romeo as an usher who for years paints Juliet's portrait from photos he takes of her unobserved. I thought this made Romeo seem pretty creepy, but Renn didn't at all. "He's a frustrated romantic, like so many of us," he said.

"Not you," I said, trying not to sound as unhappy as I felt. "You can have whoever you want."

He opened his mouth to argue but then thought better of it.

5. *Mrs. Frisby and the Rats of N.I.M.H.* His children's favorite book when they were little. It was one of my favorites too. He told me that he read it to Anna and Billy at least ten times while they were growing up. I asked him to read it to me too, and he did not long after we were married. He used different voices for the major characters, and the fact that he bothered with this, that he took his time reading it, performing it, really, using all of his considerable actor's skills, was probably the single sweetest thing he ever did for me.

*Causes he is interested in and/or donates to, in no particular order:***

1. PETA (because of Anna, not because he is against people wearing fur or eating animals, but I do think he genuinely feels bad about the animals that live their short lives on factory farms)

2. VoL (Victims of Landmines—losing a limb is one of his phobias)

3. GiRLS (Girls in Real-Life Situations—an organization devoted to finding and freeing girls from child prostitution. A worthy cause,

obviously, but the director, Tamara Snow, is someone Renn fucked while he was still married to me, I'm about 98 percent sure)

4. HHOP (HIV Hospice of Pasadena—he had a close friend who died there, a guy he met in college who tried to convince Renn that he was bi when they were still in school together, but I don't think Renn ever fell for it)

5. Cows for Life (because Renn has a soft spot for Wisconsin—both of his parents are from there. CFL is based in Madison, and their mission is to convince all dairy farmers to stop using bovine growth hormones on their herds)

6. SOCC (Save Our California Coast—I think the name probably speaks for itself. I'm not sure if Renn had an affair with anyone who works for them, but I wouldn't be surprised)

7. WWF (World Wildlife Fund, not the World Wrestling Federation. He loves the earth. He really does. Especially when he can ride around on it in a Land Rover on an African savannah)

8. Himself (for the promotion and upkeep of his Movie Star Lifestyle)

**Some of the above was also excised from the published version.

Not all of it was bad:

He wasn't selfish or condescending the whole time we were together; otherwise I would probably have left him before he left me. He had many soft spots, gentle habits, and generous moments. He loved his parents and brother, and both of his children, and treated them all well. He was also curious about the world and felt compassion and interest in people whose lives were very different from his. I don't think he would ever have been interested in me if he weren't willing to give everyone a fair chance at earning his attention. But this democratic spirit often made me jealous because I never felt like he was fully there, even when we were alone together. He was always preoccupied by some project or half-baked hope or why someone important was taking so long to call him back. His life seemed to me, the outsider housewife, to be full of suspense, of secret dealings and intrigue—it wasn't just his movies that were filled with these things. He seemed to have so many ideas and sometimes woke in the middle of the night to make a phone call or scribble in a notebook that he kept on his nightstand, a habit that woke me up because he would always click on the bedside lamp.

Regarding Monet, he also loved Modigliani, Ed Paschke, Georgia O'Keeffe, Gerhard Richter, Lucian Freud. He didn't own much art, though, which seemed a strange omission, considering how many art books he had and how much money too. He could have bought some interesting things, and there are plenty of good galleries in L.A., not to mention in many of the other places he has traveled. He had a framed charcoal drawing of two small monkeys embracing that his daughter and one of her friends drew for him that he loved, though I thought it was kind of silly. Monkeys? Why? The friend, J, had a big crush on him and used to show up at our house in low-cut blouses and no bra and take every chance she could to bend over in front of him. I think she hated me. Needless to say, the feeling was mutual.

For as long as I was with him, it felt like I had to be constantly on the lookout for other women who were trying to get too close to him. It was both exhausting and futile because he wanted the pretty ones to get too close to him. I realized later that basically every straight man wants this. I am a jealous person. I think most people are jealous, if they're being honest. But we are forced to swallow this poison alone, and sometimes it corrodes the soul. (Yes, Renn, if you're reading this, I do love melodrama.)

One good thing is that I wasn't yet thirty-six when the divorce went through. It could have been worse; I could have been his first wife's age, or even older. Even though I'm not an actress or someone who desperately needs her looks to pay the bills, it seems to me that the worst thing a woman can do is grow older. I still had several years left to have a baby, but I ended up not having one. Going out with other men after Renn, especially at first, was very strange. I thought that I needed and wanted an ordinary guy, but in truth, I wanted someone more unique. Even though Renn was ungenerous and very harsh with me by the end, I couldn't help but compare the men I dated to him. They weren't as good-looking or as interesting or as charming or wealthy. He is a man who has everything other men want. Absolutely everything, and if he doesn't, he can quickly acquire it. This is not the kind of man a sane woman should want to date. He is too impossible, knowing himself to be better than everyone else.

CHAPTER 8

A GOOD
PERSON

*W*hat I have documented here, in my fifty-third year, from June through October, on a Sony ICD-SX712 digital recorder, is intended to assist an authorized biographer after my death. Or, perhaps like Mr. Twain (he and I are hardly of the same intellectual caste, I realize), I will act as my own biographer/ghostwriter, and publish a transcript of the following as part of a posthumous autobiography. The pun seems apt, because in a way, I will be speaking from the grave. Although I won't instruct the executors of my estate to wait a hundred years to release this material as Mr. Twain did with his own, I will tell them to wait no fewer than five—long enough, I hope, for any arguments over my last will and testament to have lost their initial, most potent virulence (if there is any virulence between my heirs—maybe there won't be).

A few of the following revelations, needless to say, will not be particularly flattering—for myself or for my closest family members. It might be that none of these revelations will be released until after my children, Anna and Billy, have also passed on, if ever. But this detail is something that I will have to decide at a later date.

A. *HOW IS IT THAT . . .*

"When did you realize that you wanted to be an actor?" "Or did you always know that you would become one?" "Who are your role models?" "Who is the real Renn Ivins?" "Is there a *real* Renn Ivins?" "What are your secrets?"

They don't stop asking these questions, however many times I've already answered them, one way or another. Who, if he has a shred of sanity, is stupid enough to tell a journalist his secrets, especially the darker ones? And isn't it clear why people want to become actors? They want to be loved. They want to be rich. They want to have sex with beautiful people who will never forget them. They want revenge on all of the kids who used to pick on them. They want revenge on everyone who didn't believe in them enough or dismissed them outright, despite how pathetic or dull these dismissers' own lives were. They want to be forgiven their selfishness and thoughtlessness. If you become famous, more people than you expect will forgive you for things you probably shouldn't be forgiven for, though there is also the chance that you will never be forgiven and that your disgrace will make international headlines, ones that might generate enough profit for the people reporting the story to retire to Monaco before year's end.

Some advice: two questions that interviewers should ask but don't (except for one guy who was doing an article for *Vanity Fair* a few years ago, when *The Zoologist* was released), probably because they know that I won't answer them honestly either: "What's it like for you to grow old in Hollywood?" and "How do you think it's different for men than women?" *Grow old*—does this mean that the journalist thought I was old already? These questions aren't exactly polite, but at least they're not stupid. I told the *Vanity Fair* guy that I didn't really feel like I was getting old, only more experienced. I remember his expression, something between a frown and a smirk, and I also remember feeling angry but hiding it from him. He sensed it anyway, because what he wrote was, "Ivins seems to be suffering from the collective Hollywood delusion that if you're rich and famous enough, the rules of gravity don't apply to you." Frankly, he's wrong about this. I do feel the gravitational pull that in due time will bring all of us down, but I'm fighting it. Almost everyone I know seems to live more in fear of aging visibly than of dying from cancer or seeing their children die before they do. Maybe even more than losing all of their money, and it's as bad with men as it is with women. I have booked a few Botox appointments but so far have avoided the face-lifter's scalpel and the antiaging snake oil sold in the back of otherwise reputable magazines. Despite all of our purported brainpower and common sense, human beings are truly a sad and ridiculous species.

That sounds cynical, I suppose. But despite our fears and vanities, I do think we are capable of selflessness and love and great empathic leaps of imagination. Many of us can and do appreciate beauty. We do not want to grow old, in part because it means that someday we will not be around to appreciate the things we find beautiful. Aging also implies that we will not be loved in the same ways that we were when we were younger. So few of us like change, especially when something is being subtracted rather than added. I don't think that many of us are conditioned to lose: only to gain, to succeed.

B. *FORTUNES TOLD*

Lucy, the mother of my two children, hated the fact that I started to consult an astrologer not long after our son was born. A director I was working with at the time, one who helped me get my first Oscar nomination, put me in touch with a woman named Isis Durand who lived way out in Upland. For years, apparently, she had helped him make decisions about which projects to take on, which people to trust, which days he should try not to travel, at least not by air. "She's unbelievable," he told me. "I can talk to her for five minutes on the phone, and for days afterward, I feel like everything is exactly as it should be. Nothing else works for me like that. Not pills or pussy or money."

To be clear, I was very skeptical, because before meeting Isis, I didn't bother to read my horoscope, let alone pay some expensive psychic to tell me my future. No one could tell the future; in lucid moments, I did not doubt this. And how could it be that the constellations had anything to do with whether I would encounter unforeseen obstacles on a certain day or meet an important stranger who would make me think twice about a career goal? To make matters worse, I was married to a doctor, someone who put her faith in science and facts, little else, a quality I had initially admired in her very much.

The reason I ended up contacting Isis is that my agent received two phenomenal screenplays, and I wanted to do them both, but the director and producers for each project weren't going to wait around for me to film one and then the other. The directors were rivals, and I knew that whoever's I made my second choice would likely never ask me to work with him again. They were both extremely successful, and egomaniacal, and I was still in the early years of my career, and how I handled this would matter a lot. These things still matter a lot, but I'm no longer as vulnerable to the whims of the powerful because, to be frank, I have some of that power now too.

Isis already knew about my dilemma when I called her. It's obvious to me now that my director friend had probably tipped her off, but at the time I was too awestruck and naive to figure that out. I've known her now for twenty-five years, and aside from her advice about signing on to do that humiliating flop, *The Writing on the Wall*, she's more or less always been on the money. She's old now and often sick, but I've done my share to keep her alive. When she told me a few years ago that she had breast cancer but no insurance, I gave her most of the money for her treatments. During that time, she wouldn't meet with me in person, but she did take my calls. Her treatments have cost me almost a million dollars, but spread out over a couple of years, that's not so much money. I'd probably have paid ten times as much if I'd had to. A number of the checks that I gave her for her treatments were written out to a Dr. Selzer, but about half of them I wrote out directly to her. It could be that she's the biggest con artist out there—I have thought of this, but I really don't think she is. We've known each other too long, and I've paid her too well for her to have any complaints in that respect.

Even so, if she was conning me, it doesn't matter that much. Who knows what my career would have become if she hadn't been advising me these past two and a half decades?

Based in part on the reading she did for me not long before we wrapped on *Bourbon at Dusk*, I decided to submit it to the Cannes Film Festival's screening committee, nearly killing my relationship with Elise to make the mid-February deadline. It had been five years since I'd last been to the festival, and that year the film was one that I'd only acted in, not directed and co-written, not invested more than two years of my life in—finding the right producers, casting it, writing the screenplay with my friend Scott Jost, who unlike me is a screenwriter by profession, but mostly he edited what I'd written, though he would say that he wrote as much original material as I did.

Bourbon was a runner-up for the Palme d'Or, and so it earned a "Grand Prix," which is fine, but the French-Israeli filmmakers who won the Palme for their "gritty, neo-realist drama about child prostitution in an age of urban anomie" were possibly the most ungracious bastards I've ever had the misfortune of spending an evening with. The director said to me point-blank two hours before the winner was named, "I liked your film, Mr. Ivins, but I do not think it is good enough. I do not think that mine is good enough either, so this is not meant as an insult."

Well, let me put it this way—if it sounds like an insult, it most likely is an insult. In fairness to this guy, I think he was drunk, but five minutes later, his producer stoked the fire by saying, "I agree with Henri. *Bourbon* is a good film but not a great one. Our film is maybe very good but not great either."

It could be that they were jealous of the fact I was with Elise, who they might not have known was my girlfriend before meeting us at the festival. These two balding gnomes couldn't keep their eyes off of her, and when she was polite but not flirtatious with them, I suppose they decided to take out their sexual jealousy on me by insulting *Bourbon*. I could see these guys calling her when we were back in L.A., begging her to star in their next film. It made me sick to my stomach to think about this, especially because I would tell her not to do it and she would probably get angry. In my experience, no one I know in Hollywood has ever spoken frankly about jealousy, an emotion as natural and certainly as painful as any others that we feel. Because of this tacit code of silence, it is very hard to truly be friends with many of the people who work in film. We are a jealous, neurotic group, both disdainful of and avid to be in the public eye; always comparing ourselves to other people, and so worried about losing what we have that half of us have been hollowed out by ulcers and fear, not to mention unchecked ego, by the time we turn forty.

Later that night, Elise went on to win the award for best leading actress, and when they called her name, I felt this unsettling mix of paternal pride and amorous longing. She had never looked better than she did at that ceremony, and she is a woman who looks good every single minute of the day. Her skin, which is a honey color that I would guess a lot of people, both men and women, would run down a pedestrian for, was glowing in a way that I had never seen before, such was her extreme pleasure in being the object of so much admiration and respect. She had chosen a Dior dress for the occasion—a pure, poetic statement in mauve silk, one that hugged her tall, slender body. All night, even after we didn't win the Palme d'Or, I kept thinking about unzipping that dress, pressing my lips to her warm and fragrant neck, saying and doing the things that make her blush, things that she loves but would never admit to unless the lights were off.

She is not, however, a woman simply coasting by on her beauty until it runs out. She is sharp and very talented, her presence in front of the camera so natural that none of the seams show, which they do with lesser actors. The first time I saw her, which was in this asinine picture a friend of mine directed about two nitwits driving their dead uncle cross-country, I almost fell out of my chair. At the time, Scott and I were arguing daily over the fourth draft of *Bourbon at Dusk*, Isis was taking two or three days to return my calls, and a number of things were in flux with both the story line and the project's funding, but even without Isis's input, I knew that Elise would be the perfect woman to play Lily, the female lead. When I called her agent and had the script sent over after Scott and I had finally finished it, the agent called back the very next afternoon to say that Elise wanted the role more than anything she had wanted in her entire life. This was probably only agent-speak, but regardless of how much he was exaggerating about her response, it was clear that she was interested. The producers liked her too, which I was almost certain they would. After a quick screen test, we agreed on a salary, figured out the shoot schedule, and signed a contract. Then she was mine. For about nine weeks, anyway.

I realize that the age difference makes some people pause. But it's not my tendency to imagine failure. At the same time, I'm not a simpleton; I know that it's possible that Elise and I will not stay together until death do us part, but there seems no point in assuming that our relationship is only a temporary diversion, something to amuse ourselves with until we each find someone better. She is generous, kind, easygoing. I have never met anyone like her, and to state the obvious, I have met a lot of people. Her appetite for the world is one of the things that I like most about her. Before we went to Cannes, she hired a tutor to help tune up her college French, and once there, her sudden facility with the language surprised me and a number of other people. I've never known anyone who could speak a foreign language so well without having studied for at least a few months in the country of origin. "You must have had a good teacher when you were in college," I told her, and she gave me sort of a strange look and said, "Well, yes, I guess I did."

"I bet there's more to that story," I said.

But she only shook her head and said that she guessed she just had a good ear for languages. There probably is more to it than this, but it's not my habit to pressure girlfriends for detailed histories of their past relationships or flings. Elise would likely have told me if I'd probed a bit, but the last thing I need to do is act the jealous boyfriend who also happens to be old enough to be her father. In fact, I think I might even be a couple of years older than both of her parents. But really, so what. My body is still in very good working order. I see no reason not to be with her if she wants to be with me too.

In Cannes to celebrate her leading-actress win, I bought her a three-carat emerald ring. It was too soon to buy her a diamond, in part because everyone would have cried "Engagement!" as eager as the media is to marry its stars off, often with the tacit hope that things will soon devolve into a spectacularly acrimonious divorce.

Although I'm not eager to get married again, the thought has crossed my mind a few times. I know that at some point she does want to get married, though maybe not to me, and I haven't dared to ask if she wants kids, nor has she told me. I'd really prefer not to have another child; raising kids is one of the things that I probably am too old for, or else I just don't want to devote the energy to it again. Still, if having a baby turned out to be one of her fondest wishes, I'd probably have to give in.

C. J1 AND J2

I keep two journals—one of them, J1, to be published after my death if the executor of my estate (who is my attorney, not one of my kids) thinks enough people will want to read it. The other journal, J2, I don't and won't share with anyone. To protect the people I leave behind (and myself, sure), I start a new notebook each year and destroy the one that precedes it. This is where I write down the things that I have done or the thoughts I have had that sometimes make it hard to sleep at night. I can't talk to my psychiatrist about these things because I don't want him to think badly of me (not any more than he probably already does). Despite the risks, I need to keep this second journal because it's like a pressure valve—if it weren't there, my life would blow up.

There are entries about my relationship with Isis in J2, entries about my ex-wives and other women and my children and friends and brother. I've also written about shady things that I have witnessed and done nothing about, things I have done myself and later regretted, or, sometimes, regretted while I was doing them. I almost never read through the book before I burn it each year, always on January first—I think of this as a cleansing, a way to start over, and I always hope that each year there will be fewer entries, or shorter ones, or ones that could go in my other journal, the one for public consumption.

Lucy, I think, has seen one or two of the J2s, which is why, probably, she never believed me when I lied to her about a few things that happened while I was on location (or, once in a while, at home in L.A.). She would never admit to reading my journal, but I'm almost certain that she did—the specificity of her complaints and accusations made me realize that she had to have read some part of that year's J2. I have always tried to keep it locked up in the glove compartment of my car when I'm not at home. If I am, I keep it in a desk drawer, one in which I eventually had a special lock installed (too late, unfortunately, to keep the diary from Lucy) because desk locks, my brother Phil and I discovered while we were growing up and snooping in our father's study, can be picked with bobby pins or the kind of tiny screwdriver used to repair eyeglasses.

Each year's J2 always starts off slow—only a few entries for the first several months, but then, around June or July, for some reason, things start to shift—Isis says that for some people, myself included, the summer months are known for creating full-moon conditions for weeks on end. The full moon seems to stir up the crazy elements that ricochet through a person's life. Even the police blotters attest to this—full moon fever is real. It's a little unfortunate that I live with it for almost half the year—things don't start to calm down until November or early December for me. Last year, that was also the case, and there was no little whimper either. Things ended with a big bang—the debacle with Billy in New Orleans. Not long before I asked him to work for me on the *Bourbon* set, Isis told me that some rogue element was coming right at me, but I didn't suspect that it would be my own son.

D. *PROBLEM CHILDREN*

It took Elise and me about a week or so to come down from Cannes, during which time she was sometimes weepy and very tired. Her moroseness made me a little sullen too, or maybe it was just the jet lag. We argued more than we ever had before, more than we did during the month over the holidays that I did my kamikaze editing job on Bourbon with Fred Banes, who edited *Javier's Sons*. I knew he'd be the right guy if he had time in his schedule to work with me for about five intense weeks. He didn't, not really, mostly because his wife wanted him at home over Christmas and New Year's, but he's not divorced yet, so I think it worked out.

After we got back from France, Elise's sister Belle started calling a few times a day and wanted to talk to her for an hour or more each time, and Elise absolutely did not have the space in her schedule for this, especially with our prerelease obligations for Bourbon— the several TV and radio interviews (only a couple of which we did together, though by now our relationship was common knowledge), the magazine photo shoots, the extra features for the DVD version that I had insisted on starting early, which included interviews with principal cast members and voice-over commentary from Elise, Marek, and myself. She was also reading scripts for the project that would follow the next two she had already committed to.

If it wasn't clear to Elise, I could certainly tell that Belle was dealing with some serious emotional problems following her attempted suicide, which I did feel bad about, but there wasn't a lot that Elise could do to make her better, not being a doctor (something she didn't appreciate me reminding her of). Despite how depressed Belle was, I did not like that she was calling all the time and draining Elise's energy, which made it nearly impossible for her to enjoy her talent and good fortune, and the heartening trajectory of her career, which was suddenly soaring. These were crucial months in Elise's professional life, and if she couldn't give the majority of her attention to her work and the people involved most closely with it, her preoccupation was likely to have serious repercussions on her future prospects.

"She's my sister," Elise said during one of our arguments, tired and angry. "What am I supposed to do? Hang up on her after five minutes?"

"You could stop answering your phone every time she calls," I said.

"I don't answer it every time."

"No, but you answer it most of the time. She's taking advantage of you. She knows you feel guilty about everything you've already been able to achieve while she sits at home in Dallas with your parents and mopes."

"You don't know my sister. She's not like that."

You're either dreaming or lying, I wanted to say, but I didn't.

I have my own problems, probably not as unpleasant as hers, but there are things that keep me up at night, even after they've been written down in J2 or J1. One of them is *Bourbon*'s release date. If I waited until October or November, I'd have a better shot at positioning it as an Oscar contender. Fall is Oscar season, when the bullshit that populates the theaters over the summer has mostly faded away and people are ready, with the end of their vacations and the return to school, to see some intelligent films. But a fall release also means that there's more competition for serious moviegoers' time and money.

On top of this, there is my inability to trust anyone with the oversight of my finances. Having been burned twice, predictably, I'm nervous about entrusting my investments and the general accounting activities related to my day-to-day life to a so-called professional, but unless I want to do it all myself, I have to trust the people who work for me. Fidelity and Wells Fargo seem trustworthy, and unlike the two crooked business managers I've worked with, the first a second cousin (he was also a supposedly reputable CPA when I hired him), they are large corporations that aren't likely to bilk their clients in an underhanded way. Like any Fortune 500 company, they bilk their clients in broad daylight.

Yet another worry is my son. For one, I'm pretty sure that he still has a crush on Elise, and even though I'm not about to hand her over to him if she even wanted to go to him, which I'm pretty sure she doesn't, I can admit that a match between them, at least where their ages are concerned, makes more sense. Born only two years apart, they grew up listening to the same music, using the same slang, watching the same television shows, wearing the same brands. Billy would also be able to give her more attention than I can because he isn't dealing with publicists, agents, producers, fans, ex-wives, charity spokespeople, investment advisers, personal assistants—the list goes on and on—close to twenty-four hours a day. Basically, he could devote his life to her if this were something that she required. But the truth is, I can show Elise things that Billy cannot. I know a lot more about the world than he does, and if I were Elise and were choosing between him and myself, I'm pretty sure that I'd choose the same way she has.

She *did* choose me. I don't even have to pretend that any of this is a hypothetical situation. When Billy tried to seduce her in New Orleans last fall, when he wrote her such an earnest love poem that the paper practically dripped blood and tears, she apparently told him, "Thank you, you're sweet, but I'm quite happy with your father." I'm sure Elise was very tactful. I was not. When I finally boiled over, a day or two after I saw the poem in Elise's hotel room, I was not as calm as I should have been. I might be an actor who has won a number of major awards, but in this case, I was not able to perform the way that I should have. No punches were thrown, and I didn't call him any names either, but what I did say was, "If you ever pull a stunt like that again, you won't be able to draw one more cent from your trust account. For the first time in your life, you'll actually have to work for a living."

Does this qualify as blackmail? I don't think so. But it was a threat, and a serious one that I intended to follow up on if forced to do so. If he were to run off with Elise, why should I support him? The thing is, I realize that I can't know what he or Elise are up to twenty-four hours a day, nor do I want to, but I'd like to believe that she does love me, and that Billy has gotten his head on straight and has stopped trying to woo her away. It makes it more difficult to see him, because when I see him, obviously I'm not with Elise, and when I'm with her, I can't be with him too. He and I have never had an easy relationship, at least not since his mother and I divorced. He wasn't openly hostile after I left Lucy, but he moped around a lot and lacked the enthusiasm for life that a twelve-year-old usually has—boys his age generally want to go out and do things, they want to see their friends and play sports and go to pool parties and the mall and school mixers and amusement parks. Billy did do those things sometimes, but he wasn't a kid known for being the life of the party. His sister was quiet too, but she was so often smiling and sweet and thoughtful, making me cards with drawings of our cats and dog, or hiding cute little notes in places where I'd find them later:

> Dear Dad,
> Why did the window go to the doctor? Because it had panes!
> Love, Anna

And:

> *Dear Dad,*
>   *Did you know that coffee is the most recognizable smell in the world? Is that why you drink so much of it? Hee hee!*
>   ☺ *Anna*

If Billy and I got along better, I'd have him work with me any time that he wanted to. We could even consider starting our own production company, but of course that's now a pipe dream. One thing that I could really use him for is help starting a foundation that will give financial assistance and legal and medical aid to the victims of Hurricane Katrina. It doesn't matter how many years have passed— New Orleans still hasn't bounced back, and it's not going to for a while, if it ever really does. If *Bourbon* makes any money, once we cover our production costs, five percent of the profits will be routed to my foundation, which I've tentatively named Life After the Storm. If you make even a third of the kind of money I do and don't donate to worthy causes to any significant degree, you're a bastard.

Hollywood liberal, yes, I know, but why shouldn't I be? I have to wonder what it is the self-serving CEOs who run our country and the rest of the world are so afraid of. With their enormous assets scattered in banks and investments across the globe and their armies of hired bodyguards and vacation homes on four continents, why do they act as if they're more vulnerable and besieged by the world's miseries than the poorest forty percent here or abroad? I give fifteen percent of my annual earnings to the charities I believe in. Capitalism has been good to me—I won't dispute that—but it hasn't been good to everyone, and the number it continues to be good to shrinks every day. If this sounds like socialism or communism, so be it.

Fifteen percent of my annual earnings is a lot of money by most people's standards—almost five million dollars last year, which was a particularly good year. But then, most of them have been since I graduated from college thirty years ago.

Something else that has been on my mind—my ex-wife Melinda Byers's memoir, which is mostly about our marriage, and it has a title that I can't help but find offensive: *This Isn't Gold*. She must have been very bored and embittered up there in ugly, impoverished Santa Barbara or Big Sur, whichever house it was where she wrote that book. The terms of our divorce were generous—she will be very comfortable until she dies unless she really screws things up—but she still seems intent on trying to convince the world that she is a woman scorned, misunderstood, and generally wronged by the Fates and of course by her asshole movie-star ex-husband.

I know that I must sound bitter too. No matter that I have everything society tells us that we can and *should* have. One thing I kept thinking about after I met those two French-Israelis in Cannes was how they reminded me of something an American director I've worked with said to me about American alpha males. His words won't go away, because I'm pretty sure he's right: "One of the reasons we dominate the film world and most everywhere else is because we're bigger than most other men. I mean physically, not intellectually. We're overfed, overgrown, and overconfident, and we're so intent on winning any contest we can be a part of that if we're not smart enough to win fairly, we're strong enough to beat our rivals into submission." I had the sense, standing next to the Palme d'Or–winning director and producer, that they hated me more for being a foot taller than they were than for having made a fine film, one that doesn't feature any of the usual Hollywood crap—no guns, no drug abuse, no projectile vomiting, no car chases, no bar fights or catfights, no gratuitous cursing, no gold diggers, no midlife crises, no nine-year-olds giving their parents romantic advice. When we wrote the screenplay, Scott and I were very careful to avoid the usual stupid tropes.

Anyway, Melinda and her memoir. Isis has told me that the book has actually raised my stature in both the material and the spiritual worlds: I have acquired, at last, a fully formed soul. Because the rest of the world, if they care to look, can now see my flaws and insecurities more clearly. I have been summarily humbled, and great goodwill is coming my way as a result of this unsanctioned unveiling. I could be more skeptical about it, sure, but I choose not to be. If something like this—someone else's words rather than a doctor's prescription—brings you comfort, you shouldn't sneer at it.

Elise, who doesn't know anything about Isis, except that I talk to a psychic from time to time, thinks I should just be able to put Melinda's memoir out of my mind, as does Anna. I know they're right because there have been a lot of things printed about me that I'd prefer not to have out there. But nothing this personal, especially not from someone whom I was very close to at one time. When I met Melinda, she was beautiful, sweet, in need of rescue from low self-esteem and a bad marriage, and also endearingly starstruck, but not in the annoying way that fans sometimes are. She didn't feel compelled to tell me every other minute how much she loved my work, how much better I was than every other actor, how her parents and friends would never believe she had met me—could she take my picture? Great! How about a few dozen more?

People are buying this memoir, and they aren't buying it because they love how Melinda writes. I'm trying to feel flattered, but it's not easy. She's definitely not a writer, and she won't ever write another book, unless she gets on the children's book bandwagon, which it seems everyone, including the guy who trims the neighbors' hedges, is probably about to cash in on.

My brother says I should sue for slander, but I don't see the point. The book is already out there, living its own sorry life, having its sordid affairs, and unless every copy can be hunted down and destroyed and every reader's memory of it wholly erased, the damage is done. Why bring more attention to it? I also have no desire to stand in a courtroom with Melinda a second time and look on the weary, knowing face of a judge who is likely to think we are both spoiled children.

We are a cheating species, both male and female, whether or not we are famous. Why, I would really like to know, does this fact continue to surprise and scandalize so many people?

Some people say, Isis included, that I should thank Melinda. After all, I'm getting older, and although I keep doing respectable work and might have the kind of longevity Clint Eastwood has had, I do know that the laws of gravity apply to me, despite what that *Vanity Fair* columnist wrote. I realize that I won't always be interesting to moviegoers or journalists. I also realize that there is a date of expiration to all of these good times, one that I can't predict; probably no one can, not even Isis. And this is something I have to live with because it can't be burned away on the first day of every new year.

E. *MUST-SEE*

When you're waiting for the reviews to come out, it's like waiting for a hurricane to hit—you feel an almost unbearable tension and anxiety, but one that I think a lot of movie people are addicted to. To be talked about favorably, even fawningly; to see your name in the New York Times, the Guardian, Le Monde, La Repubblica, Der Spiegel, and any other major newspaper that still publishes movie reviews—this is one of the things people like me aspire to.

Some of the highlights—

More than 20 critics agree: Bourbon at Dusk, 4 out of
4 stars. *A masterpiece.* Bourbon at Dusk *is the year's first
must-see.*

—New York Times

*Elise Connor is a revelation, an actress of the finest caliber. A
star has indeed been born.*

—Los Angeles Times

*Renn Ivins proves that he can write and direct with the same
intelligence and suppleness with which he acts. You really need to
see this movie. As with Spike Lee's* When the Levees Broke,
*Ivins and his co-writer Scott Jost have gotten to the heart of one of
the biggest tragedies and failures of leadership in recent memory.*

—The Oregonian

Marek Gilson is in his finest form. Think Newman and The
Hustler.

—Entertainment Weekly

If you see only one movie this year, make sure it's Bourbon
at Dusk. *I can't stop thinking about it.*

—Chicago Tribune

*A truly humane portrait of a New Orleans family struggling
to survive both the communal and personal horrors of life after
Hurricane Katrina.*

—FilmCritic.com

One of the few bad ones (and try as I might, I can't forget what
this fucker wrote):

*As if the world needs more tragedy porn. Ivins does a passable
job as director, but couldn't he have cast less pretty actors? Marek
Gilson and Elise Connor spend half of the film looking like*

bewildered *Abercrombie models plunked down in the middle of* Waterworld.

—The Miami Herald

Aside from the *Herald's Waterworld* cheap shot, after I read the reviews, I felt like I wouldn't need to sleep for about two weeks straight, like I could run a two-hour marathon or grow wings and fly to the top of Mount Kilimanjaro. It is one thing to be celebrated for a film you've done a good job acting in, quite another if it's a film you've dreamed up on your own, written the screenplay for, hired the cast and crew, cobbled together the funding for, and then spent more than eight weeks in the sweltering heat of an on-location shoot and directed everyone to the best performances of their careers. This is my *Apocalypse Now*, my *On the Waterfront*, even, perhaps, my *Citizen Kane*. To celebrate, Elise and I flew up to Napa and had dinner at the French Laundry, where, in a stroke of mad generosity, I treated all the other diners to their meals. It cost me about twenty-eight thousand dollars, but I handed the waiter my credit card, and aside from making everyone's day, I probably made some friends too.

No Palme d'Or, but the Best Picture Oscar isn't out of reach. Reviews this good usually mean that it will stay in theaters for at least a month and then move on to the second-runs. After the Golden Globe nominations are announced in December, and a month or so later, the Oscars, the first-runs sometimes pick up the nominees again. I have some good foreign distributors too, and I'm confident that *Bourbon* is going to be a hit overseas. Foreign audiences love films about American tragedies. Our tragedies make their own, which are often worse, seem a little less terrible. There is also so much poetry in sadness, a very different and possibly more potent variety than the kind of poetry you find in happiness.

After Elise, Marek, and I went to the premieres in New York and Los Angeles with a number of other *Bourbon* people, we flew to London for the UK premiere, and afterward we had dinner with Mick Jagger, whom I'd met when we'd worked on a picture together several years earlier. Jagger is very worldly, self-possessed, and witty, and that night, he could not keep his eyes off Elise. I told myself that I should be used to this by now, but it's hard for me to watch other famous men ogling her, especially if they are both a rock legend and a legendary womanizer.

Sometimes I think that I'd be happier if I broke it off with her and went out with a woman closer to my age, one who isn't an actress, but I cannot see myself giving her up. I can't imagine meeting another woman as beautiful, talented, and sweet-natured. Maybe two of the three, but no more. We're either together until I die, or she will have to be the one to dump me.

Belle's calls were arriving less frequently by the time *Bourbon* was released in the States, and Elise was in better spirits than she had been for a while, so we had a good time in England. But a week after the UK premiere, Elise had to leave for three weeks in Montreal for a new project, then two more in upstate New York before she'd be back in Los Angeles, where they'd wrap the film after one final week on a Paramount sound stage. I was going to be away for a few weeks too, doing a role in a French film that Jean-Pierre Jeunet, the genius behind *Amélie*, was directing. Aesthetically, we're pretty different, but I love his films and he apparently really liked *Javier's Sons* and *The Zoologist* and now *Bourbon*. When he approached me with the role for *The Hypnotist* (*L'Hypnotiseur*), it seemed a safe bet that we'd work well together, provided I let him do all the directing, which admittedly is getting harder as I get older. I often visualize how I'd shoot a scene instead, or how I'd have written the dialogue, and this causes me something like physical distress. I'm definitely not the first person this has happened to—Clint Eastwood is someone who again comes readily to mind, and Paul Newman, two fine actors whose directorial projects often worked out too. No matter what, it's hard to take orders, especially when you think you're smarter or more creative than the boss (which I suspect a lot of people do).

E. *J2 REDUX*

Something happened just before I left for Paris to work with Jeunet that I'm not proud of. Elise was about to finish up in Montreal and head to New York, and we were using Skype to visit with each other nightly, unless she had a late shoot, and then we'd try to talk earlier. One afternoon when I had nothing scheduled that I couldn't postpone for another day or two, I ducked out to see a movie, a five p.m. matinee that I hoped wouldn't have a lot of people in it, and if I timed it right, I'd be able to slip in after the previews had started and no one would notice me. It was a German movie about a man who takes a vow of silence for a year, moves out to a remote farm in Bavaria, and tries to figure out why the Holocaust happened and then write the defining book about it. When I got up after the credits rolled, a little dazed by the film's sorrowful intelligence, I ran into someone I knew in the lobby. Seeing her there, as if conjured out of a daydream with her pretty short yellow skirt and flowing white blouse, I felt this sudden, almost sinister desire rise up from the pit of my stomach. This lovely girl was my son's most recent ex-girlfriend, Danielle, and we hadn't seen each other since last fall, not long before she broke up with Billy. The final time that I saw them together, I got a little drunk on champagne and kissed her good-bye right on the lips. I'm pretty sure that she and I both enjoyed it more than we should have, and I'm also pretty sure that one of the reasons I kissed her was because I was still very angry with Billy over that fucking poem he gave to Elise last fall, hardly more than a month after she and I had first gotten together.

The whole time Anna, Billy, Danielle, and I were together that night at Sylvia's, listening to the house band blow blue notes into the electrified air, I felt sorry for Danielle, knowing what I did about my son's behavior in New Orleans, and how it was very unlikely that she had much of a clue about what he'd been up to there. I knew that it wasn't my place to tell her, and I didn't, but I liked Danielle and had enjoyed seeing her the few times we'd all gotten together. She had always seemed smart and kind, a girl my son was lucky to have in his life. I can't say that about all of his girlfriends. One of them, a rail-thin performance artist he'd dated in college, had offered me a blow job at Billy's graduation party. Another had also offered sex in exchange for an introduction to a director I was working with at the time.

For the record, I turned them both down. But I did not turn down another offer that I should have ignored too—one made by one of my daughter's closest friends. I did not turn around and walk away when I knew what she was about to do—she was lying by the pool in my backyard, facedown on a lounge chair, her bikini top untied. I knew before she did it that she would rise up and show me her perfect seventeen-year-old breasts. I knew that she would do it because Billy was staying at his mother's house, and Anna had just left to pick up carryout at an Italian place five miles away. Jill sat up and gave me the kind of smile that's impossible to misinterpret, and we went into the cabana where I sometimes took naps or changed into my swim trunks. We locked the door and lay down on the sofa beneath the windows and almost before she could pull off her bikini bottom, I had my face between her legs, tasting the chlorine on her cunt, the salty sweetness beneath it, and then she climbed on top of me and I went for it so hard that I think my teeth were bared, scarcely managing to pull out in time, even though she swore that she was on the pill. It was all over in about seven or eight minutes. She wanted to do it again, wanted to sneak over whenever I'd let her, but after a few more times, I told her that we had to stop. I didn't want Anna to find out because I knew that she wouldn't forgive me. I knew this in part because Isis told me, but I also knew my daughter—she has a stronger moral compass than anyone I've ever met. This is what I thought, in any case, until I met her married lover a couple of months after *Bourbon's* release.

When I saw Danielle after the matinee, I didn't behave as well as I should have then either. It was such a surprise and an almost unconscionable pleasure to see her that I didn't want to let her go. I hadn't made any dinner plans, and after the power of that melancholy German movie, I wasn't ready to go home. Elise had a night shoot, and I knew she wouldn't be expecting me to call her on Skype at eight, eleven o'clock her time. After Danielle and I hugged each other hello and she shyly kissed my cheek, I asked her out to dinner.

Her face flushed. "Do you really have time?" she said. She sounded a little breathless. I think, as early as this moment, that I had already made up my mind about what the night would hold.

"Of course. I'm free as a bird." I laughed, a little embarrassed. "Sorry about the cliché. They slip out sometimes."

"I saw your new film," she said. "I think it's just terrific. Actually, I saw it twice. It's even better than they say. I've been telling everyone I know to see it."

"Thank you, Danielle," I said. "That means a lot. While we were working on it, I had a feeling that things would turn out all right."

"It might be my favorite movie, ever."

I wanted to put my arms around her again, but I didn't. "You don't have to say that."

"It's true," she said. "It's amazing."

We walked out to my car, which I had parked behind the theater. I was hoping we wouldn't be stopped by anyone asking for an autograph, but about four yards from the car, we were. I signed a paper bag from Whole Foods that a woman and her daughter presented to me, both of their faces so bashful and happy that I didn't really feel too irritated. Danielle stood a few feet away and waited for the girl to take a picture with her phone of her mother and me and then I posed for one with her and finally we were done and I got Danielle to the car and realized that it might be better to go to my place and order in so that we didn't have to worry about other interruptions. "If you don't mind?" I said. "Is your car here? Do you want to follow me to my place?"

"We could go to my place too," she said. "I only live about a mile and a half from here."

She lived in Hollywood, just off Hollywood Boulevard, in a new building with a lot of windows, and when we got inside her apartment, I was impressed. There was no clutter anywhere, and she had spent time and money on the decor—sand-colored walls, large windows, tall lamps, a refrigerator with glass doors. I felt like I'd stumbled upon a meadow in the middle of a forest—everything had been crowded and close, then in a second, it all opened up and brightened. Another effect of her beautiful, clean place was that I no longer felt too guilty about being alone with her. I felt unencumbered and relaxed. "This looks like one of the apartments you see in those Scandinavian design catalogs," I said.

"You really think so?" she asked, blushing. "I tried very hard with this place because it's my job. I don't know if you knew that I earn my living by reorganizing other people's homes."

I nodded. "I remember. You did a wonderful job here."

"Thank you."

Neither of us mentioned Billy. The entire night, neither of us said his name. I think I said "my son" or "my kids" once or twice, and Danielle probably said "him," but we didn't talk about Billy or their breakup directly. I didn't mention Elise either, though Danielle probably knew that I was still seeing her. News of our relationship continued to appear in the gossip columns and entertainment magazines, and I think Danielle read some of them, because as many people in L.A. read them as anywhere else, whether they would admit it or not.

We ordered Mexican, and it was delivered after we'd already drunk a bottle of white wine. We were sitting on her leather sofa, looking out the west-facing windows, where the sun had just set. Eight stories below, the streets pulsed with traffic and possibility and the desperate energy of a million dreams not coming true fast enough. She had put on some Nina Simone and we had slipped off our shoes and she was listing toward me and I was already half hard when I leaned in and kissed her. She let out a little cry and fell against me, her arms snaking around my neck, and I knew with the libidinous, cunning certainty that lives just below good manners and good intentions that we would not stop. Her breasts are fuller than Elise's and her hips rounder. She has a womanly body, more soft than Elise's, but not at all fat, and when I was moving inside her there on the sofa, she came so fast that it thrilled me speechless. She was so beautiful, a true grace note of my recent life, and yes, so was Elise our first time and many times after that. That I could do what I was doing while being in love with another woman is the kind of mystery that seems to bewilder and appall so many of us, even though it happens all the time. The body acts, and the mind tries to rationalize it. Danielle is a knockout and so is Elise. There are a lot of beautiful girls in the world, and sometimes when you're close to them, you don't know how you'll act.

We let the food congeal on her kitchen table and had to reheat it when we finally ate at midnight, the witching hour, and I should have been home alone in my bed, sleeping the sleep of the innocent, but this wasn't who I was and hadn't been for many years.

I didn't leave her place until almost three a.m. She wanted me to stay, but I knew that in the morning we would feel uncomfortable and have a hard time looking at each other, the realization that we had done something dishonorable, or rather, that I had done something dishonorable, rushing toward us with the usual destructive speed of regret.

Before I left, I asked her about the German movie, not sure why we hadn't talked much about it earlier—mutual nervous preoccupation, I suppose. "What did you think of The Black Forest?"

"It made me cry," she said softly. "I loved it."

"I'm glad you felt that way. I did too."

At the door of her apartment, after kissing her good-bye for a long time, I said, "I'll call you, Danielle."

I meant it, but I wasn't sure how or if it would be possible.

"Good," she said. "Because I really want you to."

Something I'm sure of: you do not know yourself as well as you think you do. Along with the J2 entry about the slipup with Danielle, one of the other entries I'd recently made had to do with the resurfacing of a fixation that I'd hoped had been eradicated with the help of my shrink.

When Billy was still in college and flew over to India to help me work on a shoot, I had a dream that he wasn't my son, and it was so vivid, I felt that it might be true. I also thought that maybe our often-rocky relationship was due to the fact he wasn't actually my flesh and blood. Even though we do look a bit alike, I was almost convinced that he had been switched in the hospital nursery by some absent-minded nurse, or maybe Lucy had screwed around on me and had had some other guy's child, but the former seemed more likely than the latter because Lucy was not the type. When I asked Isis what the truth was, she claimed that the messages were mixed—some of her spirit consultants said that Billy was my son, others said that he wasn't.

When I got home from India, I got hold of Billy's baby book and removed the piece of his umbilical cord and put it in an envelope that I planned to take to a lab where my own DNA sample would be taken and Billy's paternity would be determined once and for all. It wasn't too hard to find a discreet lab to work with (in fact, I was surprised by how many labs offered paternity tests—not exactly reassuring), but when I was on my way there, a UPS driver rear-ended me while I was waiting at a stoplight, and it seemed that this was God's or some other big spirit's way of telling me that I was being a huge asshole.

Yet ever since all of the bullshit with Billy in New Orleans last fall, I have been thinking that maybe I *should* take his umbilical cord to the lab and determine once and for all if I really am his father. If I'm not, I might sever ties with him (Lucy would never speak to me again though, I'm sure). I'd be able to stop pretending that everything between Billy and me is fine. He could keep his trust fund, and I would do my best to step out of his life. It might even be a relief to him. It's quite probable that it would be.

I went on with these thoughts in J2 for a number of pages, but the conclusion I finally came to was that it doesn't matter in the end if he's my biological son or not because I have raised him as if he were. Based on this alone, he is my son.

F. *A GENTLEMAN AND A THIEF*

This young guy I know from Sony who was in a class or two with Billy at UCLA—a nice enough kid, I thought, before I caught him in my dressing room several months ago, about to lift my sunglasses— somehow found the balls to ask if I'd let him interview me for a documentary he hopes to make about me and a couple of other actors who have worked with foreign directors. He said he wants to look at some of the differences between our American and foreign roles and make the argument that Europeans are less afraid of progressive tactics like continuous takes and extreme close-ups and allowing actors to write their own lines like Mike Leigh does (but only after a lot of discussion with his cast about each scene's goals), and Europeans also focus a lot more on character than plot. Hardly a revolutionary argument, but I was curious about what this kid would come up with and I told him that I'd give him the interview if he let me approve how he used my footage.

We taped the interview up at the Griffith Observatory, early in the morning before it got too hot and too many people showed up to walk the trails. I go there to run or hike sometimes, with George, my driver, joining me if I browbeat him enough because he spends too much time sitting when he's on the clock. I planned to get in a run after the interview if it wasn't too warm of a day. The kid, Jim Marion, was so nervous and grateful that I actually showed up that I almost had to laugh. I didn't mention the day I caught him in my dressing room because we didn't need to revisit that scene, and when he started to bring it up, I held up my hand and said, "Stop. Ancient history."

"I just wanted to say that I know how it must have looked. I really was—"

"Jim, like I said, ancient history. Ask me your first question."

"Okay," he said, pressing a button on his little handheld camera. "How was it, working with Jean-Pierre Jeunet? I heard that you were just over in France acting in his new film."

"It was a lot of fun," I said. It really was. As with *Amélie*, Jeunet filmed more than half of *The Hypnotist* in the Montmartre neighborhood of Paris where he lives with his American wife, who is a film editor. Every morning while I was there, all the mornings I've ever been there, probably, I had a delicious café au lait and a chocolate croissant that the hotel brought in from the bakery next door. So many things are made or designed with such patience and care over there. I love all of the sounds in the streets too—the motorbikes that whine like wasps; the people calling to each other in mellifluous French, laughter often following; the way high heels clack against the old cobblestones. French women take good care of themselves and dress very stylishly; they also have an attractive briskness about them that most American women do not. There was always something or someone beautiful to look at. I just wish that I could speak more and better French.

"Can you tell me a little bit about his process?"

There were a few yellow jackets buzzing around us, but I tried to ignore them, sure they would follow us if we moved. "Jeunet is a perfectionist, but he was polite when I wasn't doing exactly what he wanted me to. We had to do a lot of takes for several of my scenes, but he was so precise about what he wanted from everyone that I didn't really mind. I'm sure I learned some things that I'll use again."

"Which foreign director have you liked working with the most?"

"They've all been great in their own ways. I don't play favorites, so please don't ask me to name any."

Jim waved away a yellow jacket, which made me nervous. I had a feeling that one of us was going to get stung. "What about Polanski?" he asked. "What was it like working with him?"

"He's very professional, very smart and funny too."

"What did you think about what happened with that girl he allegedly raped and drugged back in the seventies?"

This wasn't the first time I'd been asked that question. I had my answer ready. "It was unfortunate for him and everyone else involved. He was still recovering from Sharon Tate's murder and the loss of their unborn child. I'm not saying he should be excused, but he wasn't behaving in a rational way, and I bet he'd say the same thing if you asked him."

Jim looked down at a small piece of paper he had in the hand that wasn't holding the camera. "What do you think are the main differences between foreign and American directors?"

I laughed a little. "That's a pretty broad question. There are plenty of differences just among American directors, don't you think? But I suppose one thing is that foreign directors don't usually have enormous budgets like some American directors do, so I think there's often a little less pressure from their studio and producers to do everything exactly the way the studio bosses say."

"They have more autonomy?"

"I think some of them do. So if the picture does well, they get most of the credit. If it doesn't, they also get most of the blame. But that part's the same as here. When something tanks in the U.S., the director gets the lion's share of the blame, but it might actually be his producers' faults more than his own."

Jim swatted at another yellow jacket. "Can you give me an example?"

I shook my head. "I'd rather not. But I'm sure you can find one if you do a little research." I paused. "You'd better not get too pushy with that wasp. One of us is going to get stung."

"I have that disease where you don't feel any pain."

I stared at him. "No, you don't."

"You're right, I don't." He laughed.

What is this guy's problem? I wondered, blinking with irritation. I was starting to feel a little warm too. The morning run probably wasn't going to happen.

"Sorry," he said. "Sometimes I say things that are supposed to be funny, but no one can tell that I'm joking."

"Keep trying," I said. "But only with the people who know you well."

We talked for a few more minutes, until he'd used up the forty minutes I'd allotted for the interview. To my surprise, neither of us got stung.

When we shook hands in the parking lot, Jim looked at me for a long second and said, "Do you remember when you said to me in your dressing room, 'There's a reason you're the person you are and I'm the person I am'?"

Had I really said this? It sounded a little stupid, not to mention self-aggrandizing. "No, I don't think I do."

"You did, and I couldn't stop thinking about it. I wouldn't be making this documentary if you hadn't said it to me. I was working at Sony during the day and writing screenplays at night, and feeling this rage over why nothing was happening for me."

"And because I said those words to you, you changed your life?"

"Yes, I did."

I regarded him, not sure if he was making fun of me in some backhanded way. "Well, that's good, I guess. I hope it works out for you the way you hope."

"You're a good person, Mr. Ivins," he said, very solemn.

I shook my head. What was he going to try to sell me? "I doubt it," I said.

"Everyone I know who works with you thinks so."

I studied his face, his earnestness making me pause. "I'm sure that's not the case."

"You are a good person, Mr. Ivins. You wouldn't have done this interview if you weren't."

You wouldn't be here if you weren't a good person. That "here" can be both literal and figurative. Have I made my career solely by showing up when and where I said that I would? Because that's definitely a big part of what determines a person's success. If you make a promise, you keep it. The trick is not to make the promises you can see yourself breaking. At least professionally, if not personally.

In France I kept thinking about the night I'd spent with Danielle, and when I finally called her about a week after I got to Paris, she sounded so happy that she almost started crying, or maybe she was crying but trying to hide it. I felt uncomfortable, hearing her small, girlish voice, the hope in it almost unbearable. "When are you coming back?" she asked.

"Probably in about two weeks."

"Can you come see me?"

There was static on the line, the normally clear transatlantic connection failing us. "I'd like to," I said, "but I'm not sure if I'll be able to."

"I could come to you."

"No, it'd be better if I went to your place, if we do see each other. I'll call you when I get back to L.A."

"I haven't told anyone what happened."

"I don't think it would be a good idea if you did."

"I've had a crush on you since I was twelve."

"Well," I said, looking up at the stucco ceiling of my hotel room. "You're sweet to say that."

"The whole time I was with Will, I wanted to be with you instead."

I think I winced when she said this. But something in me also unfurled. It might have been relief or maybe even exultation. "I'll try to call you when I get back."

I told her then that I had to go, and she was quiet for a second before she said, "Are you still with Elise Connor?"

"Yes."

She hesitated. "It would be okay if you saw us both. I think I could live with that."

"Danielle, I'm sorry, but I have to go now."

"Okay," she said.

"Good-bye," I said.

I waited a few seconds, but she didn't say anything. Finally, I hung up.

Isis has mimicked Jim Marion's phrase but has applied it to Danielle: she is, apparently, a good person too. She is not someone I should mess with unless I have serious intentions. I know this, but I do not know what I am going to do. About Elise, Isis has said that there is great potential for us, but it might not be in this life. I have tried to ignore this prognostication, and after she made it, I didn't talk to her for several weeks. But it won't go away; like the thought of my death, it burns in my private heart with a tiny, brutalizing flame.

G. *FALLING*

All summer and part of the fall now too, my daughter has been having an affair with a married man. He is one of the attending physicians at the UCLA Medical Center where she's doing her internship. I know this because she invited me to join them for dinner at her house, and I brought Elise along, not knowing at first what I was getting us into. Anna tried to pass off the doctor as a friend, but there was such a strange and powerful undercurrent between them all night that I knew there had to be more to the story, and of course there was. She seems to be taking this affair very seriously too, probably, in part, because it is her first, and because it is in her nature to take such things seriously.

All during dinner, I could see her affection for this guy on her glowing face—new and carnal love, the kind that makes it difficult to sleep, but that doesn't really matter because your body is releasing so many endorphins and so much adrenaline that you don't need a lot of rest. But maybe what troubled me more than her modified state was that the doctor, Tom Glass, didn't look much better off, even though he was wearing his wedding ring, brazen as the one rooster in the henhouse. My stomach dropped to my feet when I noticed it because at first I thought maybe he and Anna had eloped, but when I saw that she wasn't also wearing a ring, I figured out pretty quickly why this was the case.

"What's going on between you two?" I whispered to Anna in the kitchen while she was getting ice cream and ladyfingers together for dessert. "I know you and that man out there are more than friends."

She gave me a look that I had never seen before, at least not on her pretty face. Amused scorn—this is what I'm almost certain it was. "We're friends," she said. "But if we were more, I don't think you'd be the one to judge."

I bristled. "So you are more than friends?"

"Dad, please, they can probably hear us."

Elise was laughing in the other room. I really doubted that they could hear any part of our conversation. "Don't be silly. I can barely hear us," I said. "Why is he wearing a wedding ring?"

"The usual reason," she said. She handed me two bowls, each with a ladyfinger slanting up from a scoop of chocolate. "Would you take these in to Elise and Tom?"

"If you're working with him and having an affair, you could both be fired."

She gave me a disappointed look. "He wanted to meet you. He thinks you're great. He thinks you and De Niro are the two best actors in the world. Please don't get upset. There's no need to. Everything's fine. Really, it is."

"Where's his wife? Why isn't she here?"

"She's playing bridge."

"Bridge?" I said. "How old is she, seventy-five?"

She ignored this. "Her father used to teach it at the community center in Newark where she grew up. I guess she's very good."

"Does she know you two are friends? That he's over here meeting Elise and me tonight?"

"Dad, please. Can't we just have dessert and enjoy ourselves?"

So she was already a doctor, already in charge, like her mother had always been.

I took the ice cream into the other room and set a bowl in front of Elise and another in front of the doctor. I tried to smile, but despite my purported skills as an actor, I wasn't able to move my mouth convincingly and the doctor gave me a wary look. He was no fool. He had probably worked with his share of terrified liars, patients who don't want to admit to the symptoms they are pretty sure will spell their doom. Or other doctors who pretend they haven't made the mistakes they're being accused of. Malpractice, malignant, malign, malingerer. *Mal* as in evil, bad, dangerous. I didn't think that Tom Glass was evil, but I really did not want him calling my daughter, having sex with her, or worse (from her point of view, anyway), canceling the occasional tryst when she was so looking forward to seeing him—because his wife had changed her plans for the day, or one of his kids had broken his wrist, or his mother-in-law had dropped by unexpectedly. He had someone to sleep next to at night. My daughter did not. She had only his word, the next promised assignation, and she must have known by now that a rendezvous wasn't a given until he stood directly in front of her, clothes on their way to the floor. It all made me feel ill. I knew this man. I *was* this man. And of course my daughter realized this too. What could I really say to her? Even so, I didn't care if my displeasure seemed a double standard to her. I wanted to protect her from disappointment, from unfortunate or foolhardy choices. I did not want this walking midlife crisis with his MD and smooth talk to break her heart.

But part of me, I have to admit, liked him. He was funny, intelligent, respectful, at least in front of Elise and me. He was probably a very good doctor and a good teacher. He spoke with confidence but not arrogance. He laughed easily. He looked at Anna with admiring eyes, and I could see why she had been drawn to him. He might even have been thinking about leaving his wife for her, but did I want Anna to be the other woman who managed to steal the husband away from his wife and kids? I was pretty sure that I did not. He was also so much older than she was. If she wanted kids of her own, I had to wonder if he would oblige. If he should oblige.

Elise had a good sense of what was going on too, and when we were in the car heading back to her place, she looked at me and said, "That must have been a little strange for you."

"How do you mean?"

"Well, Renn, let me see," she said, laughing a little. "Because you left Anna's mother for another woman, and now it looks like Anna is playing the same role that Melinda did for a while."

Playing a role. I don't like that expression when it's not being used to talk about filmmaking. Life is real; it adds up to something. Yet I understand why we say it all the time. Real life is also surreal in a way that movies are not. One of the reasons I wanted to be an actor was because the best movies felt so much more important to me than my own day-to-day life. Now, ironically, they are my real life.

"It was a little awkward," I admitted. "I think Anna knows that I'm worried about her."

"He's very nice though."

"Yes, he seems to be."

"Anna's a year or so older than me, isn't she?"

"Yes."

She was silent.

"Why do you ask?" I said.

"Has she given you a hard time about me?"

"No, she hasn't." In fact, she had made a few comments about our age difference, but I didn't feel like telling Elise. It would have hurt her feelings and she might have gotten upset, and there was no reason for her to feel that way. It wasn't like I would break up with her if my daughter didn't approve, but Elise certainly had cause to break up with me. I had seen Danielle after my return from France and had had sex with her, and I wanted to do it again. I knew that if I continued to see her, it would end badly, but I wasn't yet ready to stop. It was likely to end badly no matter what. I did not want Danielle to tell me that she was in love with me, but because I have a hard time being a hardcore asshole, I brought her a couple of gifts back from Paris—a little keepsake box filled with handmade chocolates, and a necklace with a tiger's-eye pendant that I'd found in one of the antique shops on the Left Bank. I bought Elise presents too, five of them. I spent a lot of money on them both, but more on Elise.

My favorite role, I suppose, is the romantic. It's one that I play well, though romantics are dangerous—to themselves and to their lovers. Sometimes it's only their stupidity that makes them dangerous. But often it's also their selfishness.

A final note. About a week after I met Elise's married boyfriend, I got a call from Lucy, Anna and Billy's mother, saying that Billy was in the hospital. He'd been taken in because he had collapsed when he was out running earlier that day. He was dehydrated and hypoglycemic, and had apparently been out running something like twenty or thirty miles on the streets and trails near the Rose Bowl without enough water and no energy bars. A couple of other runners found him, probably not long after he collapsed. One of them had a cell phone, and they might have saved his life by moving him into the shade and getting him to swallow some water before the paramedics arrived and took him to the hospital.

I went to see him that afternoon, as soon as I could leave a meeting about a film I was hoping to direct and play the lead in starting in January, and it was only the third time since his ill-fated trip to New Orleans that I had seen my son. About a year had passed since the episode with the poem, and we still hadn't talked about it, at least not in any meaningful way. No truce had been reached, neither of us having bothered to extend anything like an olive branch, and there I was, fucking his ex-girlfriend on the sly now too. When I went to the hospital to see him, I wondered for a panicked second if Danielle might be there, if Lucy had called her too, but I told myself that everything would be all right if she was. It wasn't like I had shot and killed someone. We were all adults, capable of making our own decisions, as unwise as they might occasionally be. Elise was working, but I wouldn't have brought her along even if she had been free. I hadn't called her on my way to the hospital to tell her what had happened to Billy. To be frank, I wasn't sure when I would tell her.

Lucy was in the room with Billy when I got there. Anna was too. They had attached an IV to his right hand. He looked exhausted and was sunburned. But he was conscious and alert, and I felt a rush of overwhelming relief, as if I had just opened a window after a very long time of no light or fresh air. I went over to the bed and smoothed the hair back from his forehead. "I'm so glad you're all right," I said. "I hope you'll take it easier from now on."

Billy's voice was hoarse when he spoke. "I will, Dad. I don't know what happened. I go out all the time with only one bottle of water and usually I'm fine."

"You have to stop that," his mother said. "And you need to stop running so far, especially if it's hot outside like it was today. You're so thin, and if you're not going to drink enough water either, I'm going to have to hire a detective to keep an eye on you."

Lucy was wearing a pair of gray slacks and a white blouse with pearls. She had probably just come from the clinic after a day of seeing children with asthma and food allergies and ear infections. She looked tired but pretty, her light brown hair frosted almost blond now, and she had stayed in shape from sheer nervous will and treadmill runs at six a.m. five days a week. I hadn't seen her in over a year, maybe two, but it didn't feel like it had been that long. I went over to hug her, and then to our daughter, who smelled like something I couldn't quite place, but later I realized it was the brand of cologne that her attending physician had been wearing the night we met for dinner.

"Mom, I run almost every day, and this has never happened before. I did three half-marathons and four ten-mile races over the summer. I'm signed up to do the marathon here next March too."

"You are?" I said, impressed.

"Yes. It'll be my first."

"Wow. That's ambitious. Good for you," I said.

His mother, however, was not impressed. "Billy, I don't know. Marathons are so hard on your body. And you don't eat enough."

"I'm fine, Mom. I love running. I'm good at it."

"Says the dangerously dehydrated guy from his hospital bed," said Anna.

Her brother rolled his eyes but said nothing.

"Do you want me to go to In-N-Out and get you a burger and fries?" I asked. "Or there's a Carl's Jr. just a couple of blocks away. Whatever you want, I'll go get for you. You need to get some hearty food in your body."

Billy shook his head. "I don't eat red meat anymore."

Anna stared at him. "You don't? Since when?"

"Since May. But I still eat chicken and fish."

"I hope you're getting enough protein," said Lucy.

"Most people get too much protein," said Billy.

"That's true," said Anna.

"It is?" I said.

Anna nodded. "Yes, and it's hard to digest if you eat too much of it. That's one of the reasons why there are so many gastrointestinal disorders in our country. We eat more meat than we need."

"We eat too much gluten too," said Billy. "I've cut out a lot of bread products from my diet."

"Why?" said Lucy. "You've never had a weight problem."

"That's got nothing to do with it, Mom. I just want to be healthier."

"You're not going to be healthier if you're starving yourself."

I looked at the three of them, these people with whom I had shared a house and a life until I thought I could do better. I wouldn't say that I regret the divorce, but I do regret causing them the unhappiness and bad feeling that I know I did. I regret missing so much of my children's adolescence. I also regret that Lucy hated me for a while, and that she hasn't remarried or found someone to live with who makes her happy. Maybe she is happy on her own, but I think she could probably be happier.

"I'm sorry," I said, looking from Billy's face to the outline of his skinny body beneath the hospital sheet. He really had become a lot thinner since I'd last seen him, which had been in April on my birthday. Elise had been in Dallas, visiting her sister and parents again, which is probably why I decided to meet Billy for dinner, something we'd always done on or near my birthday if I wasn't out of town. When we met at an Italian place I like in Santa Monica, I could tell that he'd lost some weight, but he wasn't as thin as now. He was probably twenty pounds lighter than his normal one sixty-five. His eyes looked bigger and his cheekbones were more pronounced; some would have called him gaunt.

Lucy looked at me. "Why are you apologizing?"

I could feel my face starting to grow hot. "I don't know," I said.

Anna and Billy were looking at me intently too. "I don't know," I repeated. "I just wanted to say it."

"We're all sorry," said Lucy. "We're all sorry, and then we die."

"Mom," said Anna. "Don't be so dramatic."

"I'm not," said Lucy. "I'm only speaking the truth. Your father would agree, wouldn't you, Renn?"

I looked at her for a long moment, and then I nodded. "Yes, I guess I would."

In the hall, someone was pushing a cart with a screeching wheel, and when Lucy and Anna glanced toward the door, I looked down at Billy and he looked up at me, his face unreadable. "I'm sorry, Billy," I said.

"I'm sorry too," he said, and then he closed his eyes. I reached down to touch his hair, but he was lying so still that I lost my nerve.

CHAPTER 9

BILLY, WILL, GUILLAUME

*W*ithin a week after his arrival from Los Angeles, he had established his morning routine. He liked to walk from the fourth-floor apartment on the tiny rue Tiquetonne that he had found through his friend Luca's father, into the high-spirited commercial bustle of the rue Montorgueil, where he bought fresh fruit and yogurt, sometimes a croissant too, the best of his life, though he was trying to stick to a low-gluten diet, which was difficult because the bread was so good everywhere he went in Paris. After he did his shopping, he walked the few blocks from this cobblestone street of grocers and butchers and pastry makers to Les Halles and sat on a low wall near the big Brancusi sculpture of a man's head. There by the enormous sideways head, across from one of the entrances to the church of Saint-Eustache, he would eat his breakfast, even when it was very cold outside. Most mornings he got out of bed a little before eight and brewed a small pot of coffee that he drank as he dressed himself, and then he stepped out into the Parisian morning, where a few million people he would never know were disappearing into the Metro or briskly walking toward the shops and schools and offices where they would spend their day. Will couldn't have legally worked in France even if he had wanted to, at least not without the proper visa and a sponsoring employer or, perhaps, a French wife.

He had come to Paris to try on a new identity, to live a different life from the one he had in California. He thought that it might become permanent, but he did not have to decide anything now. The language, at least, was not a daunting mystery because he remembered some of his high school French, and he had started watching three or four French films a week when he decided after spending a day and a half in the hospital, recovering from a case of dehydration and heat exhaustion, that he needed to move away from Los Angeles and his parents, though he had never before wanted to do such a risky thing.

Seeing the worried faces of his mother and sister and the guilty face of his father while he was held captive in the small, sterile hospital bed at Huntington Memorial, he knew that his life would not change and he would never be happy if he stayed where he was. His father's strange, remorseful behavior, the multiple apologies for nothing specific, had unnerved him, and when his father embraced him before leaving and accidentally dislodged the IV in his hand, Will thought that he had seen tears in his eyes, something he didn't remember ever happening before. The tears had upset him more than the vague apologies, and when he talked them over later with his sister, she had said that their father was getting older and maybe was realizing how important his family was to him. Or maybe he felt sentimental because everything was going so well for him, even more so than usual—Bourbon at Dusk's reviews and receipts had exceeded his expectations, and he was probably exhausted from interviewing people to staff the Hurricane Katrina foundation he was about to get off the ground. "And of course there's Elise," said Anna.

"What do you mean?" asked Will, wary. He hadn't seen his father's girlfriend in five long months, and hearing her name, he felt a stab of anxiety and longing. Jealousy too.

"I'm sure keeping up with her wears him out." She paused. "She and Dad came over for dinner a couple of weeks ago. I invited a friend and grilled some salmon for the four of us. It was nice but a little awkward. Elise insisted on helping me with the dishes afterward because she said she couldn't let me do everything. She kept complimenting me too—on my earrings, my furniture, the drawing of the two cats I did that's hanging above the stereo. I think she feels a little weird that she's younger than me."

"Why didn't you invite me?"

"Because it was just supposed to be Dad, my friend and me, but at the last minute he asked if he could bring Elise."

"You still could have invited me."

"Billy," she said gently. "I know that you still have a crush on her. I didn't think it'd be a good idea."

He was silent. It would be useless to lie to her. Elise was still on his mind so often, and he did little to try to forget her. She had acted in six movies, and another that hadn't yet been released, and he had watched all of the six at least as many times, including *Bourbon at Dusk*, which he didn't regret working on, despite the rift it had caused between his father and himself. If it hadn't been for *Bourbon*, he wouldn't have met Elise, who had been attracted to him too; he knew that for sure, especially after the last time he had seen her, which had been the previous May, just before she left for the Cannes festival with his father. Now she would not return his e-mails and had changed her cell phone number. Because of his feelings for her, he had ruined a relationship with a different woman he knew that he should have been happy with. She was smart and patient with him and had her own small but successful business. She was also very pretty and shared his taste in movies and music. He had botched it badly with Danielle, but there seemed no remedy for this because he had fallen in love with someone else. The most unfortunate thing about all of it was that the woman he'd fallen for was his father's girlfriend, an enormous taboo if ever there was one.

"Which friend did you have over?" he finally said. "Jill? Celestine?"

"No, a friend from the hospital."

"A boyfriend?"

She shook her head, but she was smiling. "No."

"Who?"

"One of the attending physicians I work with."

"What? Are you guys allowed to socialize outside of the hospital? I thought you told me that the attendings are like your bosses."

"I can't socialize with my boss?"

"Is he married?"

She laughed in a harsh burst. "Billy, stop it. You sound like Mom."

"Sorry. You can tell me. Are you seeing this guy? I won't judge you."

Anna looked at him for a moment before looking away, her face coloring. "I think I'm in love with him, and I think he feels the same way about me. And yes, he's married."

So both he and his sister were romantic fools. He would never have imagined that she would allow herself to get involved with a married man. "Does he have any kids?"

She nodded. "Two. One's a senior in high school, the other's a sophomore."

"Almost the same age difference as you and me."

"Yes, I guess that's true."

"Where do you think this is going?"

"I don't know. Neither does he. We're just taking it one day at a time."

"Everyone says they'll do that, but I don't know anyone who actually does. Except maybe for Luca." His friend, like himself, did not need to work at any kind of steady job because he lived on inherited money, and since graduating from college five years earlier, he had spent time in France with his father and then in Australia with his mother, with intermittent returns to L.A. His profession was girls and leisure, he had said to Will, only half joking, his blithe attitude about their privileged status very different from Will's, who felt a mixture of guilt and relief that he didn't need to work at some dull job with people he wouldn't have chosen to be with otherwise, but he also felt shame that he had no real profession, no "calling," a word that had once struck him as almost religious in its gravity, as if some supreme being were summoning people and telling them, Moses-on-Mount-Sinai style, what they must absolutely do with their lives.

"I *am* taking it one day at a time," Anna insisted. "I couldn't do anything else even if I wanted to."

Now, in Paris, he was sending e-mails to Elise again, telling her where he was, asking her to join him if she was in Europe or had a reason to come to Europe. He was acting without scruples, he realized, with these ongoing attempts to woo away the girl his father seemed to love, though he doubted that Renn was being faithful to her. As far as Will could tell, his father hadn't been faithful to any of the women he had made a public commitment to, and it seemed unlikely that he would ever change this behavior for good, despite how beautiful Elise was, or how remarkable her talents.

From what Will could tell, truly talented actors had the ability to forget their insecurities, to be shameless and joyful in front of a camera and crew, to risk with a stony will other people's laughter or derision. They also had to have the feeling, whether they acknowledged it or not, that people wanted to look at them, and that these people wouldn't be able to stop looking. Elise might have been a little shy in her personal interactions with friends and acquaintances, but Will knew that she had a streak of exhibitionism in her too, as did his father. If the age difference between them hadn't been so egregious, Will might even have thought that they were a good match. And, as much as he disliked doing so, he had to admit that his father could offer her things that he could not, especially when it came to her career.

What he himself could offer her might not be as extraordinary as what his father could give her, but Will knew that without question, he would be committed to her. He could offer her sexual fidelity, which, based on all precedent, his father could not. Will also believed that he could offer her sanctuary from the world his father and she publicly inhabited, one that often had its tentacles in almost all aspects of their private lives too. Not being famous the way his father was, Will did not have paparazzi following him into restaurants and stores or waiting on the street outside his house. He did not have a cell phone that rang twenty-five times an hour. He was his own person in a way that his father was not.

And so he persisted. He had never done such a thing before, never tried to poach some other man's girlfriend. Despite his adherence to talk therapy's dictum that doctors not tell their patients what to do, the previous summer Will's therapist, Dr. Shepherd, had bluntly said: "You need to direct your energies elsewhere. You'll only make yourself unhappy if you keep pursuing her. If she wants you, she'll come to you. But even if she does, you must still consider your father's feelings."

Paris, two-thousand-year-old glittering city of lights, the Louvre, and the lovelorn, was the trapdoor through which he had plunged, hoping to escape from his disapproving therapist, his parents, his disappointments and jealousies. That he had escaped from some but not all of these things was a relief, but the heaviest burdens had remained with him. Before he left, he had told no one that he was going to France—not his sister or parents or the few friends he saw regularly—because he would not have been able to say how long he planned to stay or why exactly he was going, and he imagined them asking, Won't you be lonely, not knowing anyone there (except for Luca's father, who was busy with his own life)? His father had friends in Paris, and Will knew a couple of people from college who lived there too, but no one well enough to call a friend. It seemed best not to think too long about his motives because this was the first time in years, aside from his pursuit of Elise, that he had done something with spontaneity and an almost giddy sense of adventure. Hemingway, Fitzgerald, Stein and Toklas, Josephine Baker, Alexander Calder— other adventurous souls had also escaped the sock garters and girdles and prudishness and fearful, unquestioning mediocrity of their hometowns for Paris's salons and august boulevards, its verdant parks where art seemed to be created as effortlessly as California smog. He was not an artist, but it was possible that he would become one, or at least become something other than the floundering, directionless son of a famous man.

It startled him how easy it was too, once he set his plans in motion: he packed two suitcases, transferred money to an account he opened with the BNP, and gave away his houseplants to a neighbor. He had no pets and paid his monthly building assessments and utilities electronically. Luca was in L.A. when he left, but had put him in contact with his father, who had a friend willing to lease her apartment to him while she was away in Buenos Aires on diplomatic assignment. Will planned to return to L.A. in March for the marathon, but he would likely go right back to Paris afterward and run in the marathon there in April, running being the one activity that consistently filled him with a sense of elated contentment. During his runs, the near hopelessness of his feelings for Elise did not plague him. He didn't know why he couldn't simply force himself to stop wanting her, but his appointments with Dr. Shepherd had led him to the conclusion that he was a self-indulgent child. Also, that he was probably afraid of mature commitment, with the occasional sacrifices it required—it was safer to want someone you couldn't have because you might fail to keep someone you could. Hence Danielle. Hence Sherrie and Luz and Melissa and Rian.

It was during his third week in Paris, at the end of January, that Elise acknowledged the two e-mails he had sent since arriving in France.

> Dear Will,
>
> I am happy for you. Paris is a beautiful city and I hope you're doing well there. I'm sure you'll be great in any of the marathons you run. I'm sorry you haven't heard from me since we saw each other last May. I think you understand why it's hard for me to be in touch with you. It would crush your father. Be well, Elise
>
> P.S. If things were different, I would come to Paris and have dinner with you. I think I should tell you that your father proposed to me a couple of days ago. I haven't said yes yet but I'm thinking about it.
>
> P.P.S. Btw, thanks for your nice words about my Oscar nomination. I still can't quite believe it. I know I'm not going to win, but I'm so excited to be nominated. One of us will win something though, I'm sure, with Bourbon getting eight (!) nominations. It feels like a dream sometimes. I wake up thinking about it in the middle of the night all the time now.

After reading her e-mail, which arrived just before midnight when he was about to go to bed, he put on his coat and went out into the quiet streets, where snow had started to fall, and walked across the city for three hours. It was a Tuesday night, and there were few people on the sidewalks and not many cars moving either. In his grief-stricken state, he still recognized that it might be dangerous to be out so late by himself in a city he didn't know well, but he kept going and it made him feel better to be risking something, to be aware that his life might be taken from him if he didn't care about it enough. He crossed the Seine and went southwest toward the locked gates of the Musée Rodin, then southeast to the tower in Montparnasse, before he turned north again and walked up through the crooked streets of the Latin Quarter, where more people were out than in the other neighborhoods he had passed through. He recrossed the Seine and walked to the Louvre, which at night looked especially like the impenetrable fortress-palace that it used to be, and then home again to rue Tiquetonne. He spoke to no one and felt his body's strength and youthfulness and wondered why he could not stop wasting his life. He did not know why he couldn't find anything that he wanted to do for a career, why his sister and mother both knew that they wanted to practice medicine or why his father had thought that he would be good and lucky enough to make a living as an actor. (And now he had those eight Oscar nominations. They weren't a surprise, but Will had not felt very happy for his father when he found out about them, and his bitterness had bothered him more than the nominations themselves. How long would he and Renn be mired in this competitive struggle? It was horrible and pointless too—this was his father, not some grade-school classmate—but he did not know how or when it would end.)

Aside from a few months of thinking seriously about becoming a lawyer, and a number of business ventures since college that he had invested money and only a little time in, Will had never felt that he had been called to do anything in particular. If he were meant to be a playboy or a jet-setting dilettante, he thought that even these dubious callings would have made their appeals to him by now.

What he was most interested in doing, more than anything before, was running. Aside from the one bad day when he had ended up in the hospital, he had a knack for it. His body burned oxygen efficiently and surprised him with its endurance, and this corporeal fitness filled him with optimism and strength. He was using minimalist running shoes now too, ones that he had gradually introduced into his workouts; he had reconfigured his stride to put less stress on his joints and had read and studied books by expert runners. There were people, ordinary in most other ways, who ran hundred-mile races, people who routinely ran fifty miles in a day. Some of them looked like greyhounds, their faces lean and intense and inquiring. When he ran through the streets of Paris toward the Bois de Boulogne or in the opposite direction toward Père Lachaise and the eastern reaches of the city, he felt that he was running toward some great happiness. This sense of well-being lasted for an hour or two after his runs, sometimes longer. While he was walking off Elise's troubling e-mail he wished that he could run instead, but at night, it wasn't a good idea. Many of the ancient streets were poorly lit, and if he tripped and fell, he might have injured himself badly enough that running wouldn't be possible for weeks.

He slept until ten the morning after his snowy, lovesick wanderings. When he woke up, it felt like he was on the verge of catching a cold, but after he drank two cups of coffee and ate a croissant, he felt better. Sitting by the Brancusi head, a sculpture whose eerieness Will had seen make a small boy burst into noisy tears two days earlier, he realized how lucky he was, how lucky he'd always been. His good fortune burned in the pit of his stomach, its heat spreading upward until he felt his face turn warm. He had to stop thinking about Elise and find someone else to be with. He would reply to Elise's e-mail and tell her that she would not be hearing from him again. That he was sorry he had been so pushy and ignored her request that he leave her alone after the day they had spent together in Santa Barbara, where he had met her for lunch and they had walked together on the beach for two hours, she letting him hold her hand and kiss her several times. He had written another poem (it was actually the fourth poem that he had written for her, but he had not sent the second and third, believing them to be terrible). He had sent this new poem to her after the one phone conversation they had had in late April, during which she had told him that he must stop trying to see her, but he sensed that she was ambivalent, that he might need only to keep trying a little longer and she would yield to his wish to see her again.

And then, at last, she had. The second poem he sent to her was a little longer than the first, and he had ended it with the final three lines from James Wright's "A Blessing":

> Suddenly I realize
> That if I stepped out of my body I would break
> Into blossom.

She had called him after receiving the poem and said that she loved it. That she remembered the Wright poem from college, and it had been one of her favorites, and how had he known this? He hadn't, he said, but it was one of his favorites too. Then she had started crying, and he felt both guilty and gratified. It seemed that she really did care about him, that she was confused and maybe a little disoriented, but they would probably be fine. Even if his father disinherited him, he would survive, and perhaps this was what needed to happen so that he would stop sleepwalking and finally find his place and purpose in life.

"I think about you too," she said. "I don't mean to, but I do."

"I want to see you, as soon as we can arrange it."

"I've never done this before. I'm not lying."

"I know you're not."

Four days later, seeing her in Santa Barbara, an hour and a half up the coast from L.A., where they met because they weren't as likely to run into his father or any of his and Elise's friends, Will felt that he couldn't take a normal breath for several minutes. She wore a straw hat and sunglasses and did not want to be recognized because now she was being recognized all the time. If someone snapped their picture and posted it on the Web, or worse, published it in some sleazy gossip rag, "Star Steps Out with Boyfriend's Son," it would be catastrophic for them both. It was he who took their picture—with his phone, several photos of them together on the beach that she felt wary about letting him take because, he assumed, she worried about his father somehow getting hold of his phone and finding the photos. Or worse, Will sending them to him, trying to force her hand.

He had rented a room at an inn in Ojai, but he didn't tell her about it in advance. When he mentioned it to her after they had been walking on the beach for a while, his desire to be alone with her close to intolerable, she had stopped suddenly and withdrawn her hand from his. "I can't," she said.

"Yes, you can," he said, heart sinking.

She shook her head. "If I do, I'm going to screw everything up."

"No, you're not," he said desperately. "Everything will be fine."

"I need to go home. I'm sorry, Will, but I do."

"If you felt like you didn't need my dad to help you with your career, would you go with me to Ojai?"

She looked at him. "Please don't say things like that."

"You don't need him. You're famous now. You're going to Cannes in a week, and things will just keep getting better for you." She was going to Cannes with his father, and it made him almost sick to bring it up, but he did not know how to change her mind about Ojai. The room was actually a small villa with its own kitchen and housekeeping staff. It cost more than a thousand dollars a night, and he could not bear the thought of her not seeing it. The thought of staying there by himself was even worse.

"He's my boyfriend, Will," she said. "Not someone I'm using to get ahead with my career."

"Then why did you come up here?"

"I don't know," she said. "Because I wanted to."

He had not been able to change her mind, even after she kissed him good-bye a final time next to her car, even after she saw that he was about to cry and had looked away. If he had been the type of person who liked romantic movies that did not end happily, he might have felt that his disappointment was almost something to cherish. But he had not particularly enjoyed The English Patient or Casablanca or Dr. Zhivago. He wanted the hero to get the girl and keep her. He wanted Cinderella and The Princess Bride and Sleeping Beauty. He wanted, he realized, a fairy tale.

Three days after the first e-mail from Elise in Paris and two days after his reply that he would not bother her anymore, she sent another message:

> Dear Will,
>   I turned down your father's proposal. I know that I'm not
> ready to get married. I'm only twenty-five, and I told your father

that I think we should just keep dating for a while and see how it
goes. He was disappointed, but he said that he would live with it if
he had to. I didn't tell him this, but I also think he's been seeing
someone else. Maybe it's only my faulty sixth sense making
trouble for me, but I can't shake the feeling that he's preoccupied
by something (or someone) that has nothing at all to do with his
work or *Life After the Storm.*

Please keep all of this between you and me. I'm sure you will,
but I thought I should say it anyway. Take good care over there in
France, Elise

He read the message over and over, wondering what Elise was
trying to tell him, if there was a subtext at all. His parents and sister
knew that he was in Paris now, and he had talked to Anna in the past
week, but she had said nothing about his father proposing to Elise.
She probably didn't know and wouldn't know unless Will told her,
because he could not see their father talking to her about it if his proposal had been rejected. Elise's refusal was enough to make him call
his father; Renn had left him a voice mail four days earlier, which
Will had so far ignored. Just checking in, his father had said. Hope
everything's fine.

He tried his father's cell phones, leaving a message on both, before he reached him when he tried calling a second time. "Is everything all right?" his father asked. "You sounded a little agitated in
your messages."

"Why didn't you call me back after you listened to them?"

"I would have, but I'm at a shoot right now. It's only eleven
thirty in the morning here. What's it over there? Six thirty?"

"Eight thirty."

"Oh. Well, I would have called you in a couple of hours."

His father sounded no different than usual. He even sounded a little buoyant. Had Elise changed her mind since e-mailing him and accepted the proposal? The thought made it harder to breathe. Maybe his father had seen his mistress, if he had one, which Will assumed he did. Elise was likely to be right about this. Women often seemed to be able to tell when something was going on; his mother had known too, though she had tried, often unsuccessfully, not to bring up her suspicions in front of Anna and him while still married to their father.

"Sorry that it's taken me a few days to get back to you. I was just wondering how you were doing."

"I'm fine," his father said, a wary note in his voice now. "Everything's fine."

"That's good."

They both were silent until Renn said, "I hope you're not overdoing it with your running."

"I'm not," said Will. "It's harder to get overheated in the winter anyway."

"But you could still overdo it."

"I could, but I don't."

"Have you made any friends over there yet?"

"Dad, I've only been here a couple of weeks."

"What do you do all day?"

"I go for runs. I shop for food and go to museums. I'm going to start taking a French class at the American School too."

"Any more thoughts about law school?"

Will could hear someone talking in the background, then an eruption of laughter. He knew that his father would have to go in a minute, and they had said nothing at all to each other. But he didn't know what he had expected—his father to confess to an affair? To admit that Elise didn't want to marry him, at least not yet? Few people he knew, especially his father, were ever forthright about these sorts of things, unless they were being filmed for a reality show or calling in to *Loveline.*

"I'm still thinking about it," said Will, "but I don't know if I want to be a lawyer."

"Billy," said his father, almost soothingly. "Just try something. Take a leap and apply to Cordon Bleu if you're planning to stay in Paris for a little while. Learn how to do magic tricks and work as a clown at kids' parties. I don't know. Just do something, and maybe it'll stick."

"Whatever I do, it's going to be about running."

"Running," his father said slowly. "Running away. To Paris or Johannesburg or Riyadh or Warsaw."

Will said nothing.

"Well, I hope you're taking care of yourself. No girlfriend yet, I suppose."

"No."

"I'm sure it won't take long."

"What about you? Do you have a new girlfriend?"

His father hesitated. "No. I'm still with Elise."

"Oh. Well, I guess you are."

"What do you mean, you 'guess'?"

"I don't mean anything. I was just talking."

"That's the problem," said his father, half under his breath. "All right. I have to run. Maybe we can talk more later."

"Okay," said Will. "I'll be awake for a few more hours."

His father did not call back that night or the next, but aside from his resenting Renn a little for his silence, it was a relief. He waited to reply to Elise's e-mail too, not sure if he should respond at all because he had told her that he would leave her alone, and if he waited long enough, maybe she would e-mail him again. It would almost feel like he had the upper hand for an hour or two, but he wasn't sure what that meant or what good it would do him to have it, especially considering that they were more than six thousand miles apart.

He had not been lying about the French class at the American School. He had stopped by there on one of his many long walks and signed up for a class that would meet on a Tuesday night for the first time, which was a few days after Elise's e-mail and the phone call to his father. He did not have high hopes for the course, but when he walked through the door of the classroom and chose a seat two rows from the front and along the wall, he was pleased to see two pretty women there, one of them a student, the other their teacher, both probably not much older or younger than he was. He had not yet written Elise back. He had forced himself to wait until after the first French class, but he had spent more time than he should have staring at the printouts he had made of the photos he had taken of her during their afternoon in Santa Barbara. These were the second copies; the first he had handled so much over the past several months that they had become grimy and wrinkled.

One good thing since coming to Paris, aside from how it had cleared his head about a couple of things and made him feel less inert, was that he had gained back some more weight since he had been in the hospital. He was close to one fifty-five again, about six or seven pounds short of his normal weight. He had not intended to get as thin as he had before the October collapse, but his appetite had so often been poor, and even though he knew that he was losing too much weight and his mother was constantly harassing him about it, he had had trouble forcing himself to eat enough to make up for all of the calories he was burning. The chocolates and pastries and baguettes and croissants in Paris, along with the many good restaurants where actual French people rather than tourists ate, had restored the color to his face. An added benefit, related or not, was that he no longer seemed to be losing much hair, and the places where it was thinning did not seem to be as sparse as they had been in L.A. He wondered if he might be imagining this, but it didn't seem like it.

The teacher was a blond woman named Camille Moreau (*Madame Moreau, s'il vous plait*, she said to her students). She was petite and trim with large dark eyes, and the night of the first class, she wore a flattering beige shirtdress cinched at the waist. Her heels were the same color as the dress, and she wore a double strand of pearls and small matching earrings. Will had trouble keeping his eyes off her, but if she noticed, she did not seem to mind. The only time he spoke directly to her, however, was when she asked for his name. "Comment vous appelez-vous, Monsieur?"

"Will," he said, his voice breaking.

"Will?" she said, smiling slightly. "Ici nous avons les noms français. Maintenant vous vous appellez Guillaume. D'accord?"

"Yes." His face burned. "I mean *oui*."

"Bienvenue à la classe, Guillaume. Vous êtes américain?"

"Oui." She spoke a little quickly, but he thought that he understood her. He was American, and it seemed he had a new name. Before now he had been Billy, then Will, and now in France, he had become the more complicated (all of those vowels, he thought) and possibly more distinguished Guillaume.

"Vous venez de quel état?"

He hesitated, working up the nerve to reply. He could feel his face reddening.

"Which state are you from," someone a row away translated unnecessarily.

"I'm from California, from Los Angeles," he said.

"Ah, très bien, Guillaume. Beaucoup de soleil là-bas, n'est-ce pas?"

"Oui," he said. "Beaucoup. We do get a lot of sun there."

"En français, Guillaume! Alors, et vous, madame?" the teacher said, looking now at the other pretty woman in the class. "Votre nom?"

"Jorie," she said. "Je viens de Boston."

"Jorie," said Madame Moreau. "Alors, c'est un nom assez français. Très bien."

Will glanced at Jorie, but she did not turn her face toward him, her head with its long black braid tilted slightly downward, but he could see her in profile, her cheeks pink, their teacher's attention making her blush too.

The classroom had three overhead rows of fluorescent lights that were so bright Mme Moreau had turned off the middle row within a minute after entering the room, a book bag on her shoulder and a black wool coat thrown over one arm. No one complained about the dimmer lights, but Will did not think that anyone would, especially if the complaint had to be made in French. There were a dozen students all told; most of them close to his age, a few a little older. He felt contented in this uncluttered classroom, looking at his nicely dressed teacher, waiting to learn from her. He had not been a student for so long and felt hopeful and welcome sitting alongside his classmates: four Americans, three Koreans, three Canadians, and one Japanese couple, as if whatever he would learn over the next eight weeks would change his life.

Yet once the class ended, everyone quickly scattered into the cold night. He had hoped that someone might suggest a drink or a late dinner, but no one did, and he did not feel bold enough to suggest it himself. He was slow gathering his papers and putting on his coat, but when he saw that Mme Moreau was waiting for him to leave the room before she locked the door, he hurried to wrap his scarf around his neck. She nodded to him on their way out and said,

"Bonne soirée, Guillaume. A jeudi." Thursday seemed far away, but it would have to do. He couldn't think of a question to ask to forestall her departure, especially one in French, and left the building feeling like a fool.

It was stupid to think that he could make friends in one evening, that his classmates would find space for him, unprompted and trusting, in their lives. He wasn't sure if he wanted to go back to the class on Thursday, even if it was the only consistent social contact he could expect. "Aren't you lonely in Paris?" his mother had asked the one time they had spoken since his arrival. Anna had asked too. "Who do you talk to? Cashiers?" He had talked to Luca's father a few times, and they had met for dinner twice. Mr. DeGrassi had also told him that he should drop by his apartment any time that he wanted to. Maybe he would like to watch TV or play chess or read some of his magazines or books? He had many in English. But Will was reading a book of his own right now, his stepmother's memoir of her marriage to his father.

In the window of a book and music store that took up close to an entire city block near the Seine, he had been startled to notice a display that featured both Melinda's and his father's faces. Beneath the photo were several stacked books, all identical, the French title more melancholy than the American: *Quelques-uns de mes regrets*. Some of her regrets, though Will wondered if the word would be more accurately translated as sorrows.

He wasn't sure why he hadn't bought Melinda's book in L.A. right after it had been published, but he supposed that part of his reluctance was because he did not feel like reading about his father, even if much of what Melinda had written was undoubtedly critical, though he did wonder what she had written about Anna and himself, if anything. Anna hadn't read the book either, as far as he knew.

That morning, however, he went into the Fnac to buy a copy

but soon realized that they would only have the French translation. He asked the clerk for the English version anyway, but as he suspected, it wasn't there. The clerk told him to try Shakespeare & Company across from Notre Dame, and after he rode the Metro east to this small, crowded store with its resident cats and laid-back salesclerks, he quickly found This Isn't Gold. They had three copies, all of them, to his surprise, signed by Melinda. Had she done a book tour? Apparently so, and he had missed her by only four days. He wondered if she was still in Paris but wasn't sure how to contact her, and he also didn't know if he wanted to. He hadn't seen her in several years, not since his father had divorced her and she had retreated up the coast to Big Sur to nurse her wounds and allegedly to drink, which she had also done while she was married to Renn but not to the embarrassing extent, as far as Will knew, that a few particularly mean-spirited gossip columnists had accused her of.

As he remembered her, she had been kind to him and his sister, and often fun to be with. Despite their guilt over liking Melinda, which he and Anna knew upset their mother, they couldn't help themselves after the first few months of trying to ignore Melinda's attempts at friendship. Their young stepmother had known which rock bands they liked and seemed genuinely to like them too. She had let them eat pizza three nights in a row and have ice cream for lunch or breakfast when their father wasn't home. She had not tried to make them talk when they didn't feel like it, but when they did, she had told them tasteless, hilarious jokes and had given them surprise gag gifts like Silly String and a machine that made fart noises and Halloween masks at times of the year nowhere close to October 31. She had cooked them special meals and braided them friendship bracelets that their school friends had envied and wanted for themselves. She had told them about her childhood and what had seemed to her an interminable adolescence, the boys she'd had crushes on in high school who hadn't noticed her, the sports she was too unco-ordinated to play, the way her mother, off-kilter since Melinda's father left when Melinda was seven, had sometimes made her give the dog and her little brother a bath together in a steel tub in the front yard on hot summer nights, something that had embarrassed her almost as much as it had delighted her.

The first sentence of her book saddened Will, but he had half expected this: *Every little girl wants to grow up and marry a prince, and I guess that I was no exception.* The whole book saddened him, and he felt like finding her and telling her that he'd had no idea that she had suffered as much as she had. No surprise that he hadn't much noticed her misery though—he had been a teenager most of the time she'd been married to his father—but he still felt bad that she seemed to have lived through a hellish era of jealousy and self-doubt and emotional abuse, if her accounts of Renn's treatment of her were to be believed. He had to assume that there was some, if not an inordinate, amount of truth to them. He remembered his father and her arguing several times and Melinda crying once or twice, but he knew that she had tried to hide their disagreements, had smiled after Renn had left the house in a huff, had told them they could go out to eat or she would teach them how to drive her car, which was a Jaguar and beautiful, even though they hadn't yet gotten their learner's permits. If their father had known about these lessons, he would have been angry.

What she wrote about Anna and him was generous: that she had thought they were sweet kids, well behaved for the most part, a few temper tantrums but that was to be expected. They had always remembered her birthday and had once baked her a banana cake, which was her favorite, and it had been a good cake too. (How had his mother felt, he wondered, reading this passage? He and Anna had never told her about the banana cake, and Will knew that she had read Melinda's memoir, even though she had not wanted to discuss it with him, other than to say that some of it had surprised her. Some of it had upset her too, though she had anticipated as much.)

He wondered if Melinda regretted publishing the book now that it was out all over the world. If she regretted the fact that she would now never be able to reach Renn again, because in the rarefied realm where he lived, as she had put it in one section, "very few people had kitchen privileges." She had probably made him an enemy for life, if he hadn't felt that they already were enemies. All that his father had said to him about Melinda's book was, "It's out there and I have to live with it. Or rather, now I have to ignore it. It'll die down though. After a few months, most books drop out of sight, especially the trashiest ones."

"You hope," Will had said.

His father had given him a considering look. "Yes," he'd said, "but I'm ninety-eight percent sure I'm right."

Will had allowed an entire week to pass without replying to Elise's message about the proposal she had turned down. During his silence, she had not sent him another message. He went for his runs, did his shopping and eating, went to the Centre Pompidou twice to stare at the Basquiats, and attended his second French class on Thursday evening. He looked at his pretty French teacher and the pretty girl from Boston, and no one tried to talk to him either before or after class, other than one of the Korean students who had said hello to him and everyone else, nodding his head agreeably and laughing when one of the Canadians started to sing "Frère Jacques" before the teacher arrived. In these first two classes, Will had refreshed some of his school French, and could now ask with more confidence where a Metro station was or if he could have ice cubes with his Coca-Cola.

He had already known how to ask these questions, or at least he had thought he did. Jorie spoke better French than he did; his accent was embarrassingly discordant to his ears, the trademark American honk that made Mme Moreau purse her lips as she tried to suppress a smile, or so it looked to Will. He could not get the soft, gliding vowels and consonants to flow from his mouth, though some of the vowels were surprisingly nasal. Mme Moreau had told the class on the first night that if they could master the vowels, they could master the language. There were thirteen French vowel sounds, and some of them were difficult, but with practice, they would be able to speak très bien, comme un Français. Right, thought Will. As if. As if I'll be able to speak one word of French and pass myself off as a native.

The weekend after his second French class, he wrote to Elise.

> Dear Elise,
>   I wasn't sure what to say about your last note, and I also wasn't sure if you'd want to hear from me again. I hope that you're doing fine and that my father is too. You're on my mind a lot. I know that this has to stop, especially because you've said it has to. I am having a good time in Paris, though I do wish that I knew a few more people.
>   One thing that I've been thinking about lately—I haven't really understood why you've ever given me the time of day, from day one, but I think that maybe you sense that we're alike in some ways. At least I think we are. You have a conflicted relationship with one of your parents, as do I. (I guess a lot of people do, but still . . .) I think sometimes that we both worry we'll never be happy. (Am I wrong about this? I don't think I am—why else did you seek me out the few times that you did? You don't seem like someone who likes making trouble for herself—if you did, I think we might already have slept together.)

I've grown up in Hollywood but have never been important there. You didn't grow up there and are suddenly very important but you're probably wondering how long it will last or if you deserve it. I don't really like people looking at me, which is one of the reasons I never tried too hard to go into acting. I also didn't want to compete with my father. It's not like I could hope to do as well or better than he has either.

All right, I think I've probably said too much.

Love, Will

She did not reply the next day, nor did she write to him the day after that. He checked almost hourly except when he was running; he even checked in the middle of the night a few times, because he worried now that his assumptions had offended her. He wished that he could take back the message, his complacent attempts to psychoanalyze her, to impose his own shortcomings and hang-ups on her. Maybe she had changed her mind about the proposal too. Maybe she and his father had already set a date and she was busily making preparations for a June or July wedding in Monterey or Santa Barbara (the thought of a wedding in Santa Barbara made him feel ill)—buying an elaborate and expensive dress, scouting reception locations, going over the guest list (would he be invited? He had to assume that he would be—his father did not like controversy, at least not more than was necessary, and so of course he would invite both of his children and expect them to be prominently there).

He called Anna to find out what he could, but she didn't answer and he didn't feel like leaving a message. He thought about calling his mother too, but since his breakup with Danielle more than a year ago, things with her had been strained. He knew that his mother loved him very much, but sometimes she suffocated him with her affection and her desire for him to do something happily with his life that would also make her happy. He could say, however, that he was no longer unhappy, that Paris with its many architectural marvels, its well-dressed residents and their unabashed worship of beauty and pleasure, seemed to have a place for him, or at least it didn't appear to mind another visitor, seeking who-knew-what. Inner peace? If you were at peace, Will thought, how could you fail to be at least a little happy?

Yet he had only been there for a month; how would he feel during the next month and the one after that? Would his solitariness, with the exception of his French classes and Mr. DeGrassi, weigh too heavily on him?

How lucky he was to have these problems. He could admit that. Out of the extraordinarily varied and astounding number of miseries that people suffered each day, he knew that his privileges were extreme, that his was by most, if not all accounts a charmed life.

His French class on Tuesday evening, the third meeting, was an unaccountably ebullient affair. Mme Moreau arrived with a silk rose tucked behind an ear and set about naming different types of common flowers, several of which she pulled from her handbag before proceeding to go over the words for the various articles of clothing she and the class were wearing. There seemed no order or reason to the lessons she had planned for them—if she had planned anything—but Will didn't mind. Despite her refined appearance, he wondered if maybe she was a little kooky. The thought made him smile, which she noticed. "Pourquoi vous souriez, Guillaume?" she asked, fixing her dark eyes on him.

"Je ne sais pas," he said, blushing. He really didn't know why he was smiling. It was the only thing he could think of to say.

"Alors, vous êtes content? Avez-vous une raison pour votre bonheur à partager avec nous?"

He hesitated, groping for the correct words. He did feel happy, but again, he wasn't sure why. "J'aime cette classe. C'est ça."

"Moi aussi, j'aime bien cette classe." She smiled, and her right eye twitched. He didn't think she was winking at him but it almost looked like it.

He wanted to hide his face behind his scarf (une écharpe, they had just learned), it was burning so hotly now. But within a few minutes, after Mme Moreau had begun going over the names of various professions, she had another question for him. "Guillaume, qu'est-ce que vous faites dans la vie?"

What did he do (for a job, a vocation, an occupation, a career— what was his raison d'être)?

He could feel a stab of heat in his armpits. "Maintenant, je suis aux vacances. Pas de travail." His life in Paris was a vacation. He wasn't sure what else it could be called.

"Bien, mais après vos vacances, qu'est-ce que vous ferez?"

What would he do afterward? He really didn't know. The question, like the one before it, lay between them like something dead. It had to be acknowledged, despite how much it bothered him to do so. "Je vais faire un film."

There was an immediate, electric murmur of curiosity among his classmates. He would make a film? Oh fuck. He wasn't sure where that had come from. He was sweating now in earnest.

Mme Moreau was looking at him, wide-eyed and lovely, her face a study in surprised delight. "Vraiment? C'est extraordinaire. Comment ferez-vous un film?"

He wasn't sure how, or if, he would do it, but there seemed no reason to admit this. "Mon père est Renn Ivins. Je travaille avec lui de temps en temps." He had said it, the one thing that he had intended to keep from everyone he met in Paris. My father, the movie star. My father, the hero, which was also the name of a French film Will had seen as a kid. It was a dopey movie, one that his own father would not have been likely to sign on for if they had approached him for the American version instead of casting Gerard Depardieu again.

"Renn Ivins," exclaimed Mme Moreau. "J'adore Renn Ivins! C'est votre père? C'est vrai?"

Will nodded. "Oui." Weren't Europeans supposed to be blasé about fame, at least compared to Americans? Apparently this did not apply to all of them.

More questions started coming, from the teacher and a few of his classmates, some in French, some in English. Was Renn Ivins also in Paris, and would he visit their class? Did he have a black belt in karate? Had he really carried an actual tarantula in his pocket in *Death Valley by Nightfall*? No, no, no. Did Will know Harrison Ford too? Brad Pitt? George Clooney? Scarlett Johanssen? Yes, sort of, sort of, no, but that'd be nice.

After several minutes, Mme Moreau finally held up her hand and said that they needed to move on, but perhaps Will would tell them more about Hollywood and his father in a future class. The atmosphere in their classroom had changed, probably permanently, the air altered by the introduction of something powerful—desire, curiosity, hope that their lives would somehow be transformed for the better because they were spending a couple of hours each week with a film star's son. Will had not felt this atmospheric shift since college, when in a film class about the French New Wave a guy whose name he couldn't remember kept sitting next to him but was often too shy to talk to him, though two weeks before the end of the semester, he had asked if Will might get his father's autograph for him. He hadn't done it. The request had annoyed and embarrassed him, al though he realized later that his embarrassment was for this nervously smiling guy who thought that autographs actually meant something. What would he do with it besides stare at it from time to time? And what exactly was the point of that?

Girls had made the same request, and sometimes Will had brought them the autograph, especially if he wanted to get them into bed. For the first few years of college, and almost all of high school, he had used his father's name to get pretty girls out of their clothes. He had slept with quite a few women, probably well over a hundred, though he had stopped keeping track after fifty. He had had sex with young actresses who hoped to get to his father through him; he had slept with the daughters of other actors, and some of his sister's friends, including two of her closest—Jill and Celestine, who had sometimes come over and hung around his room when they knew that Anna wouldn't be home. He had had sex with much older women too; a couple of them were actresses his father's age who had made passes at him at parties or spotted him on the street and told him to get in, they would drive him home, but usually it was after they had taken him to their homes first. He had lost his virginity at fourteen to a twenty-three-year-old woman who acted on a soap but dropped out of sight two years later, lost to drugs and alcohol, he had heard. He had slept with her on five different occasions, until his father, not nearly as outraged as Will expected, caught wind of their affair and told him that it would ruin the actress's career if word got out that she was fucking a fourteen-year-old. Word did eventually get out, but only a little, and it didn't matter very much—she was already an addict by then, as far as Will knew.

It wasn't until he got back from a semester abroad in Scotland that his self-disgust became a force that he couldn't ignore anymore, even when he was drunk. He decided to stop having sex until he found a girl who liked him, not just his father. Some of the girls he'd slept with had seemed to like him for who he was, but these were the older women and they were so busy, and he was only a puppy, one of them had said, and surely he would grow tired of her and then where would she be? It was best not to get too serious; he was so young and would meet so many women in his life. After he stopped the gratuitous fucking his senior year in college, he eventually found real girlfriends, two of them women whose parents were in the movie business too, but few of his relationships lasted for more than three or four months, until Danielle, who had stayed with him for more than a year, but then, of course, he had fallen in love with Elise.

Now he was in Paris, living a monk's life, and it wasn't so bad, but all of that would change very soon if he wanted it to, he realized. After Mme Moreau dismissed them for the night, the Japanese couple and Jorie, the girl from Boston, stayed in the classroom until they could follow Will out, and when Jorie and the Japanese man both called his name, he knew that they would ask if he wanted to go out for dinner or a drink. When he turned around and looked at their smiling, flushed faces, he felt an unexpected surge of gratitude, no scorn or weariness at all.

"Yes," he said, when they asked if he wanted to have dinner with them. "There's an Italian place near here that I've wanted to try. Would that be all right?"

Yes, it would be. Jorie nodded, her blue eyes glowing. The Japanese woman, dressed in a pink down coat and matching hat, giggled and nodded too. Her boyfriend smiled and offered his hand. "Yoshi," he said. "You might not remember from the first day. Yannick in our class."

"I do remember," said Will, smiling.

Outside it was snowing for the third time in six days and the city glistened, its streetlamps casting a muted golden light over the covered sidewalks, the air cold against their hopeful faces. Elise had still not replied to his e-mail. That was all right, at least for now. His classmates, he knew, would be happy to do whatever he wanted. It would all be so easy if he allowed it to be that way.

CHAPTER 10

EVERY GIFT YOU'VE EVER GIVEN

r. Greenbaum, a patient who had been admitted with a severe case of bronchitis during one of Anna's recent internal medicine rotations, had grabbed her wrist while she was listening to his lungs and said, "On any given day, do you know how much time the average person spends worrying about things he can't control?"

"No," said Anna, startled but curious. "I don't think I do."

"Neither do I," said the patient with a smile that featured a chipped front tooth, "but it has to be a lot. Half our lives, don't you think?"

"I sure hope not," she said.

"You're still young," he said. "You don't worry that much right now, but it'll catch up with you."

After she left Mr. Greenbaum's room, she kept thinking about his question. Was it an hour a day that the average person fruitlessly worried? Probably more, but she didn't have much time for worrying during these last few months of her internship year at the UCLA medical center that had been named after Ronald Reagan, which she wasn't thrilled about, having learned in childhood from her liberal parents that Reagan's policies had done a lot to put the poor even further behind the rich. (Plenty to worry about there, she thought, wondering if Mr. Greenbaum or any of her other patients had made the same connection.) When she worried, she tried to do it early in the day because if she started to think about the problems in her life, or the potential for new problems, late at night, it sometimes kept her up for a while after she had turned off the bedside lamp, and she needed every minute of sleep that could be wrung out of her short nights. Rising at five thirty in the morning, sometimes at five, did not come naturally to her, and she rarely could get to bed before eleven, even when she left the hospital by seven thirty. On Sunday, the one day that she could sleep in, she did not wake up until well past nine unless the phone rang, but everyone she talked to regularly knew not to call before ten. Except for Tom Glass, who called whenever he wanted to because he was the one person she would willingly lose sleep for, and his free moments were unpredictable. She had been seeing him for close to seven months when Mr. Greenbaum asked his unanswerable question, and sometimes it was as if it were only the first month of their affair—she still felt giddy around him, and a little anxious. He was the one source of anxiety that she might take up at any hour of the day because she could not stop worrying that he would no longer want her if she said or did something foolish.

When they saw each other at the hospital, her desire to be close to him was sometimes unbearable—she wanted to touch his hair, the curls that had grown back from the previous summer's severe pruning, and it was also difficult for her to stop looking at his mouth, the full lips that had kissed hers and so many inches of her body

LITTLE KNOWN FACTS **241**

more times than she would have been able to count. Seven months of clandestine meetings, and he was now talking about moving in with her after she finished her internship year; he would leave his wife and sons for her, but he was certain that his sons would like her once they got to know her and would have little trouble adjusting to his less frequent presence in their lives because they weren't home that much now anyway, one with his driver's license and the other with friends who had driver's licenses. His boys, Trevor and Nathan, would come and stay with them from time to time anyway, though Trevor was going to college in the fall, so it would only really be Nathan who stayed with them, but maybe Anna would ask her downstairs tenant to move out so that she could take over the whole house, if he did leave his wife?

If he left his wife. Despite being such a small word, if had a lot of power.

He was much calmer than she when they worked side by side, doing their daily rounds. It seemed that way to her, at least. He had sworn to her that she was the first and only intern he had ever been romantically involved with, but she continued to wonder if this was true. How was it that he did not feel more nervous when they were at work, especially because if she wanted to, she could have gone to the hospital administrators and made things uncomfortable for him? He must have been confident, however, that she would never do such a thing. And she wouldn't. She loved him and couldn't imagine doing him harm even if one day he told her that he didn't want to see her anymore. People changed their minds; it happened all the time. And if he did dump her, she would not be so lame as to pine for someone who didn't want to be with her.

From the beginning, however, he had made an effort to see her at least once a week, sometimes twice. He told her that he would have come to her every day if it had been possible, and sometimes when they were in her bed, he said that he had dreams about her at night and was afraid that he talked in his sleep, because on some mornings his wife would hardly speak to him and there was no other logical reason for her remoteness that he could think of.

"Other than the fact you've been married for nineteen years?" Anna teased.

"How could she possibly be tired of me?" He laughed, this Dr. Heart-of-Glass, as her friend Jill called him, this faithless wretch, this man she was witlessly crazy about. Her mother, having been left years ago for the other woman, did not know that he was married. Her mother wanted to meet him, having gotten wind of the fact, from Anna's brother, Billy, that there was a new man in her life, Billy having blurted something about Tom over the phone from his possibly beautiful new life in Paris.

"But if you were talking about me in your sleep, wouldn't she say something? How could she not?" she asked.

Tom gave her an almost pitying look. "You have no idea what isn't said in a marriage, especially ones that have dragged on for years."

This seemed to her a bleak view of couplehood, and so much in step with the many marital clichés that comedians had made their reputations on for years. But a small, mean part of her liked it when he talked so unflatteringly about his marriage. What was keeping them together? Laziness over the upheaval and tedium a divorce would doubtless entail? Worry over how their children would respond? Surely their marriage would give out soon if things were as dull and pointless as he said.

But that's what every woman who falls for a married man thinks! Her common sense was usually awake and ready to spout off if she let herself hear it. Surely you're not so stupid/naive/deluded to believe . . .

She did know better, but it didn't matter. A person would believe anything if she wanted to badly enough. She had seen it in her patients, the wan, ailing souls—inveterate smokers, sweets-addicted diabetics—who did not believe that they were going to die. Every person, no matter how bright, seemed to think that he would be the exception to the rule. "This is the human condition," one of her other attending physicians had said, Dr. Fitch, who normally she found to be a grouch but on this day had been warmer than usual to her and her classmates. "What you see will break your hearts," he had said. "But hope is also what saves some of them. We doctors aren't supposed to say that, but it's true. Drugs and surgery don't cure everything."

Some mornings when she woke before her alarm went off in the predawn hours, it startled her to realize that she had done it—she had become a doctor. All of those years of studying and worrying that she should study even more had at last come to fruition—the innumerable hours spent poring over textbooks, memorizing every muscle and bone in the body, every abstruse biochemistry formula. She had lost so many hours of sleep before her biggest exams, certain that she would forget everything when the test paper was in front of her, but this had never happened. She had done well in her classes and was now doing well in her rotations, tacitly vying with Jim Lewin over who was the quickest to make the most feasible diagnosis (him, usually), who had the most winning bedside manner (her always, though Jim tried), and who told the best jokes to put their patients at ease (neither—it was usually only the attending physician who made the patients laugh, but Anna was getting more confident, knowing that she had made a favorable impression on the attendings with her compassion but also with her brains).

Jim and she were pals anyway, more so than they had been during med school, in part because she had set him up with her

friend Jill the previous fall, who seemed to like him for real and apparently was not cheating on him, which was unusual for her. Ac-
cording to Jill, Jim was hot in the sack and was well hung and what
more could a girl reasonably ask for? Anna had almost shrieked when
Jill told her this; she did not want to know what lived behind Jim's
fly, but now, of course, whenever she saw him, she thought about
Jill's words and wondered if maybe she had been wrong to dismiss
his earlier crush on her without giving him a try first.

The thought of having sex with Jim was a little ridiculous
though—he was such an earnest dork, and she could only picture
him in his doctor's smock with a stethoscope around his neck, not
naked and passion-inflated. Jill claimed that he had done some kinky
things to her with this same stethoscope, another disclosure that
Anna did not want to consider, but it did make her laugh. She was
glad that Jill seemed to have fallen for him and hoped it continued to
go well. (If not, poor Jim would be crushed—she could see it clearly.)
They both deserved to be happy.

Her own happiness, however, was elusive—when she knew
that Tom was coming over because he was in the car and on his way
(though even this was sometimes no guarantee), she felt as if she
would never again ask for anything else. Even if he wouldn't be able
to see her again for a month or more, it would be all right, as long
as she could see him that night for an hour, even a half hour. When
he gave her a tiny platinum ring on a fine silver chain for Christmas,
saying that she had his heart (but his wife had his balls, Jill and
Celestine had later joked), she had thought that she might burst from
happiness, and that this happiness would last because he had given
her tangible proof of his feelings. Whenever he stashed a note beneath her pillow saying that he already missed her, his initials
enclosed in a penciled heart, she believed that she needed only to
bide her time and he would leave his wife and move in with her.

She knew that this was how Melinda, his father's second wife, must have felt when she was living through the suspenseful year before he had left Anna's mother for her. Her father, she had come to suspect, was probably never going to be satisfied, unlike herself, she hoped, even though he was with the extraordinary Elise, who was so young, but Anna liked her and hoped that her father had finally met the woman he would settle down with for good. Why she wished this, she didn't know, only that it seemed that she would feel better about him if he did.

Because there was something a little strange, possibly sordid, going on with him right now, something she did not want to think about because if her hunch was correct, it would mean that he was having an affair with someone she knew and had previously liked quite a bit. If he was seeing Danielle, her brother's ex-girlfriend, on the sly, she did not want to get mixed up in it because she knew that she would have to decide whether to tell Billy, and if she did tell him, the two men, their relationship already strained, would probably argue ferociously and maybe not talk to each other again for a long time, if ever. Billy would probably wonder if the affair had started before their breakup and also feel wronged because their father had Elise and he did not.

Danielle had called Anna the day after Valentine's Day, just to say hello, she claimed, because they hadn't talked in so long and Danielle missed her. When Anna told her that Billy had moved to Paris, she did not seem surprised to hear this, though she pretended to be, and this, Anna realized in retrospect, was the first red flag, because from what Billy had told her, he and Danielle were not in contact. The second red flag, a much bigger one, was the sudden barrage of questions about Billy and Anna's father—where was he now? and if he was out of town, how long would he be gone? Danielle had recently crossed paths with him at the Griffith Observatory, where they had both gone for an early-morning hike, and she wanted to send him something in the mail, information about her business for someone that he said might be interested in hiring her to reorganize his home.

Her story sounded as if she were reciting it from a script.

Didn't she have a website? Anna asked. And couldn't the potential client contact her himself?

Well, yes, of course, but Renn had asked her to send the brochure directly to him, and she wanted to oblige him.

Then another question, a complete non sequitur: What did Anna think of Elise? Were she and Renn happy?

Anna had hesitated before answering, suspecting that Danielle's interest wasn't innocent. "They seem very happy whenever I've seen them together," she said warily.

"That's great," said Danielle. "Elise seems like she's a nice person."

"She is."

Her brother's ex wavered, taking, what sounded to Anna's ears, a long and shaky breath. "How serious do you think they are?"

Anna faltered. "I'm not sure. Pretty serious, probably. Why?"

"Oh, nothing. Just curious. In that interview in *Time* last week about Life After the Storm, your dad didn't say anything about their relationship." She laughed self-consciously.

"He doesn't like to talk about his personal life. I'm sure Billy told you that when you guys were dating." Anna paused. "Look, Danielle, is everything okay? Why are you asking me about Elise and my dad?"

"I'm sorry." Danielle laughed again. "I guess I'm just in a nosy mood. I'm sure you're busy. Congratulations on being a doctor now too. I bet you're great at it."

"Thanks. I do like it."

"I'd better let you go. Sorry to bother you with my questions. It's nice to hear your voice."

"Yes, you too."

"Good-bye, Anna. Sorry again," said Danielle, hanging up abruptly, leaving Anna to hold on to the phone for a few seconds, wondering what was going on.

The next morning Anna called Tom to tell him about the disquieting conversation with Danielle. She managed to catch him while they were both still driving to the hospital, she from Silver Lake, he from Marina del Rey, but he didn't take her distress over Danielle's call as seriously as Anna thought that he should have. "Your father can pretty much do whatever he likes and probably has for years," he said.

"So you're saying that it's okay if he's sleeping with my brother's ex?"

"No, that's not what I'm saying at all, but if we're going to be honest with ourselves, I don't think that either of us is in much of a position to judge him right now."

". . . no, but I still don't think—"

"I bet your father would say the same thing, sweetheart."

Normally she loved it when he used endearments, but this one sounded patronizing. "I suppose he would," she said dryly.

Tom laughed. "Don't worry so much. Your father's a big boy, and I assume that this girl your brother used to date is old enough to take care of herself too. I'd do my best to stay out of it if I were you. You don't have proof of anything, and I don't think it'd be a good idea to go looking for any either."

"Sorry to bother you with this, Tom." She was irritated but tried to keep her voice even.

"It's not a bother. I'm intrigued. You must have known that I would be."

Tom had asked her to introduce him to her father a month after they had started seeing each other, but she had waited a few months more before inviting her father over for dinner, during which time she tried to decide if she was more nervous about Renn guessing that Tom was something other than a friend, or about whether Tom was having an affair with her mostly because he wanted to get to her father. She had talked it over with Jill and Celestine, the only two people who knew that she was seeing Tom, and they had both thought she was being paranoid. "I think it's pretty ballsy of him to want to meet any of your family members, whether your dad's a movie star or not," said Celestine. "I also doubt that he'd spend all this time wooing you and risking his marriage just to get to your dad. It's not like he wants to be an actor, right?"

Jill said, "Unless you think Tom is bisexual and wants to get your dad in the sack, I don't think you have anything to worry about. It's probably just a mancrush. No big deal."

Tom had told her that he been a fan of her father's films for about twenty years, and after *Bourbon at Dusk* was released and so generously reviewed, and there was the attendant publicity about the foundation for Katrina survivors that he had started, it was almost like Tom thought that her father deserved to be canonized. But she too loved that he had started Life After the Storm and thought that at some point she and Tom might be able to get involved by volunteering for a week or more in the clinic Renn planned to open in or just outside of New Orleans in the next several months.

Her father, no surprise, had figured out almost immediately after he and Elise had arrived at her house that Tom was Anna's lover, and he was more upset by this fact than she had imagined he would be. He told her bluntly that she was wasting her time getting involved with a married man, that he would likely disappoint her, that she could do a whole lot better, didn't she understand what a tremendous catch she was? Beautiful, incredibly intelligent, and also such a decent, down-to-earth young woman? And of course she had money, but her father didn't mention that. He had to believe that Tom had it too, though probably not as much as Anna did. Why in the hell was she selling herself short by hanging around with this guy who was also so much older than she was?

She had looked at her father, an aging man who was dating a woman almost thirty years his junior. Compared to that, the nineteen-year age difference between her and Tom felt much less egregious. Anna had smiled and said, "Dad, you can't be serious about the age gap. Come on."

It had taken a few seconds for this to sink in, but then, to her amused surprised, he had blushed. "I suppose you're right, but really, Anna, I don't recommend it. I wish there was only a few years' difference between Elise and me, but obviously, that's not the way it worked out."

And now, despite his prized young girlfriend, it seemed that he was stepping out on her, with his own son's ex-girlfriend. Danielle had sounded anxious, even a little desperate, when she called. It wouldn't have taken an experienced psychologist to figure out that there was a subtext to the phone call that could not have been innocent. When Anna called her father after her shift at Reagan ended for the day, he did not pick up. She didn't say why she was calling, only that he should call her back. By ten thirty that night, he hadn't yet called back. She tried him again, but he still didn't pick up, and she resigned herself to brooding until she could question him about Danielle, though she would try to do it in a roundabout way. Nevertheless, she could not see him giving her a straight answer no matter how she phrased her question.

Tom was right that she should not get involved, and that given enough time, it would all blow over, if anything was going on in the first place. Her father would eventually tire of Danielle, and provided that she didn't do anything drastic and brainless, the affair would simply end and neither Elise nor Billy would have to find out about it. Anna didn't really understand why it bothered her so much, but she thought it might be because she was involved in something dishonest herself, though as Jill had said not long before Anna had started seeing Tom, it was he who had to answer to his wife and children, not Anna.

A convenient way to see things, certainly.

And not Anna's usual way of going about her business either. How much she had learned about herself in the past several months, how many previously held assumptions about her character now had to be revised! Before she had met Tom Glass, affairs had always sounded to her like puerile self-indulgence, the most common adult cliché. There were plenty of single men and women to go around, weren't there? Who really needed to get involved with someone who was married? She could not imagine falling for a man who lied to his wife on a regular basis, especially if the lie was told so that he could go off and have sex with another woman. How could she love a liar? How would she ever be able to trust him not to do the same thing to her? And if he had kids, wasn't it just the most lowlife, selfish thing in the world to be risking their well-being and happiness by keeping a mistress? How could it possibly be worth it?

Ah, self-knowledge. She really had had no idea what lay beneath the veneer of her good intentions and good opinion of herself before she had started her internship. In more ways than one, Tom Glass was educating her.

The next morning around nine, when she was already two hours into her workday at the hospital, her father called her back. She could feel her phone vibrating in her lab coat's pocket, and knew that it was him. As soon as she could get away from her group with the excuse that she needed to use the bathroom, she went into a visitors' bathroom and called him back.

"Is everything all right, Anna?" her father asked. "I would have called you back last night, but I was out so late that I didn't want to wake you up."

Hearing the concern in his voice, she nearly lost her nerve. "I'm fine, Dad. I'm sorry if you were worried about me."

"Are you okay?"

"Yes," she said, pausing. "I was just wondering about something. A couple of days ago Danielle Dixon called me, Billy's ex-girlfriend. You remember her, I'm sure."

There was a distinct pause before he said, "Yes, I remember her."

Other than the pause, there was nothing telltale in his voice. She had to keep in mind that he was an actor, that he was probably capable of bluffing his way out of anything. "Have you seen her lately?"

"No," he said. "Not since that night at Sylvia's more than a year ago."

"Really? She said you ran into each other at the Griffith Observatory not long ago."

He was silent for a moment. "I haven't seen her at Griffith. Why would she say that?"

"I don't know. Is there any reason that you think she would?"

"Why was she calling you?"

"She said it was because she missed me." Anna paused. "She had a number of questions about you too."

"Anna, that's strange. I have no idea why she'd be calling to ask you about me."

"Don't you want to know what her questions were?"

"No, I don't."

"She wanted to know where you were and how long you'd be gone. She asked if you and Elise were happy, which you can imagine I found rather odd. She also said that you had a friend who might be interested in hiring her. I guess she's still doing that job where she organizes people's homes."

"I don't remember telling her that I had a friend interested in hiring her. Maybe it's something we talked about that night at Sylvia's."

He was not convincing her. She could hear something in his tone now—vagueness or guilt, maybe both—that made her feel almost certain he was lying to her.

"Dad, it sounded to me like she's seen you recently and that she wants to see you again. It was like she expected you to call her on Valentine's Day or something, but you didn't."

He laughed. "That's absurd. I hardly know her. Why would I call her on Valentine's Day?"

She was getting irritated with the way that he kept turning her questions back on her, and she needed to rejoin the other interns, who were probably wondering what had happened to her. She asked him one more question: "Is something going on between you two?"

"Anna, you can't be serious," he said, laughing again. "You know that I'm with Elise. I just asked her to marry me."

"You did?" said Anna, taken aback. A third marriage? It seemed a foolish move on her father's part. Elise was bound to get restless, if he didn't first. "Did she say yes?"

"Not quite. She wants to stay with the status quo for now, but I think we'll probably get engaged and wait a couple of years to marry."

"Well, congratulations, Dad. I have to get back to work, but maybe we can talk tonight if you're free."

"That could work, but I might fly down to New Orleans later to check on a few things for the foundation. Janice wants to move us into the rest of the building where our offices are because the other tenant is about to move out. I'm not sure it's necessary, but she's convinced it is. Our rent would nearly double, and I think for now that it's best to stay where we are."

Janice was the woman, a longtime heavyweight in nonprofit development, whom her father had hired to oversee his fledgling foundation. Anna had met her once the previous fall when she was first hired and thought that Janice seemed nice enough, if not also a little sycophantic around her father. It was nothing that she hadn't seen dozens of times before, but it still made her uncomfortable, as if someone she had just met was walking around, unaware that his pants were unzipped.

"You could just tell her no. You've raised most of the money so far, haven't you?"

"I have, but I feel like I should go down there so that at least she knows I considered it."

This seemed a little ridiculous, but Anna didn't say anything. If he didn't want to rent the whole building, he need only say no and Janice would of course have to demur. She had not known her father to be hesitant about such things before. Was he having an affair with Janice too? It wasn't likely, but it also wasn't impossible.

When had she become such a paranoid, as Tom had said yesterday? Her own transgression had to be responsible for this new and troubling desire to police her father, which was a preposterous undertaking. And it was not her place to police him anyway. Elise could do it, if she even had those tendencies, which she probably did. Anna could not think of any woman she knew who would have felt comfortable sharing her husband or lover. It was the same with her lesbian friends. Jealousy was a universal human weakness, though maybe it was sometimes a strength, in that it was supposed to help you hold on to what or who was important to you.

"Well, if you do go down there, Dad, I hope you won't let her rope you into anything. You're the boss."

"Yes, I know. Don't worry about me. I shouldn't have said anything."

When she rejoined the other interns in her group in the neurology wing, Jim Lewin raised his eyebrows and said, "Everything okay, Dr. Ivins?"

"Yes," she said, glancing at her watch. She had been gone for almost ten minutes. But their attending physician was missing now too.

"Dr. Gutierrez excused himself a minute or two after you left us. You're off the hook," said Jim. He paused. "Do you know if Jill likes Beethoven? I was thinking of getting tickets for the symphony. There's a matinee on Sunday, and they're doing *Eroica*. I'd really like to go if you think she'd like it too."

"She'd love it," said Anna. "That's sweet of you." The symphony was one of the many things that she and Tom could not do. Too public, he had told her apologetically, as most things were. People knew him—his patients, other doctors, his and his wife's friends, some of whom seemed to hold season tickets to every sporting and cultural event within a hundred-mile radius of Los Angeles. Even if they could have escaped up the coast to San Francisco or Napa, Tom would have still worried that he might run into someone who knew him and his wife. His wife was a realtor and knew as many people as he did, possibly even more.

When Anna had told Celestine about how narrow the possibilities for their dates were, her friend had said, "Just make sure the next guy you have an affair with doesn't have any friends." She laughed. "But isn't the whole point of an affair the sex? I've always thought that it was."

Unlike Jill, Celestine had not asked to be set up with one of Anna's doctor friends. She preferred to date athletes and actors, and working as a media escort for a PR firm with dozens of clients, she met quite a few. Celestine was pretty, charming, and fit, though she had suffered on and off since age fourteen from bulimia, and had never been very confident about her looks or intelligence (despite having graduated cum laude from Loyola Marymount), even after the athletes and actors she was attracted to had started noticing her.

Celestine's comment about affairs, flippant as it was meant to be, had made Anna wince inwardly. Despite the ring pendant and the hypotheticals about moving in with her and having his sons visit, she wondered sometimes what Tom was really doing with her. Maybe it was just the sex that he wanted. And the cachet of having met Renn Ivins in person, of having successfully romanced his daughter, a competent new physician and very easy, as it turned out, to seduce.

If she were to talk with her mother about Tom and admit that he wasn't exactly a boyfriend, nor was he truly available in any traditional sense, she knew that her mother would be gravely disappointed. If only Billy had kept his mouth shut! He thought that she was stupid for seeing a married man, but he was hardly one to judge. Aside from her mother, no one in her nuclear family had any right to pass judgment on anyone else's love life. Billy with his futile crush on Elise while he pretended to want to move in with Danielle; her father with his long, storied history of philandering; herself with her married lover. In the sixteen years since her parents' divorce, it wouldn't have been inconceivable if her mother had dated a married man. Or else had wanted to date a married man, but had chosen not to. Her mother had been single for the past two years, as far as Anna knew, and although she probably had the occasional offer, she seemed to prefer to remain alone. It sometimes bothered Anna that Lucy had not remarried or at least found someone with whom she wanted to live, while at the same time their father went from wife to girlfriend to wife as easily as if he were changing his socks.

Since Billy had slipped up the previous week, their mother had called her three times and left messages, saying in a wounded voice in the last one that she knew how busy interns were, but couldn't Anna find two or three minutes to call her back? Or was she too occupied with her new boyfriend in the off hours to talk to her mother?

After this third pitiful message, Anna returned her call. It was almost nine thirty, and her mother didn't like her nonwork phone to ring after nine p.m. because she said that it made her think that someone was calling with bad news, but Anna called then anyway. Tom had come home with her at seven thirty and had stayed until nine fifteen, a rare event because when he visited her on a work night, he usually couldn't stay for more than forty-five minutes to an hour. Tonight they had had sex, as they always did, and then eaten dinner, a pizza that Tom had ordered before they took off their clothes, requesting that the delivery person not arrive for forty minutes. He beamed at her after he had made the call and said, "See how organized I am?"

"You're great," she said, not really meaning it, but he didn't appear to notice. He was looking at her breasts, which were still encased in her bra, a lacy white one that she had bought several months earlier and taken care to keep from turning a dingy gray, which she could only do by hand-washing it.

"I try," he said, snaking his arms around her back, unclasping the bra. He pressed his face to her breasts and kissed one, then the other. She wished that she could resist him. When he was in her bed, this was the only time her fear that he would leave her ever fully dissipated.

He was a strong man of average height, with silver hair on his chest to go with the sprinkle of silver on his head. He had hair on his back too, but none of it was gray. Tonight his back was smooth when she put her arms around him, and she liked that he had gone to the trouble to shave it off. His chin and cheeks were rough though, the day's whiskers chafing her breasts. She shivered and pulled at the curls on his head, whispering that she wanted him to enter her right away, but he rarely ever would. He liked to make her wait, to plead with him a little. It was something he was very good at.

"When do I get to meet him?" her mother asked. "What's his name?"

Anna sighed inwardly. What if her mother knew him and knew that he was married? "Tom," she said, hoping she wouldn't ask for his last name.

"Is he a doctor too?"

"Yes."

"Is he one of your classmates?"

There was no point in lying. She knew that Lucy would find out the truth one way or another. "No, he's one of the attendings."

Her mother faltered. "Really? Anna, I hope he's not one of your attendings."

"He is."

"Oh, God. You should not, under any circumstances, be dating him."

Anna said nothing.

"Anna, really, it's a terrible idea. You've worked so hard to get where you are. If something happened to you because of him, I'd have to report him. Or kill him."

"Mom, nothing's going to happen."

"Are you in love with him?"

"I don't know," she lied.

"Oh, Jesus. You are."

"I said that I don't know."

"At least tell me that's he's not married."

She felt the pressure of anxiety in her chest. But was it really any of her mother's business? "He's not."

"Good," said her mother. "I guess it's not as bad as it could be." She paused. "You're sure he's not married?"

"Mom, please, let's talk about something else. How are you?"

"Isn't there someone else you could date?"

"I'm sure there is, but I'm dating him. Are you thinking of going to see Billy? He said that you said something about it when you talked to him the other day."

"I might. I haven't been to Paris in about five years, and I'd like to see how he's doing. He sounds happy on the phone. I think it was probably a smart idea for him to go over there for a while, but I do wonder what he'll do next."

"Maybe he'll be a boulevardier for the rest of his life. There are worse things."

Her mother laughed. "What a word, sweetie. Did you learn that in college?"

"I don't know. Probably," she said. "Mom, I'm sure Dad would tell you this himself, but I know you don't talk to him that often and it might leak into the papers. He told me a couple of days ago that he asked Elise to marry him."

There was a long pause in which Anna could hear a bird sing-
ing; several mockingbirds lived in her mother's neighborhood, and
a few of them sang day and night. Finally she said, "He did?"

"Yes," said Anna.

"Did she say yes?"

"No. But he thinks he'll get her to agree to a long engagement."

"God, that man will never learn. Why can't he see that the girl
doesn't want to marry him?"

"Because he doesn't want to believe she's rejected him. No one
rejects him."

"Oh, Anna." Her mother sighed.

"What? You've said it yourself about a thousand times."

"I know, but it's different when I say it."

"It is?"

"Yes, you know it is."

Before they hung up, her mother said, "I want to meet Tom.
Would you bring him over for dinner next Sunday? That's your day
off, isn't it?"

"He's going out of town for a few days. It'll have to wait." Another lie.

"Then the Sunday after next."

"I'll ask him, but I don't know if he'd feel comfortable. He already thinks that you wouldn't approve because we work together."

"You've talked about me with him?"

"Yes, of course."

"I want to meet him. If I have to come to the hospital when
you're both working, I will."

"That would not be a good idea."

"Then bring him over to meet me."

"I will when he feels more ready."

"Has your father met him?"

"Mom."

"Has he?"

She exhaled. "Yes, he has."

"Oh, Anna, and you haven't brought him over to meet me yet? He wanted to meet the movie star but not me?"

"No, that's not it at all." Though it was, and her mother knew it. Anna had only been willing to introduce Tom to her father because she hoped that her father's glow would burnish her too, and the two men had gotten along well, Renn saying when she spoke to him a few days later that even though he hated to admit it, he thought that she and Tom seemed happy together. But of course they hadn't been seeing each other very long and affairs were different from other relationships and Tom had a wife and kids and if Anna could walk away now, she should. The conversation had ended shortly thereafter, Anna feeling like her father had jinxed her. But she felt that way about so many things that happened now: the affair was turning her into an obsessive-compulsive.

"You're breaking my heart," her mother said. "Both you and Billy. He has a girlfriend in Paris now, but he won't tell me much about her other than that she's an American too."

"If you go to visit him, I'm sure you'll meet her."

"Maybe. But he might not want to introduce me to her either."

"He will." She hesitated. "Mom, Dad met Tom because he stopped by to see me one night when Tom was over for dinner."

Her mother was silent for a moment. "Really?"

"Yes." There were many ways that her mother could find out that this wasn't true, but it was a mercy lie and they were sometimes necessary. This, at least, was what Anna told herself.

"Oh. Well, okay," said Lucy, the relief in her voice obvious.

"I'd better go, Mom. Another busy day tomorrow."

"They'll be like that for as long as you keep working."

"Yes, I'm sure they will."

She could not sleep that night and lay awake for two hours before she got up to take an Ambien. She was lying to her mother because of Tom. Her father was lying to her because he was having an affair with Danielle—Anna could not help but feel convinced of it. She was making a muddle of her life right now, and her father was doing the same with his. Yet she wondered if her mother was any better off, sitting alone in her big house, worrying too much about her and Billy and the ex-husband who had cheated on her and left her for someone else after fifteen years of marriage.

When she was finally feeling the sleeping pill's effects, Mr. Greenbaum and his question about how much time people wasted worrying drifted into her consciousness. He reminded her of a friend she had had in college who had since disappeared from her life. He was someone she had briefly dated, but he had turned out to be very religious, and after a month, she knew that they would probably always be incompatible. Nonetheless, he had made one vaguely religious comment that she still thought about from time to time. They had gone to a birthday party for a mutual friend, and on the walk home, he had said, "Don't you wish that you could go into a room and see every gift you've ever given set out on a table? If you've given a lot of presents in your life, think of how cool that would look. All of those gift-wrapped packages, the bows and the cards too. I'd love to see that. Maybe that's what heaven is, a place where you get to see all of the nice things you've done for other people. You'd get all of the thank-yous that you should have gotten when you were still alive too. That has to be what heaven's like. Forget the angels playing harps and the white robes and hushed voices. I want to see a lot of colors. I want to relive the best parts of my life."

Anna wondered where he was now, this boy who had considered joining the Catholic priesthood. Maybe he had become a priest; maybe he was living an honorable life, one without much private tension or disorder and few lies or dark secrets. Maybe he was happy wherever he was now, but she doubted it. Other than Jim Lewin and Jill (though how could she be sure?), she couldn't think of anyone she knew who was happy, not for more than an hour or two at a time.

CHAPTER 11

HOLLYWOOD ENDING

*I*f my son felt that he had to run away from home, I suppose there are worse places to run to than Paris. I'm relieved that he didn't choose some remote region in China or an Alaskan outpost where modern conveniences and medical clinics are scarce. One of my fears, ever since I saw that movie about the boy who moves to Alaska and dies a wretched, lonely death because he accidentally ingests a poisonous plant, is that Billy will somehow come to a similar end. This is wholly irrational, I know—Billy doesn't even like to camp—but one's fears are hardly ever rational.

Despite Paris's much admired charms, it's hard for me to believe that my son will stay there for very long. My hunch (and hope) is that he will miss Los Angeles and his sister and friends here, his spacious condo and the energy of our sprawling dreamscape, if not also his father and me. I'm hurt that he wanted to leave and did so without any kind of warning—one day he was here, the next he wasn't, and he left no note with any sort of hint about where he had gone and why. I realize that children leave behind their parents and childhood homes all the time, but both of my kids have lived in southern California their entire lives, having chosen to go to college here too. And usually when people leave, they give you a forwarding address or allow you the chance to say good-bye.

About Billy's big move, my friends say, "It's about time, isn't it? Wasn't it bound to happen sooner or later?" I know they're right, but the comparison I make (only to myself) is this: his departure is like a cancer diagnosis. Despite the fact most of us have heard the sobering statistics—one in two people will suffer from some form of cancer before they die—when the diagnosis comes, it's still a shock.

The irony is, my son and I seem to have grown closer across the distance of one entire continent and the Atlantic Ocean. He calls me every week now, or I call him and he calls back within a day or two. There are no more unreturned phone calls, no more plaintive or frustrated or angry pleas for him to call me back before I contact his building's doorman and ask him to confirm that Billy is still alive. In the three months that he has lived in France, his attitude appears to have changed from bad to mostly good. He has told me twice that he loves me without me saying it first. He has started writing a screenplay (though he told me not to tell his father if I talked to him, because he did not want Renn to know anything about it until after he had finished it). He has a new girlfriend, a woman named Jorie who apparently is also taking time off from her regular life in the States to study art and learn French and finally make a real attempt at appreciating beauty. That's how Billy has phrased it, at any rate. "There's beauty to appreciate in California," I told him after he said this.

His reply: "I knew you'd say that. But in France it's different. The French practically invented beauty, at least in its modern conception."

"You sound like a philosopher now," I said. "I guess Paris is working for you."

"It's not just working," he said quietly. "It's saving me. I was going crazy in L.A. Things are a lot better now, but I had to get out of there to realize just how depressed I was."

"Are you still running too many miles?" I asked him another time.

"No," he said, "but I do run almost every day, and compared to what some people run, fifteen or twenty miles isn't that much."

"You don't need to run more than a few miles at a time to stay in good shape if you're already eating healthy."

"I don't do it just to stay in shape. I do it because I love it. I'm not changing my running regimen, Mom. We don't need to keep discussing this."

This is a little hard for me to accept, considering that it wasn't very long ago that I got a phone call from Anna telling me that her brother was in the hospital because of what he had done to his body on his morning run. It has since been pointed out to me repeatedly that he is a grown man, that his collapse was a fluke, he can make his own decisions, he can take care of himself, etc etc. As a doctor, I've heard this sort of petulant defense more times than most people probably have. I know that in Billy's case, I'm not dealing with a fool, nor do I think he has a death wish, but it's hard not to worry about him, and if something were to happen to him, it would be a little more difficult to get to Paris quickly than down the road to Huntington Memorial.

Billy's original plan was to return home to run the marathon in March, but he has now decided not to, probably because of Jorie, though he said it was because he wants his first official marathon to be the one in Paris, which is only a couple of weeks away. I have my plane ticket and will be there for those 26.2 grueling miles through this most historic city's winding streets. I don't really understand why people think it's a good idea to run so far all at once. The concrete and blacktop we have covered so much of the earth with are two of the worst possible surfaces for the human body to spend time bouncing up and down on. Whose idea was it that people should compete in races like this? When what we now call the marathon was first run in ancient Greece, it was out of necessity, not because people needed something to amuse themselves with.

I understand Billy's desire to escape his California life, if only because he wants to look upon another vista for a while, another view of what a life can be. It's not that the French have lives so much more healthy and mindful than our own, but I know that many of them do still take their time when it comes to some of the more important daily rituals—they buy their food from small local grocers and bakers and butchers, they take their time at the dinner table too, and they often dress themselves with an artistic flair (they are not known for wearing sweatpants and gym shoes to restaurants and movie theaters and doctor's appointments, among other obligations that require them to appear in public). Something else: they read poetry. The last time I was in Paris, I was stunned to discover how large the poetry section was in one of the bookstores I browsed—as big as or bigger than the self-help sections in most American bookstores. Truly, this was a revelatory moment, and unaccountably, I felt my eyes well with tears.

That said, they do have race riots and poverty and plenty of criminals who rape and steal and destroy. They are subject to the same human failings that we are, but I do think that Billy is right to say that he is learning about beauty during his time in Paris. There is the Seine and its many bridges, structures that look like they were stolen from a fairy tale; its enormous but unbelievably intricate municipal buildings; its dozens of museums (a whole museum devoted just to Picasso, another to Rodin, a third to Dalí, and each of them so very good)—all of this available whenever he walks out his front door. Paris has been here since the days when Christ allegedly walked the earth, its marketplaces thriving long before the Crusades began, before Saint Augustine wrote his *Confessions*, a time when America did not exist, not in the incarnation that the European invaders began to create after their arrival on its alien shores.

Paris, needless to say, is quite different from L.A., which in comparison is a newborn city, though they are similar in one crucial way—both are places where people believe they will be able, with a little good luck, to step into the lives they are destined for.

Something has happened since Billy moved overseas that was as unexpected as his sudden disappearance: I met someone. Or, I should say, I re-met someone. This man went to USC for his undergraduate degree too, and Renn and I were friends with him for a year or so, but then we lost touch because I think Michael had a bit of a crush on me. Renn thought so, in any case, and eventually stopped inviting him out with us. It's a bit surreal to remember that there was a time when Renn worried about losing me to some other man. But he did worry, and this era lasted for several years, until a little while after Billy was born, when Renn became so busy and sought-after that people like Harrison Ford (gorgeous *and* funny) and Warren Beatty (gorgeous too, but his much-publicized playboy ways alarmed me) were regularly dropping by to hang out at our dinner table.

Now, three decades later, Michael appeared before me one morning a few weeks ago when I was at a bagel place on Colorado Boulevard where I sometimes buy a cup of coffee on my way to work. "Lucy?" he said. "Lucy Wilkins?"

He was standing behind me in line, and I almost jumped when I heard my maiden name. When I turned around to see who the voice belonged to, I know that my mouth opened involuntarily when I saw who it was. "Oh my God," I exclaimed, much too loudly. "Michael Kinicki?"

There was one person standing in between us, a tired-looking

blond woman in running clothes who was frowning at the chalk-
boards over the cash register, the ones that listed the café's menu in
Day-Glo colors. I stepped around her and walked into Michael's open
arms, his body's warmth enveloping me. He looked fit and happy
and had kept himself trim, I would later learn, from years of swim-
ming mile after mile in his health club's lap pool four days a week,
his hair still a little curly and now attractively gray. He paid for my
coffee and bought us both oatmeal and asked me to sit with him
while we had breakfast. I had to call in to ask the receptionist to
reschedule my first appointment, which I almost never do, but I
didn't want to leave him so soon after finding him again. It felt then
like I had been waiting a very long time for his reappearance, even
though I don't think I had thought about him in years.

"You look fantastic, Lucy," he kept saying as we ate our oatmeal.
The compliment made me blush, but I loved it. What woman doesn't
want to be told she's beautiful, especially by someone she also finds
attractive? I've never been the type of woman who gets angry when
someone whistles at me or tells me I'm pretty. I'm confident in my
intelligence, but there are plenty of days when I don't know if I'm
still physically attractive. I don't feel pretty as often as I'd like to, this
being one of the more insidious effects of aging because it can't
be treated the way brittle hair or dry skin might be. When I was
younger, I didn't know if I'd care what I looked like after I reached a
certain age, but I know now that I will care about it until I die or else
senility sets in.

"I heard you're a doctor," he added. "Congratulations."

"For a long time now," I said, smiling into his cheerful, suntanned face. "Even longer than the Cold War's been over."

He laughed. "The Cold War? You don't hear too much about it
these days."

"No, I suppose not. But you were a history major, weren't you?

I thought you'd get a chuckle from the reference." I laughed a little, embarrassed. I was trying to impress him, the impulse there as aggressively as anything I'd felt in months.

"Poli-sci," he said. "Close."

"Let me guess, you're an attorney?"

He nodded, his smile a little sheepish. "I am. Sad but true."

"That's all right," I said. "As long as you're not working for Monsanto or defending the Mafia."

"No, not even close. I'm an immigration lawyer, but I represent the underdog, not the INS." He paused and looked down at the table, picking up his coffee mug before raising his eyes again. "You know, I was going to look you up again when I heard about you and Renn."

"You mean our divorce?" I shook my head, smiling again. "Everyone heard about me and Renn. His fans were mad that he'd left one nobody for another nobody. They were hoping he'd dump me for Meryl Streep or Madonna or something. You can guess how much fun that whole ordeal was."

"I'm sure it was awful, but you don't look like it did any damage."

"That's because I had a job to go with the kids and the philandering husband. My work kept me sane." I paused. "Are you married?" He wasn't wearing a ring, but that didn't mean much.

"I was, but we've been divorced for four years."

"I'm sorry to hear that." But the truth is, I wasn't.

He sprinkled more brown sugar on his oatmeal and stirred it into the few spoonfuls that remained in his bowl. "Don't be sorry," he murmured. "It was a long time coming. Sandy and I wanted to wait until both of our kids were in college, but it should have happened right about the same time you and Renn separated."

"I tell people that it was Renn's midlife crisis, even though we were both still in our thirties."

"Midlife crises keep happening earlier and earlier. Some people even have two. Sandy and I were almost fifty when our divorce went through. You didn't remarry?"

"No."

"Didn't feel like it?"

"No, I guess I didn't. I was busy raising Billy and Anna and working full-time. I didn't have much extra time to go out on dates. I did see a few people though, on and off."

I had dated about a dozen men between the divorce and now, not too many, I don't think, considering it had been more than sixteen years since I'd signed the divorce papers, but getting my hopes up a dozen times—even more, because there were a few men I was drawn to who ultimately weren't available—it was difficult and often demoralizing.

"Your kids are out on their own now, aren't they?" Michael asked.

"Yes. Anna's a doctor now too, but she's doing family medicine, not pediatrics like me. Billy's living in Paris, being a dilettante."

"Lucky guy."

"I think he's writing a screenplay now. I have no idea if it'll be any good, but who knows, maybe he'll surprise me and the rest of the world too. I didn't think his father would be much of a writer, but *Bourbon at Dusk* turned out pretty well. You probably saw that it was nominated for Best Picture and Best Original Screenplay."

Michael nodded. "I thought for sure it would win in one of those categories, but at least Renn got Best Director. Didn't Marek Gilson also win for Best Actor?"

"Yes, he did."

"I thought the girl was better. I'm surprised she didn't win."

"I was too, but she was lucky to be nominated. There were a lot of good movies last year."

My feelings about all this were complicated. It certainly wasn't the first time Renn had gone to the Oscars and won. He had been nominated three times while we were married and had won twice, once for Best Actor and once for Best Supporting, but despite how much hype and anticipation surrounds this awards show each year, I did not look forward to it at all. For one, it was such an enormous hassle to prepare for. Which designers to use for Renn's tux and my dress? Who should do my makeup and hair, and his makeup and hair? Which after-party invitations to accept? Which congratulatory phone calls to return first, because everyone we knew, everywhere on earth, it seemed, was calling to say how happy they were for us, how excited, and how Renn just had to do his next picture with so-and-so (so-and-so was calling too, of course; multiple so-and-so's).

Renn couldn't get a solid night's sleep after the nominations were announced (which meant that I couldn't either), because he could not stop thinking about whether he would win, or would it be one of the other heavyweights? Surely he was as good as they were, wasn't he, if he had been nominated at all? I think that he probably was as good as they were, except in a few movies that couldn't have been saved no matter how well he performed, like that absurd stinker where he played the transsexual opera singer. I could not believe it when he chose that project. It was after we were divorced, and he and his second wife were on the skids by that time too; I think his judgment must have been impaired. I sat in a theater in West Hollywood and watched him in this movie with all of the absurd wigs and the caked-on makeup and laughed in disbelief almost the whole time. What enormous hands and feet he had, especially in those yellow pumps. How ugly a woman he was! Several other people in the audience tried to shush me, but I couldn't stay quiet for the life of me or anyone else. If they had known him the way I did, they'd have laughed so much that their stomach muscles would have ached for days afterward too.

As for this year's Oscars, I watched them by myself at home, a bowl of air-popped popcorn in my lap, a glass of white wine on the table next to the sofa. Anna was busy at the hospital and had told me that they wouldn't give her the evening off because they were too swamped from a recent E. coli outbreak, but I think this might have been a fib. She probably wanted to watch the show with her boyfriend instead of me, whom I still haven't met. I felt a little uncomfortable watching the red-carpet coverage before the ceremony began; they kept showing Renn with Elise Connor, the commentators practically drooling on them. Whatever else she might be, she is a remarkably pretty young woman. She also seems sweet, and my thought all along has been that Renn, probably as old as her father, is out of his depth. And in fact she seemed to have figured this out too, because she broke up with him a week or so after the Oscars. It took me a little while to find out what was going on, but eventually Anna told me her suspicions, which her father would not confirm when she talked to him about the breakup. I, however, was surprised that even he would do something as selfish and contemptible as carrying on with his son's ex-girlfriend, if Anna's suspicions are correct. I still care about the man, but long ago I lost any illusions I might have had about his judgment where his personal life is concerned. He seems quite capable of rationalizing any decision he makes that involves his penis.

At the bagel café, before Michael and I parted ways, he asked for my number, and with his eyes on his feet, he asked if I would like to go out for dinner sometime. "Yes," I said, feeling my heart leap. "I'd love to."

"I'm so glad," he said, raising his eyes to meet mine. "Maybe this weekend if you're free?"

"Yes," I said. "This weekend could work."

He kissed my cheek before we got into our cars, and all day I kept thinking about him and what it would be like to kiss him. I had trouble keeping a smile off my face, especially when a patient's worried mother was speaking to me about her inability to get her six-year-old son to stop eating dirt from the garden. I almost said, "Maybe he's pregnant. Pregnant women sometimes crave dirt." But obviously this would not have gone over well.

The next day, Michael called around six in the evening and asked me out, saying that he would pick me up at seven thirty on Friday rather than have me meet him at the restaurant. During the three days between his call and our date, I felt almost lightheaded with anticipation. But I didn't want to feel this way; chances were, the date would not be as good as I hoped. It was possible that he would spend the whole evening talking about his ex-wife or his recent pitiful blind dates or some embarrassing health problem that he thought I would be interested in because I'm a doctor. These are all scenarios from other dates I'd been on in the past few years, ones with colleagues' divorced brothers or cousins or businessmen I'd met online who weren't anywhere near as charming in person as they were in the e-mails they'd sent before we met. There had also been a few men who had spent the whole date grilling me for every detail I would divulge about my ex-husband: What was Renn Ivins really like, and wasn't it just the coolest thing to be married to him? The first time this had happened, I'd been so stunned that I'd laughed. "No, it wasn't the coolest thing," I said. "We got a divorce."

For some reason, this had not sunk in. "Sure," the man said, "but wasn't it still cool to be married to him for a little while?"

It mystifies me how some people really don't seem to have any idea what's polite and what's jaw-droppingly insensitive. Michael, fortunately, did know what was polite. He arrived at the house exactly at seven thirty and had a bouquet of red roses with him, the pink tissue paper and matching ribbon carefully arranged by a real florist, not some underpaid worker at the grocery store. He smelled very nice and seemed so happy to see me that I felt a lump rise in my throat. I think my children assume that I haven't remarried because their father did such a number on me that I can't bear the thought of legally binding myself to another man. But this isn't the case. I haven't remarried because the one or two men I've dated since the divorce whom I could imagine a future with eventually stopped wanting to see me. I think they thought that I was still hooked on Renn, even though (after a year or two), I no longer was, and I tried to make this clear to them, but they weren't convinced.

Other, less suitable men haven't been as quick to leave. In some cases, I've had to tell them that I was no longer interested in going out with them. It isn't easy to do this, no matter how bored or irritated you've become with the man. People assume that being the one who rejects is infinitely preferable to the contrary, but it isn't. I have never enjoyed upsetting other people, even those I suspected were only after my money or the perverse pleasure it brought them to say they were dating the woman Renn Ivins had married before the other woman he married and divorced.

In fact, this other woman, Melinda Byers, has recently performed a small miracle. She has made me feel something akin to sympathy for her. Her memoir about her marriage to Renn, *This Isn't Gold*, isn't as stupid and trashy as I expected. It's actually somewhat interesting and often thoughtful. There were parts that made me angry and other parts that I found wildly self-indulgent and ridiculous, but on the whole, reading it made me feel oppressively sad.

Then, within a couple of days of having finished it, perversely, I began to feel almost happy. This woman, my most hated enemy for a time, had actually worried that Renn would leave her and come back to his children and me. She had suffered over this, had apparently lost sleep thinking that he should follow his conscience if it demanded his return to his family because she apparently felt guilty for having taken him away from us (her parents had also divorced when she was young), but at the same time, she wanted most fiercely for him to stay with her. This emotional schizophrenia has to be partially responsible for why he began to distance himself from her within a year of marrying her. Their marriage must never have been a peaceful one. I know that my kids liked her, and at the time, their affection for her really upset me, but I would rather that she have treated them well than have ignored or openly disliked and mistreated them. I might have said a number of ugly things about Renn in front of Anna and Billy, but I tried not to complain as often about Melinda. It was sometimes very hard to hold my tongue and I didn't always succeed, but most days, I think I did.

I should say this—I probably wouldn't have reacted the way that I did to This Isn't Gold if it had been published a few years after their divorce. My wounds would still have been too fresh, my schadenfreude over their marriage's failure too great—but with more than ten years between their divorce and now, I've mellowed. I know that I couldn't have done anything to change what happened to Renn's and my marriage. It was not my fault that he left. The fact is, he had too many attractive opportunities, too many available women lying directly in his path with their legs open and their brains closed for business. He was out of town too often too. If a marriage is going to last, I think that you need to be physically near your husband more than a few days a month.

Michael, I learned during our first date, had been living in Boulder for the past twenty-five years but had moved back to southern California, to Pasadena, in fact, where I live, a couple of years earlier, and he told me over lemon linguine and an avocado and shrimp salad that he never wanted to leave California again. That's good, I thought, smiling at him. "Is your ex-wife still in Colorado?" I asked.

"Yes," he said. "She's from there."

"What about your kids?"

"They're both still in college. One's at Rice, the other's at Colorado State."

"Then grad school?"

"I'm not sure. If so, they'd better get scholarships. I'm cutting them off after undergrad." He laughed. "Maybe not, but that's what I tell them. They're good kids. I'm lucky."

"I'm sure they are. Mine are too. Usually." I smiled. I could not stop smiling.

"Yes, usually," he murmured, reaching across the table to take my hand. He held it until our waiter came by to ask if we wanted dessert and Michael looked at me and I nodded, smiling again, a little overwarm from the white wine we'd ordered with dinner. He ordered chocolate cake and I asked for raspberry sorbet, which arrived with a small chocolate shortbread cookie; I could have eaten about twenty of them, they were so delicious. When we were done, there was no awkwardness over the check, and watching him remove a credit card from his wallet, I thought, Thank you for coming back into my life. Please let this be easy.

On our way back to his car, he asked if I felt like driving over to the Santa Monica pier, and I said yes, surprised by his suggestion. I hadn't been there since Anna and Billy were kids, and when Michael and I made our way from his car to the entrance, I realized that I was glad to be there again, among the shy teenagers on first dates, the adults milling around with their small children, and the workers, some cheerful, some weary, who manned the carnival games and called out to passersby. Michael steered me out to the end of the pier, and after a couple of minutes of staring at the waves, he put his arm around my shoulders and pulled me close because I was shivering through my thin coat. I felt him hesitating, but after a few seconds, he kissed me. We kept kissing for what must have been a long time, as if we too were teenagers, and in a way we were, this being our first date, and the giddy, nervous feelings no different for us than they would have been if we were still sixteen. When he pulled his face away from mine, it looked flushed, and I thought, I can take him home with me. I can take this man into my bed and he can spend the night and we don't have to worry about our parents or anyone else finding out.

He drove me home after we kissed at the end of the pier for a little while longer, a chilly breeze off the Pacific eventually forcing us back to his car, where he kissed me again before taking us to my house. I had put clean sheets on the bed before he picked me up that evening, thinking that it was unlikely anything would happen, not so soon, but I knew now that I must have been thinking all along about inviting him inside, and I was almost faint with the suspense of it all. I wondered if I should say something about my expectations, but I wasn't sure what they were. All I knew at that moment was that I wanted him, and he seemed to want me too. He gave me a shy, expectant look when he pulled into my driveway and I put my hand on his arm and said, "Turn off the car and come inside."

I could almost feel him breathing behind me as we walked into the house, and I felt then that he was going to be good, and let me say this: he was. He really was.

We didn't bother with the lights; I turned around to look at his face and he put his arms around me and right away I could feel him pressing against my stomach. I already thought that I might love him. This probably sounds a little ridiculous, but it is nonetheless true. The truth is, when we were in college I had had a crush on him too, but I loved Renn by that time and didn't want to run around on him because this has never been my nature and I also felt that I might be imagining Michael's interest. Or that he would stop liking me once I made myself available to him because he would think I was a floozy for cheating on Renn.

That first night Michael stayed with me, it had been almost two years since I'd had sex with anyone, not the longest I've gone without companionship since the divorce, but close. He told me that it had been a while for him too, but he didn't elaborate and I didn't ask. He stayed until the morning, when I had to go to the clinic and see patients until one o'clock, and before I had finished my appointments for the day, he had already called to thank me for a "wonderful night." He wondered if I'd be free again that evening, "if you're not too sick of me," he said, laughing self-consciously, and I called him back as soon as I got out to the parking lot and told him yes, he could come over around six and I would make dinner for him.

The fears that assailed me before we went out on that first Friday night: that our date would not turn out well, that too many years had passed since we had last known each other and we were now too different from who we had been in college, that we were nothing more than two lonely, aging people desperately trying to relive the happier days of early adulthood, when all possibilities were still open to us, seemed to be, to my profound relief and joy, unfounded. We might have looked older and weighed a little more and also been veterans of one failed marriage each, but his essential kindness, his sense of humor, his generosity and willingness to laugh, were still intact. I felt like he had been dropped out of the sky by some benevolent djinn.

But it worried me to feel so happy. If you're used to nothing much happening, except for minor crises and disappointments, it's hard not to be suspicious of your sudden good fortune.

When I eventually told Michael that I was going to Paris in a few weeks to see my son, he asked haltingly if I might let him . . . well, if he might be able to join me? He didn't have to tag along with me the whole time if I didn't want him to, but he hadn't taken a vacation in a year and a half and he hadn't been to Paris in many years, and what a romantic city it was. What did I think?

"Yes," I said without a second's hesitation. I had been hoping that he would ask because I hadn't yet worked up the nerve to invite him myself. We had only been seeing each other for two weeks when I brought it up, and though we had spent about ten nights together during those two weeks, I worried that I might be rushing things by asking him to join me on a vacation all the way across the continent, on the other side of the Atlantic. When I confessed this to him, he said, "Don't be silly, Lucy. You're a grown woman and I'm a grown man. We can do whatever we want. I want to go, if you really don't mind."

"Of course I want you to come. I just wasn't sure if I should ask."

"You should always ask for what you want," he said. "No one can read your mind."

"No, I suppose not."

I called Billy the next day to tell him that I was bringing a friend with me to France, and he seemed genuinely curious. "A boyfriend?" he asked.

"A man friend," I said.

"Really? That's nice." He paused. "You're not planning on staying with me, are you?"

I laughed a little, grateful, I suppose, for his directness. "I wouldn't dream of it."

"If you want to, you could, but the second bedroom is about the size of a large coat closet, so you'd definitely be better off staying at a hotel."

"Billy, we've already made reservations at George V."

"Damn. Who's paying?"

"I think we'll probably split it."

"Is this guy after you for your money, like that loser from a couple of years ago?"

"Michael has his own money." He seemed to, but I wasn't sure if it came from his law practice because half of his cases were pro bono and I don't think the paying cases were likely to make too many people rich. He had alluded to some property he owned in Colorado, and I suspected that this was where his money came from. He kept picking up the checks when we went out, and I did not sense any nervousness on his end when the servers delivered these checks, some of them easily more than I spent on a week's worth of groceries, to our table, like I had with other men who did not want to pay or were worried that they couldn't afford to pay. His house was near the Rose Bowl and beautiful; he had traveled all over the world and dressed attractively but was not flashy with his wardrobe. If he didn't have much money, he was doing a stunning job of obscuring this fact.

I did wonder what was wrong with him, though; when it came to love, my cynicism was deeply ingrained. There had to be something. But maybe it would be something I could live with. I hoped that my flaws were ones he could live with too.

"I want to ask you something," said Billy. "Do you have any idea what's going on with Dad? He's not returning my calls. Since he and Elise broke up, we've talked only once, and that was before I knew she'd left him. I don't think Anna has talked to him that much either. Less than she usually does, anyway."

"I haven't talked to him in a long time. I called him after the Oscars, but he didn't call me back. I haven't tried him again, but I will if you'd like me to."

"Yeah, if you don't mind. Maybe he'll talk to you."

"I don't like that he's not calling you and Anna back." I tried to keep my voice even, but it rose a little. Renn was such a jerk sometimes.

"Me, I get, but I don't know why he won't call Anna," he said.

"Why wouldn't your father call you? Because of Elise Connor? Is he thinking that you're still pining for her?" I knew about this because Anna told me, not Billy. Never Billy. He does not like to talk to me about his love life, especially when something is wrong with it, which seems to be a lot of the time.

He was silent.

"You aren't, are you?" I said. "God, Billy, I hope not. She's not—"

"No," he said, cutting me off. "I'm not pining for her. She's dating Marek Gilson now, anyway."

"She is? How do you know?"

"Because she told me. She e-mailed me."

"Aren't you happy with your new girlfriend? I thought you were."

"I am happy. Jorie's great. You'll see when you meet her. Everything here's fine. My screenplay is half done, and I think it's good. It might even be something I'll be able to sell, or else I'll make it myself."

"You shouldn't use your own money if you—"

He exhaled. "Mom, don't worry. That's still a ways off."

"What's its title? Do you have one yet?"

"Yes, but I don't know if I'll keep it. Right now it's called *Little Known Facts*."

"I like that."

"Thanks. I'm still considering it though."

"What's it about? You know I have to ask."

"To be honest, it's about me. You, Dad, and Anna too, but I'm disguising everyone and a lot of the things that have happened to us."

"Oh, I hope so," I said, taken aback. I shouldn't have been surprised by this revelation, but I was. I can't say that I was pleased about it either because, well, my conscience was hardly clear. To state the obvious, Billy and Anna's formative years were not the most idyllic on record.

"Don't worry, Mom. You won't look bad, if people even figure out that it's about us."

"I'm sure some of them will," I said, knowing this was true.

We said good-bye a minute or two later, our conversation almost as worrying as many of the calls we'd had before he left. I did not know what sort of tone he would take in his portrayal of his father and me in *Little Known Facts*, and I could also imagine him frittering away all of his money on a project that would bomb, if he even managed to film the whole thing and find a distributor for it. I wanted to be glad that he was working on something that seemed to fill him with a sense of urgency and purpose, but he knew as well as anyone that the film industry is as mercurial as they come, and even if he did have talent, it wasn't very likely that he would become a successful filmmaker. Even if his father helped him during every step of the process, there was still no guarantee that Billy would succeed at this new undertaking. And quite a few people would also dismiss him out of hand, saying that he was simply another example of a child riding a famous parent's coattails.

I have never been very graceful about stepping back and letting my children make their own mistakes. Why watch them fail, I've always thought, when I can do something to help them succeed instead?

The answers the pop psychologists give us: because failure builds character. Because it teaches humility and discipline and gratitude for whatever successes a person might eventually achieve. Because it is the right thing to do.

Yes, I suppose so. Most of the time I have forced myself to let my children make their own mistakes. Or else they have insisted on making them, ignoring my advice. Billy more than Anna. Billy about ninety percent more than Anna, if truth be told.

Along with my unease over his screenplay, there was also his father's silence. Renn had to be up to something. I called him a little while after Billy and I got off the phone. He didn't answer. It feels sometimes like I am always on the phone or thinking about being on the phone or trying to ignore the ringing phone. It is much worse for my ex-husband, who has two or three cell phones and a landline, and his agent, personal assistant, and publicist also taking calls for him. I kept trying him until he picked up, about four more calls and five hours later, nearly midnight, when I should already have been asleep for an hour or more, especially because it was one of the few nights when Michael and I hadn't gotten together.

When he finally picked up, I offered a halfhearted apology for calling so many times, but then without preamble, I said, "Why aren't you talking to your children?"

"What do you mean?" he asked. "I have been talking to them, but Life After the Storm is taking up a lot of my time. I'm in New Orleans right now, actually."

"Renn," I said. "If Billy's telling me that you're not returning his or Anna's calls, I know something's going on. Our son doesn't usually complain about a lack of phone calls from you or me."

I could hear him sigh. "Nothing's wrong," he said. "I'm swamped, that's all. More so than usual. The foundation is taking up every free moment; I'm working on a new screenplay with Scott Jost, and I just signed on to act in two new pictures later this year."

"I heard that you and Elise broke up a little while after the Oscars."

He hesitated. "Yes, we did."

"I was sorry to hear that."

"Thanks," he said flatly. He sounded tired, his usual bluffness when we spoke on the phone, rare as our conversations were these days, absent. I felt a little guilty about grilling him, but I wanted to know what was going on, if he had gone out with Billy's ex-girlfriend, if he was still going out with her.

"Are you seeing someone new?" I said.

He let a few seconds pass before answering. "No, not really."

"I'm seeing someone," I murmured. I hadn't intended to tell him this, but his reticence was annoying me, even though I had no right to any kind of disclosure from him anymore.

"You are?" he said, waking up a little. "Do I know him?"

"You used to." I paused. "It's Michael Kinicki."

"Who?"

"Michael Kinicki. We were friends with him for a little while at USC. You remember him, don't you? You thought he had a crush on me."

"Was he the guy who dated your roommate and always left his dirty underwear in the bathroom after he took a shower? Didn't he also carry around a corncob pipe and say it was his grandfather's?"

"I don't remember him carrying a corncob pipe. I don't think he left his underwear in our bathroom either." I remembered the pipe but not the underwear.

"He did. You used to complain about it too."

I didn't reply.

After a moment, Renn said, "What's he doing now?"

"He's an attorney. Immigration law."

"Oh. How long have you been seeing him?"

"Not very long."

"Well, good for you."

"You need to call your children," I said.

"I will," he said.

"Tomorrow."

"Lucy."

"Yes?" I said. Just like that, I felt nervous. I recognized his tone as the one he had used the few times he had confessed to cheating on me.

"Billy isn't going to want to talk to me if he finds out that his ex-girlfriend is living with me right now. That's one of the reasons I haven't called him or Anna lately."

"What? Do you mean Danielle?" I said, my voice rising involuntarily. "Why is she living with you? She has her own place, doesn't she?"

"She does," he said slowly, "but if I tell you something, I don't want you to talk about it with anyone else, not Anna or Billy or Michael Kinicki. No one. I'm not kidding."

"You can tell me," I said, even more nervous now.

"I can't be alone anymore, not at my house. Since Elise and I broke up, I haven't been able to sleep unless I take pills, but I'm all right if someone is there with me. I wake up in the middle of the night if I'm by myself and feel like I'm about to have a panic attack. The first few times this happened, I took some Valium, but I didn't want to have to keep taking it because it was happening almost every night. Danielle has been accommodating. She's a very kind person."

"Is she with you in New Orleans right now?"

"No. I don't have as much trouble when I travel. Oddly enough."

"You're going to have to tell Billy soon if you intend to keep her there for any period of time."

"I know."

"You should probably tell him right away. He seems happy with his new girlfriend, and he loves Paris. I don't know if he'll take it that hard."

"I think he would. We had some trouble over Elise, and things between us are still pretty shaky."

"I know. But you still need to tell him soon. Ask Isis what she thinks," I say, letting a note of derision enter my tone. "I'm sure she'd agree with me."

He falters. "Are you mad at me, Lucy?"

"I might be after you talk to Billy, depending on how he handles it, but right now I'm not."

"Professionally, everything is better than it's ever been for me, but somehow I keep fucking up my personal life."

"It doesn't help if you have an affair with your son's ex-girlfriend while you're supposed to be in a monogamous relationship with one of the prettiest girls in Hollywood, who also happens to be younger than your own daughter."

"I know," he said morosely. "But I can't seem to stop myself from acting like an asshole."

"More therapy," I said. "Or try castration."

"You're not funny," he said, laughing anyway. "Speaking of Anna, have you met her friend yet?"

"Her boyfriend?"

"If that's what you want to call him."

I froze. "What does that mean?"

Renn hesitated. Maybe he felt bad about telling me something that he knew would upset me, but I doubted it. He was probably only trying to figure out how to deliver his bad news with the greatest dramatic effect. "He's married," he said. "I suppose she didn't tell you that."

My stomach dropped. "He is?"

"Yes."

Goddamn it, I thought. *Goddamn it, Anna.* "She told me he wasn't," I finally said.

"Well, I guess she lied to you."

"Yes, I guess she did." I paused. "She told me that you met him. What did you think?"

"I liked him. He's very charming. If he weren't someone else's husband, I'd say that he and Anna might be a good match."

"How old is he?"

"A lot older than she is."

Wonderful, I thought. Another aging philanderer shopping for sex in a much younger age bracket. What a surprise. "How much older?"

"About twenty years, I think."

"Jesus."

"Exactly."

We really screwed things up, I wanted to say. No, forget that. What I wanted to say was, *You* really screwed things up. But I said nothing. I was hurt and angry, my daughter having told me a bald-faced lie to hide the fact that she was carrying on an illicit affair with a man who was supposed to be mentoring her, with a man who was not supposed to be taking advantage of the pretty young interns who were entrusted to him for one of the most crucial periods of their formation as physicians. I wanted to drive to wherever this opportunist lived and spit on his shoes.

But even more than this, I wanted to flee to Michael's house and walk straight into his arms and not have to face the truth of what my faithless ex-husband had just revealed about our lovely and intelligent daughter, our precious second-born, the last child we would ever have together. I didn't care if Michael had once carried around his grandfather's corncob pipe or left his dirty underwear in Karen's and my bathroom. We were all of twenty-one when we'd first known each other, innocent of most of the frustrations that life would eventually deliver to us, unaware of most other people's sorrows, and so arrogant in our attempts to take over the world, to make an impression on someone other than our most willing admirers, if we had any admirers to speak of.

I said good-bye to Renn and went into my bedroom and lay down on the bed in the dark. What I wanted, I realized then, was a Hollywood ending. Every single day, I wanted a Hollywood ending with its hero who saves the people he loves from their worst fears, whether it be violent death via nuclear bomb or murderer's gun, or a lonely death after a life lived in fear of romantic humiliation. There are countless ways to be unhappy, so many more, it seems to me, than ways to be happy, which could be one of the reasons why happiness is so elusive. If there are ten million ways to be miserable, there are maybe a million ways to be the opposite, if we're lucky.

Renn, with his global reputation for being a Good Samaritan now that Life After the Storm has been successfully launched, with his acting talent and many awards and beautiful lovers and millions and millions in the bank, somehow has managed not to be happy. Our children, despite their own talents and good fortune, also seem to be struggling, though Billy appears to be happier than he has been in a long time, and for this I am grateful.

The choices we make and the choices that we allow to be made for us: these are the raw materials that compose our lives. Some days it feels to me as if I am stepping out of a dark theater into the brilliant sun of early afternoon—for a few moments I can't see anything, and when my ghostly surroundings start to reclaim a more corporeal form, I worry that they won't be recognizable. Because at times, they aren't.

I can only hope that I have loved the people closest to me more than I have harmed them. This is something, however, that I don't think anyone can know for sure.

ACKNOWLEDGMENTS

*L*isa Bankoff at ICM, Nancy Miller at Bloomsbury, and Sheryl Johnston: if it weren't for you, this book would live nowhere but on the hard drive of my soon-to-be-obsolete laptop. Thank you for your kindness, generosity, and extraordinary guidance.

David Elliott: writer, friend, Hollywood sage—thank you for finding the time in your dawn-'til-dusk schedule to offer your expert advice and critique.

Cara Blue Adams, Stephen Donadio, and Carolyn Kuebler: you have offered me and many other writers the professional and spiritual equivalent of life support.

Thank you to everyone at Higgins Lake for letting me hide out in the bedroom to work on the last two chapters: Adam, Marilyn Berling, Sarah Walz, Andy Tinkham, Amy Tinkham, and Eric Stromer.

Paul and Linae Luehrs, Kate Ellis, Tony Ellis, Gary Kaufman, Melissa Fraterrigo, Pete Seymour: thank you for answering my many technical questions.

Adam McOmber and Chrissy Kolaya—thank you for listening (and for laughing, often).

Thank you, friends and family: Melanie Brown, Dolores Walker, Denise Simons, Noelle Neu, Elizabeth Eck, Kate Soehren, Dorthe

Andersen, Melissa Spoharski, Leonard Sneed, Ann and Tom Tennery, Dave Wieczorek, Mark Turcotte, Bill Fahrenbach, Alison Umminger, Gregory Fraser, Mike Levine, Paulette Livers, Debby Parker, Ruth Hutchison, Kim Brun, Kathleen Rooney, Francis-Noel Thomas, Jane Goldenberg, Angela Pneuman, Laura Durnell, Michelle Plasz, Robin Bluestone-Miller, Anita Gewurz, Meredith Ferrill, Cindy Martin, Marlene Garrison, Mona Oommen, Melissa Underwood, Melanie Feerst, Lauren Klopack, Dave Ramont, Dave Sills, and the magnificent Mr. (Bill) Weber.

And thank you to my parents, Susan Sneed and Terry Webb. Persistence, joy: two of the many things that I've learned from you.

READING GROUP GUIDE

*T*hese discussion questions are designed to enhance your group's conversation about *Little Known Facts*, an insightful novel about the dark side of Hollywood celebrity.

ABOUT THIS BOOK

Will knows he shouldn't complain; as the son of movie star Renn Ivins, he has lived an extremely privileged life. His sister, Anna, is a driven medical student, and his mother, Lucy, a successful doctor. Why Will suffers from paralyzing inertia remains an open question. He can't seem to choose a career or commit to a long-term relationship, even though his current girlfriend, Danielle, is beautiful and caring.

Renn tries to help Will by inviting him to New Orleans, where he is directing an Oscar-worthy drama about Hurricane Katrina. But Will falls hard for Renn's lead actress, Elise, who happens to be Renn's new girlfriend. Back in L.A., Anna is starting to keep secrets of her own—she is falling for her boss, Dr. Glass. And Lucy, Will and Anna's mother, has to bite her tongue to keep from criticizing her ex-husband in front of her kids. She does, however, have more discretion than Renn's second wife, Melinda, who is about to publish a tell-all memoir about their brief marriage—and Renn's frequent affairs with his co-stars. Even as Renn considers proposing to Elise, he finds himself straying, yet again—this time with a woman who was once involved with a close family member. Fortunately, this person is a continent away. By the novel's end, Will might go into the family business after all: he has a great idea for a screenplay based on the tumultuous history of his family.

FOR DISCUSSION

1. *Little Known Facts* opens with an epigraph from Robert Bresson's *Notes on Cinematography*: "Let feelings bring about events, not the contrary." How does this quotation relate to the novel to come? Which characters successfully follow their feelings into events, and which characters only seem able to feel in the wake of crisis?

2. When Renn describes his two children, Will and Anna, he says, "the two of them couldn't be more different if one of them had been raised by wolves, the other by nuns" (133). Discuss the similarities and differences between Anna and Will. How does each approach love, career, and family? Are these two siblings really as different as they seem? Why or why not?

3. Discuss Will's alternate names: "Billy" from childhood, and "Guillaume" in Paris. How does Will react to each of these names? How do his changing names reflect his evolving identity?

4. Consider the narration of *Little Known Facts*, with chapters alternating among various points of view. Which character's perspective

seems the most lucid? Which is the most self-deluded? Why do you think Lucy gets the last word in the novel?

5. Discuss Jim Marion's interactions with Renn Ivins, during his work as a propmaster on set and while he shoots his documentary. How does Jim feel about Renn, and how much or how little does Renn understand about their odd relationship?

6. Consider the notes for This Isn't Gold, the tell-all memoir by Melinda Byers, in chapter 7. What is the tone of these unpublished notes? How do the notes likely differ from the published book, judging by Renn and Lucy's reactions to the memoir?

7. Discuss Elise's rise from a Texan college student to a Hollywood star. Who has helped her most in her career? How does her career ambition seem to affect her romantic choices?

8. Anna realizes, "Jealousy was a universal human weakness, though maybe it was sometimes a strength, in that it was supposed to help you hold on to what or who was important to you" (254). Discuss how Anna, Will, Renn, and Lucy all struggle with jealousy. In the end, who is able to hold on, despite jealous feelings, and which relationships shatter under the pressure of jealousy?

9. In chapter 8, we hear directly from Renn Ivins, through notes he's recording for a biography to be published after his death. How do Renn's own words differ from his family's impression of him? Is he more self-aware than family and fans imagine him to be? Why or why not?

10. Discuss Lucy's search for happiness, and her efforts to ensure that her children will lead happy lives. How does Lucy eventually

find contentment? How has she succeeded, or failed, in her efforts to love and protect Anna and Will?

SUGGESTED READING

Christine Sneed, Portraits of a Few of the People I've Made Cry; Steve Almond, God Bless America; Jennifer Egan, A Visit from the Good Squad; Bruce Wagner, Dead Stars; Monica Ali, Untold Story; Curtis Sittenfeld, American Wife; Joyce Carol Oates, Blonde; Emma Straub, Laura Lamont's Life in Pictures; Mackenzie Phillips, High on Arrival; Elmore Leonard, Get Shorty; Michael Tolkin, The Player